"You're saf

The mud sucked at his boots as he hauled her to the bank of the river and collapsed in the muck, her body falling alongside his, her breathing labored, his own chest aching as he fought to draw in air. With the blinding stars dancing across his vision, he rose up on an elbow and glared at the quivering woman lying beside him. Her lips were incredibly blue in a face that was amazingly white. He pressed his wet body over hers, trying to warm her.

"What the hell did you think you were doing?" he growled, his heart pounding wildly in his chest.

"I was going to save you."

He threaded his fingers through her tangled hair. She'd lost her bonnet. She was damn lucky she hadn't lost her life. "You little fool," he rasped in a voice rift with emotion. "You brave little fool."

His mouth swooped down to cover hers. Her cold, quivering lips parted slightly, and he thrust his tongue through the welcome opening like a man desperately searching for treasure.

And treasure he found.

By Lorraine Heath

TEXAS DESTINY

LORRAINE HEATH

AVONBOOKS

An Imprint of HarperCollinsPublishers

Rom

65394082

This is a work of fiction. Names, characters, places, and incidents are products of the author's imagination or are used fictitiously and are not to be construed as real. Any resemblance to actual events, locales, organizations, or persons, living or dead, is entirely coincidental.

Texas Destiny was originally published in the United States in 1997 by the Penguin Group

TEXAS DESTINY. Copyright © 1997 by Jan Nowasky. All rights reserved. Printed in the United States of America. No part of this book may be used or reproduced in any manner whatsoever without written permission except in the case of brief quotations embodied in critical articles and reviews. For information, address Harper-Collins Publishers, 195 Broadway, New York, NY 10007.

First Avon Books mass market printing: June 2018

Print Edition ISBN: 978-0-06-285231-1
Digital Edition ISBN: 978-0-06-204660-4

Cover illustration by Victor Gadino
Cover photography by Image 1st LLC.
Cover photograph © nanjan / iStock / Getty images (wagon)

Avon, Avon & logo, and Avon Books & logo are registered trademarks of HarperCollins Publishers in the United States of America and other countries.

HarperCollins is a registered trademark of HarperCollins Publishers in the United States of America and other countries.

18 19 20 21 22   QGM   10 9 8 7 6 5 4 3 2 1

For Curtis
When it was most needed, you gave us
all a strong shoulder to lean on.
How proud I am that you are my brother.

Acknowledgments

I have often heard that a writer's life is a solitary one. To those who proved the myth untrue, I offer my sincerest appreciation. Without your help and guidance, this story would not have been written.

Jennifer Sawyer Fisher, who saw the potential and encouraged me to reach for it.

Robin Rue, who views detours as opportunity.

Chris and Jim Armstrong, for providing medical information as well as answering my questions about weapons and the Civil War.

Alan Beaubien, for going above and beyond when sharing his knowledge on the Civil War.

Susan Broadwater-Chen, for extensively researching mail-order brides and sharing all that she learned.

Stef Ann Holm, for taking the time from her own writing schedule to offer assistance with my research.

The reference librarians at the Plano Public Library, for their exhaustive research on mail-order brides.

The many readers who have taken the time to

let me know that my stories and characters have touched their hearts, just as their letters touch mine.

And Jack Thomaston, who not only shares his knowledge of horses, any time, day or night, but who also graciously forgives me when I steal away his wife, Carmel, so she can critique my work.

Thank you, all.

A Letter from Lorraine Heath

My Dear Reader:

In February of 1993, I got *the call*: a publisher wanted to publish one of my stories. I'm beyond ecstatic that as I celebrate twenty-five years since I officially embarked on a writing career, Avon Books is making *Texas Destiny* available to readers again in paperback.

As often happens when an author is researching one fact, she runs across another that captures her imagination. While writing *Parting Gifts*, I needed to know how my heroine would treat a gunshot wound in 1881. The Internet wasn't yet the resource trove it is now, but through my local library I discovered a book written by a physician in 1890 that would provide the information I needed. It was housed in a locked chamber at the University of Texas Southwestern Medical

School Library in Dallas, and I was granted access to it. Cloistered in that room, as I was carefully turning pages, I ran across a chapter referencing the psychological trauma experienced by soldiers who survived their faces being mutilated by exploding shrapnel during the Civil War. Some committed suicide after gazing in a mirror while others lived in solitude to spare people the sight of their disfigurements.

I immediately envisioned a man choosing a life of solitude. Hence, Houston Leigh was born. Unable to leave him isolated and alone, I decided to send him to fetch someone's mail-order bride. And what better conflict than for that someone to be his older, handsome-as-sin brother? As the Leigh brothers came into being, they changed me as a writer.

Texas Destiny holds a special place in my heart. The first book in the first series that I ever wrote, it taught me the joy of creating characters I would be able to share with readers in multiple stories.

Houston and Amelia also hold a special place in my heart. They are both scarred by war: a hardened man who has turned away from the world and an optimistic young woman who finds reasons to be grateful for the smallest of pleasures.

It's been a tad over twenty years since I introduced these characters, but I hope this story will still resonate with readers. In 2015, it was ranked #4 on NPR's list of Top 100 Swooniest Romances.

Whether you're new to *Texas Destiny* or taking a return trip through the pages, I hope you enjoy Houston and Amelia's journey toward love and well-deserved happiness.

Wishing you many happily-ever-afters,
Lorraine

Chapter One

September, 1876

*H*is was not a face that women carried with them into their dreams.

Houston Leigh skimmed his thumb over the black eye patch before tugging the brim on the left side of his hat down lower. The right side showed little wear, but the crumpled left side carried the oil and sweat from the constant caress of his hand. Although the day was warm, he brought up the collar on his black duster.

Irritated with the world at large, his older brother in particular, Houston leaned against the wooden structure that had the dubious distinction of being Fort Worth's first railway station and gazed into the distance at the seemingly never-ending tracks.

He hated the railroad with a passion.

Fort Worth had been fading into obscurity, turning into a ghost town, before the citizens extended the town's boundaries so the railroad could reach its outermost edge. It had taken nothing more than a whispered promise to change the fading cow town into a thriving boomtown that the elected officials boasted would one day be known as the Queen of the Prairie.

The Queen of the Prairie.

Houston groaned. His brother had taken to calling his mail-order bride that very name, and Dallas had never even set eyes on the woman.

Hell, she could be the court jester for all Dallas knew, but he'd spent a good portion of his money—and his brothers' money—building this woman a palace at the far side of nowhere.

"We just need to get one woman out here and the rest will follow," Dallas had assured his brothers, a wide confident grin easing onto his darkly handsome face.

Only Houston didn't want women sashaying across the windswept prairie. Their soft smiles and gentle laughter had a way of making a man yearn for the simple dreams of his youth, dreams he'd abandoned to the harshness of reality.

Houston had known men who had been disfigured less. Men who had taken a rifle and ended their misery shortly after gazing into a mirror for the first time after they were wounded. Had he been a man of courage, he might have done the same. But if he had been a man of courage, he wouldn't have been left with a face that his older brother couldn't stomach.

He saw the faint wisp of smoke curling in the distance. Its anticipated presence lured people toward the depot the way water enticed a man crossing the desert. Turning slightly, Houston pressed his left shoulder against the new wood.

Damn Dallas, anyway, for making Houston leave his horses and come to this godforsaken place of women, children, and men too young to have fought in the War Between the States. If Houston hadn't been stunned speechless when Dallas had ordered him to come to Fort Worth to fetch his bride, he would have broken Dallas's other leg.

He still might when he got back to the ranch.

He heard the rumbling train's coarse whistle and shoved his sweating hands into his duster pockets. His rough fingers touched the soft material inside. Against his will, they searched for the delicate threads.

The woman had sent Dallas a long, narrow piece of white muslin decorated with finely stitched flowers that he was supposed to have wrapped around the crown of his hat so she could easily identify him.

Flowers, for God's sake.

A man didn't wear flowers on his hat. If he wore anything at all, he wore the dried-out scales of a rattlesnake that he'd killed and skinned himself, or a strip of leather that he'd tanned, or . . . or anything but daintily embroidered pink petals.

Houston was beginning to wonder if Dallas had broken his leg on purpose just to get out of wearing this silly scrap of cloth. It wouldn't do to anger the woman before she became his wife.

Well, Houston wasn't going to marry her so he could anger her all he wanted, and he wasn't going to wrap flowers around the crown of his brown broad-brimmed hat.

No, ma'am. No, sir.

He hadn't stood firm on many things in his life, but by God, he was going to stand firm on this matter.

No goddamn flowers on his hat.

He squeezed his eye shut and thought about breaking Dallas's other leg. The idea's appeal grew as he heard more people arrive, their high-pitched voices grating on his nerves like a metal fork across a tin plate. A harsh whisper penetrated the cacophony of sound surrounding him.

"Dare you!"

"Double-dare you!"

The two voices fell into silence, and he could feel the boys' gazes boring into him. God, he wished he'd never shut his eye. It was harder to scare people off once they'd taken to staring at him.

"Looks like he's asleep."

"But he's standin'."

"My pa can sleep while he's sittin' in the saddle. Seen him do it once."

"So touch him and see."

A suffocating expectation filled the air with tension. Then the touch came. A quick jab just above his knee.

Damn! He'd hoped the boys were older, bigger, so he could grab one by the scruff of his shirt, hoist him to eye level, and scare the holy hell out of him. Only he knew a bigger boy wouldn't have jabbed him so low.

Reluctantly, Houston slowly opened his eye

and glanced down. Two ragamuffins not much older than six stared up at him.

"Git," he growled.

"Heh, mister, you a train robber?" one asked. "Is that how come you're standin' over here so no one can see ya?"

"I said to git."

"How'd you lose your eye?" the other asked.

His eye? Houston had lost a good deal more than his eye. Trust boys to overlook the obvious. His younger brother had. Austin had never seemed to notice that his brother had left the better part of his face on some godforsaken battlefield.

"Git outta here," Houston ordered, deepening his voice.

Blinking, the boys studied him as though he were a ragged scarecrow standing in a cornfield.

With a quickness they obviously weren't expecting, he stomped his foot in their direction, leaned low, and pulled his lips back into a snarl. The boys' eyes grew as large as their hollering mouths just before they took off at a run. Watching their bare feet stir up the dry dirt in the street leading away from the depot, Houston wished he could run with them, but family obligations forced him to remain.

In resignation, he repositioned himself against the wall, slipped his hand inside the opening of his duster, and stroked the smooth handle of the Colt revolver. The thought of breaking Dallas's leg no longer held enough satisfaction.

Houston decided he'd shoot his brother when he got back to the ranch.

AMELIA CARSON HAD never been so terrified in all her nineteen years.

Afraid the train might hurtle her onto the platform before she was ready to disembark, she clung to her seat as the huffing beast lurched to a stop. The wheels squealed over the wobbly tracks, the whistle blew, and the bell clanged as the engine settled with an ominous hiss. The pungent smell of wood smoke worked its way into the compartment as the passengers flung open the doors, forgetting their manners as they shoved each other aside in their hurry to scramble off the train. Amelia had never seen such an odd collection of people crammed together in one space.

Women with throaty voices and low-necked bodices had graced the compartment. A few well-groomed men had worn tailored suits as though they'd been invited to dine with a queen. Only the guns bulging beneath their jackets indicated otherwise. Some men, smelling of sweat and tobacco, had squinted at her as though contemplating the idea of slitting her throat if she closed her eyes. So she'd rarely slept.

Instead, she had spent her time reading the letters that Dallas Leigh had written to her. She was certain the bold, strong handwriting was a reflection of the man who had responded to her advertisement indicating she had a desire to travel west and become a wife. He was a hero—inasmuch as the South could claim a hero in a war that it had lost. He had been a lieutenant at seventeen, a captain at nineteen. He owned his land, his cattle, and his destiny.

He had wrapped his proposal for marriage

around dreams, dreams of building a ranching empire and having a son with whom to share them.

Amelia knew a great deal about dreams and how frightening it was to reach for them alone. Together she and Dallas Leigh could do more than reach for the dreams. They would hold them in the palm of their hands.

Countless times during her journey, she had envisioned Dallas Leigh waiting for her in Fort Worth, impatiently pacing the platform. Once the train arrived, he would crane his neck to see into the cars, anxious to find her. She had imagined him losing his patience and barging onto the train, yelling her name and knocking people out of the way, desperate to hold her within his arms.

With her dreams rekindled and her heart fluttering, she gazed out the window, hoping to catch sight of her future husband.

She saw many impatient men, but they were all rushing away from the train, yelling and shoving through the crowd, anxious to make their mark on the westernmost railhead. None wore her handiwork wrapped around the crown of his hat. None glanced at the train as though he cared who might still be on board.

She fought off her disappointment and turned away from the window. Perhaps he was simply being considerate, giving her time to compose herself after the arduous journey.

She pulled her carpetbag onto the bench beside her and opened it. With a shaky breath, she stared at the conglomeration of ribbons, flowers, and a stuffed brown bird that her betrothed had labeled a hat. Since she had no portrait to send him, he had sent her something to wear that he could identify.

She was grateful . . .

She stared at the hat.

She was grateful . . . grateful . . .

She furrowed her brow, searching for something about the hat for which she could be grateful. It wasn't an easy quest, but then nothing in her life had been easy since the war. Suddenly she smiled.

She was grateful Mr. Leigh had not met her in Georgia. She was grateful that she didn't have to place the hat on her head until this moment, that none of her fellow passengers had ever seen it.

She plucked it out of her bag, settled it on her head, and took a deep breath. Her future husband was waiting for her.

She just hoped none of the cowboys still mingling at the depot took a notion into their heads to shoot the bird off her hat before Mr. Leigh found her.

Standing, she stepped into the aisle, lifted her bag, and marched to the open doorway with all the determination she could muster. She smiled at the porter as he helped her descend the steps, and then she found herself standing on the wooden platform amid chaos.

Tightening her grip on the bag, she eased farther away from the train. She felt as though she were a shrub surrounded by mighty oak trees. She had little doubt that even the hat was not visible among all these men asking directions, exchanging money and paper with a purpose, and shouldering each other aside.

She considered calling out for Mr. Dallas Leigh, but she didn't think she could lift her voice above the horrendous yelling that surrounded her. She had expected Texas to be quiet and un- settled, not reminiscent of all the carpetbaggers who had come to stake a claim in the rebuilding of Georgia.

She shuddered as the blurred memories, im- ages of Georgia during and after the war, rushed through her mind. With tremendous effort, she shoved them back into their dark corner where they couldn't touch her.

The men and women began to drift away. Ame- lia considered following them, but Mr. Leigh had written that he would meet her at the train station in Fort Worth. The sign on the wooden framed building proudly boasted "Fort Worth." She was certain she had arrived at the correct depot.

Slowly she turned, searching among the few remaining people for a man wearing a hat that bore her flowers. What if he had been here? What if he had seen her and found her lacking? Per- haps he had expected her to be prettier or made of sturdier stock. She had always been small of stature, but she was competent. If he'd give her the chance, she could prove that she was not afraid of hard, honest work.

She dropped her carpetbag and the platform rattled. Tears stung her eyes. She wanted so little. Just a place away from the memories, a place where the nightmares didn't dwell. She squeezed her eyes shut, trying to sort through her disap- pointment.

No man would send a woman tickets for a

journey and then not come to meet her. Somehow, she had already disappointed him . . . or a tragedy had befallen him, preventing his arrival.

People referred to portions of Texas as a frontier, a dangerous wilderness, a haven for outlaws. Newspaper accounts drifted through her mind. She latched onto one, and her imagination surged forward. Outlaws had ambushed him. On his way to Fort Worth, on his way to meet her, he had been brutally attacked, and now, his body riddled with bullets, her name on his lips, he was crawling across the sunbaked prairie—

"Miss Carson?"

Amelia's eyes flew open as the deep voice enveloped her like a warm blanket on an autumn evening. Through her tears, she saw the profile of a tall man wearing a long black coat. His very presence was strong enough to block out the afternoon sun.

She could tell little about his appearance except that he'd obviously bought a new hat in order to impress her. He wore it low so it cast a dark shadow over his face, a shadow that shimmered through her tears. Although he wasn't wearing her flowers on his hat, she was certain she was meeting her future husband.

Brushing the tears away from her eyes, she gave him a tremulous smile. "Mr. Leigh?"

"Yes, ma'am." Slowly, he pulled his hat from his head. The shadows retreated to reveal a strong, bold profile. His black hair curled over his collar. A strip of leather creased his forehead and circled his head.

Amelia had seen enough soldiers return from

the war to recognize that he wore a patch over the eye she couldn't see. He had failed to mention in his letters that he had sacrificed a portion of his sight for the South.

His obvious discomfort caused an ache to settle within her heart. Anxious to reassure him that his loss mattered not at all, she stepped in front of him. With a tiny gasp, she caught her breath. She had expected the black eye patch. She was unprepared for the uneven scars that bordered it and trailed down his cheek like an unsightly frame of wax melting in the sun. With fresh tears welling in her eyes, she reached out to touch his marred flesh. His powerful hand grabbed her trembling fingers, halting their journey of comfort.

"I'm sorry," she whispered as she searched for words of reassurance. "I didn't know. You didn't mention . . . but it doesn't matter. Truly it doesn't. I'm so grateful—"

"I'm not Dallas," he said quietly as he released her hand. "I'm Houston. Dallas busted his leg and couldn't make the journey. He sent me to fetch you." He reached into his pocket and withdrew her embroidered cloth. "He sent this along so you'd know you'd be safe with me."

If his knuckles hadn't turned white as he held the linen, Amelia would have taken it from him. He had shifted his stance slightly so only his profile filled her vision.

A perfect profile.

"He mentioned you in his letters," she stammered. "He didn't say a great deal—"

"There's not much to tell." He settled his hat

on his head. "If you'll show me where your other bags are, we can get goin'."

"I only have the one bag."

He leveled his brown-eyed gaze on her. "One bag?"

"Yes. You can't imagine how grateful I was every time we had to get off the train that I only had the one bag to worry over."

No, Houston couldn't imagine her being grateful for one bag. He allowed his gaze to wander slowly over her white bodice and black skirt, taking note of the worn fabric. Wouldn't a woman wear her best clothing when she met the man she was to marry?

Hell, he'd worn his best clothing, and he'd only come to fetch her.

He wrapped his fingers around the bag and lifted it off the ground. Judging by its weight, he figured she was hauling nothing but air, and they had plenty of that in West Texas.

She needed to be carrying all the things that they didn't have at the far side of nowhere. Hadn't Dallas told the woman anything about the ranch when he wrote her? Hadn't he told her they were miles from a town, from neighbors, from any conveniences?

Two bullets. He was going to fire two bullets into his brother.

"I'm ready to go," she said brightly, interrupting his thoughts.

No, she wasn't ready to go. Only he didn't know how to tell her without offending her. Without thinking, he removed his hat to wipe his brow. Her green eyes brightened, as though she were pleased with his gesture, as though she thought he'd done it for her benefit as a gentleman would. He fought the urge to jam his hat back on his head and explain the situation to her from beneath the shadows. "Did Dallas mention how long the journey would take?"

"He wrote that it was a far piece. I thought of a piece of cloth that I might use for quilting." She spread her hands apart slightly and her smooth-skinned cheeks flamed red. "But that's wrong, isn't it?"

Three bullets. He was going to shoot three bullets into his brother.

"It's at least three weeks by wagon."

She lowered her gaze, her eyelashes resting gently on her cheeks. They were golden and so delicate—not thick like his. He wondered if they'd be able to keep the West Texas dust out of her eyes.

"You must think I'm an idiot," she said quietly.

"I don't think that at all, but I need you to understand that this is the last town of any size you'll see. If there's anything you need, you need to purchase it before we leave."

"I have everything I need," she said.

"If there's anything you want—"

"I have everything," she assured him. "We can leave for the ranch whenever you're ready."

He'd been ready three hours ago, consciously packing and arranging all his supplies so he left half the wagon available for her belongings—only she didn't have any belongings. No boxes, no trunks, no bags. He cleared his throat. "I . . . I still need to pick up some supplies." He crammed his hat on his head, spun on his heel, and started walking. He heard the rapid patter of her feet and slowed the urgency of his stride.

"Excuse me, Mr. Leigh, but how did my fiancé break his leg?" she called from behind him in a voice sweeter than the memory he held of his mother's voice.

He turned to face her, and she came to a staggering stop, the bird on her hat bobbing like an apple in a bucket of water. Balling his free hand into a fist to prevent it from snatching off the bird, he wished now that he'd given Dallas his honest opinion on the damn thing when he'd asked him what he thought of it. "He fell off a horse."

Her delicate brows drew together. "As a rancher, surely he knows how to ride a horse."

"He can ride just fine. He took it into his head that he could break this rangy mustang, and it broke him instead." He spun back around, increasing the length of his stride. If Dallas had just listened to him, heeded Houston's warning, Houston would be back at his own place smelling the sweat of horses instead of the flowery scent of a woman, hearing the harsh snort of horses instead of a woman's gentle voice. He wouldn't have to watch a stupid bird nod. He wouldn't be carrying a bag, wondering what the hell she didn't have.

Four bullets. And even then he wasn't certain that thought could sustain him through the hell that tomorrow was sure to bring.

Chapter Two

Amelia followed the towering man as his long, even strides stirred up the dust and took them past several storefronts. His spurs jangled, his coat flapped around his calves, and he pulled his hat farther down on the left side.

He stepped on the boardwalk, sending the harsh sound reverberating around her. He seemed as impatient as she was to begin the journey, and she wondered why he hadn't thought to purchase his supplies before she'd arrived. She could only be grateful that he wasn't the man she'd come to Texas to marry.

He hesitated before shoving open the door to a hotel. He moved back slightly, waiting for her to go inside. She felt as though she were still on the train, traveling headlong toward a destination she wasn't even certain was right for her.

"Why are we going in here?" she asked.

His jaw tightened as three people barged past him. "I figure by the time we're done gettin' the supplies, it'll be too late to travel today, and considering how many people got off that train, I figure we ought to get the rooms before we get the supplies."

"A very wise decision," she acknowledged as she slipped past him and entered the hotel. People crowded the lobby, closing in around her. Fighting the urge to run, she struggled to draw in air. As long as she could breathe, she could live.

Houston dropped her bag to the floor. "Wait here while I see about some rooms."

She watched him walk to the front desk, tugging on his hat. She was greatly disappointed that Dallas Leigh had not met her. She had hoped to become better acquainted with him before they exchanged their vows. But she had little hope of that happening now. Once she arrived at his ranch, she was certain they would be married. She'd have no opportunity to change her mind, return to Fort Worth, or travel home.

Home. How easily the word slipped into her mind. How difficult to remember that she no longer had a home or a family. Everything of importance, everything that meant anything to her at all was carefully packed away in the bag resting near her feet, along with the marriage contract Dallas Leigh had asked her to sign. His wording had been practical and straightforward, a guarantee that he would take her as his wife if she journeyed to Fort Worth, a guarantee that she would take him as her husband if he provided her with the funds with which to travel.

She did not begrudge him his caution. He knew as little about her as she knew of him. Trust, like love, would come with time.

As the scowling man returned to her side, she

could only hope that Dallas's moods were not as dark.

"This way," he grumbled as he snatched up her bag.

She followed him through the lobby and up a distant set of stairs. At the top landing, he took a right and charged down the hallway. He inserted a key into the lock, turned it, and flung open the door. He stepped back and waited for her to enter the room.

Amelia walked into the small room. The bed beside the window immediately drew her attention. Dallas had sent her tickets that allowed her to sleep in a berth. She had taken one look at the small compartment and traded in the tickets, using the refunded money to purchase him a wedding gift—a gold pocket watch, second hand.

During her journey, she had snatched sleep here and there, sitting up, whenever she'd dared to sleep. She'd almost forgotten what it felt like to sleep in a bed.

She faced the man standing in the doorway. He was holding his hat, presenting her with his right side.

"I need to take the wagon and animals to the livery and let the hostler know I'll be keeping them there overnight. I thought you might want to"—he waved his hat helplessly by his thigh—"do whatever it is ladies do when they get off a train. I'll meet you in the lobby in an hour, and we'll go get those supplies."

"Where is your room?" she asked.

"This was the last room. I'll stay at the livery."

"That hardly seems fair. You're paying for the room—"

"You're gonna sleep with the horses?"

"I've slept with worse." Amelia dropped her gaze as the heat rushed to her face. She should explain that statement, but she couldn't. She didn't want to give freedom to the blurred memory lurking in a shadowed corner of her mind. "I simply meant . . . I am most grateful for the room, but if you wished to share it—"

"That wouldn't be proper."

She forced herself to meet his gaze. "Won't we be sleeping together while we travel?"

The cheek that was visible to her reddened as he turned his hat in his hands. "No, ma'am. You'll sleep in a tent, and I'll sleep by the fire." He settled his hat onto his head. "Tonight I'll sleep at the livery. I'll be back in an hour. I'd appreciate not havin' to wait on you."

Before she could remind him that she'd had to wait on him at the depot, he slammed the door closed. She didn't know whether to laugh or cry. Three weeks. She would be in that man's company for three weeks, and if the past fifteen minutes were any indication of what she could expect on the journey, she anticipated an extremely lengthy three weeks.

She closed her eyes. Grateful, grateful, grateful. He had to possess some redeeming quality. She opened her eyes and smiled. She could be grateful that he appeared to be a man of few words, and she was incredibly grateful that he'd left.

He no doubt thought she had the brain of a gnat, and perhaps she did: traveling from Geor-

gia to Texas in order to marry a man she knew
only through correspondence. What if she had
misjudged the tone of Dallas Leigh's letters?
What if she had created in her mind a man who
did not exist beyond her imagination?

Since the war, she had received offers to better
her life, but none had carried the respectability of
marriage. To the victor go the spoils. Her father's
plantation, his wife, and his daughters had been
the spoils.

Shuddering, she squeezed her eyes shut and
wrapped her arms around herself. She was too
tired to hold the memories and fears at bay. Too
tired.

With longing, she gazed at the bed. She would
sleep for just a few minutes. Then she would wash
away the dust of her journey and meet Houston
Leigh in the lobby. She imagined it would be
quite interesting to watch him bargain for supplies. With his temperament, she had little doubt
he would end up paying double for anything he
wanted.

She eased onto the bed, sighing with contentment. The mattress, as soft as a cloud, sank beneath her weight.

Heaven.

Just a few moments of heaven.

HELL'S FURY HAD surrounded Houston for so
long that he couldn't remember if he'd ever
known heaven's touch. He was afraid that if he
wasn't careful, he'd drag the woman into hell
with him.

He'd already hurt her feelings. He knew he

had. Otherwise, she would have met him in the lobby.

He was angry at Dallas, and he had taken his anger out on the woman. He hadn't meant to, but in looking back he could see that he had.

He stood outside her door, practicing his apology. He couldn't recall ever giving an apology, and the best words to use wouldn't come to his mind. An apology to a woman should be like the piece of cloth she'd sewn for Dallas: flowery, dainty, and pretty.

Hell, he didn't know any words like that. She'd just have to be happy with the words he knew, sorely lacking though they were.

Thank God, he wasn't the one she was going to marry. He'd spent the whole morning thinking about what he would say when he met her. When he'd seen the tears glistening within her green eyes, shame had risen up and sent every word he'd practiced scattering like dust across the prairie. Shame that it had taken him so long to gather his courage and cross that platform to greet her. Shame that he hadn't considered how she might feel standing alone in a strange town waiting for a man who wasn't going to come.

At the livery, he'd thought about how he might explain the supplies. Their purchase was sure to be a delicate matter. After all his thinking and word gathering, she hadn't met him.

Now he was having to think of an apology.

He just wanted to be back at the ranch, where he could walk alone and think alone. He didn't want to answer questions, or consider another's feelings, or remove his hat.

With a heavy sigh, he removed his hat, knocked lightly on her door, and waited, the apology waiting with him, ready to be spoken as soon as she opened the door.

Only she didn't open the door.

She was either angrier than he figured or she'd left. If she'd left, he'd be the one with four bullets in his hide because Dallas always hit what he aimed at.

Earlier, without thinking, he'd placed the key to her room in his pocket, leaving her without a way to lock her door. What if someone had stolen her? Women were rare . . . so rare . . .

He knocked a little harder. "Miss Carson?"

He pressed his good ear to the door. The blast that had torn through the left side of his face had taken his hearing from that side as well. He heard nothing but silence on the other side of the door.

Gingerly, he opened the door and peered inside. The late-afternoon sun streamed through the window, bathing the woman in its honeyed glow. Curled on the bed, asleep, she looked so young, so innocent, so unworthy of his temper.

He slipped inside and quietly closed the door. He crossed the room, set his saddlebags on the floor, and sat in the plush velvet chair beside the bed. He dug his elbows into his thighs and leaned forward.

Dear God, but she was lovely, like a spring sunrise tempting the flowers to unfurl their petals. Her pale lashes rested on her pink-tinged cheeks. Her lips, even in sleep, curved into the barest hint of a smile.

He had spotted her right off, as soon as she'd arrived at the door of the railway car. Beneath that godawful ugly hat, the sun had glinted off hair that looked as though it had been woven from moonbeams. The smile she had given the porter as he'd helped her down the steps—even at a distance—had knocked the breath out of Houston.

He still wasn't breathing right. Every time he looked at her, his gut clenched as though he'd received a quick kick from a wild mustang.

She wasn't at all what he'd expected of a heart-and-hand woman. He'd expected her to look like an old shirt, washed so many times that it had lost its color and the strength of its threads. He knew women like that. Women who had traveled rough roads, become hard and coarse themselves, with harsh laughter and smiles that were too bright to be sincere. Women who knew better than to trust.

But Amelia Carson did trust. She was a heart-in-her-eyes woman. Everything she thought, everything she felt reflected clearly in her eyes. In her green, green eyes.

The warm depths reminded him of fields of clover he'd run through as a boy. Barefoot. The clover had resembled velvet caressing his rough soles. For a brief moment, he actually relished the thought of holding her gaze.

His brown eye could serve as the soil in which her green clover took root.

What an idiotic notion! The next thing he knew he'd be spouting poetry. He shuddered at

the thought. Wearing flowers and spouting poetry. His pa would have tanned his hide good for
either one of those unmanly actions.

He watched her sleep until the final rays of the
sun gave way to the pale moonlight. He shivered
as the chill of the night settled over him. Standing, he reached across the woman and folded the
blankets over her. A warmth suffused him, and
he imagined drawing the blankets over her every
night for the rest of his life.

Only that privilege belonged to his brother.
Houston had witnessed the document Dallas
had drawn up, something as close to a marriage
contract as he could arrange without the "I do's."
For all practical purposes, Amelia Carson belonged to Dallas.

Which was as it should be. Dallas had spent
a month thumbing through the tattered maga-
zine he'd found when they'd driven the cattle to
Wichita, Kansas, in the spring of seventy-five.
Houston knew desperation for a son had driven
Dallas to write his first letter to Amelia.

He could only wonder what had compelled her
to reply, to accept his brother's offer of marriage.
He settled back in the chair. It wasn't his place to
wonder about her. He didn't have to like her. He
didn't have to talk to her. He didn't have to be nice
to her. He just had to get her to the ranch . . . and
by God, that was all he planned to do.

THROUGH A WAKING haze in which dreams still
lingered in the corners of her mind, Amelia snuggled beneath the blankets, relishing the comfort

of the soft bed. She had no recollection of drawing the blankets over herself, but she welcomed their protection against the chill permeating the room.

Complacent and rested, like a kitten that had spent the better part of the day lazing in the sun, she stretched languorously, inhaled deeply, and froze.

The aromas of bacon, coffee, and freshly baked bread teased her nostrils. Slowly she opened her eyes, expecting the harsh glare of the afternoon sun to streak across her vision. Instead, the soft glow of early-morning light cast its halo over the furnishings, directing most of its attention on a small cloth-covered table set in the middle of the room. The sunlight shimmered over an assortment of covered dishes.

Amelia's mouth watered at the same time that alarm rushed through her. She hadn't heard anyone come into the room.

Unexpectedly, she detected another scent, much fainter than the food causing her stomach to rumble, fainter, and yet in an odd way more powerful. Leather and horses.

She spotted saddlebags leaning against a chair near the bed. Cautiously, moving only her eyes, she allowed her gaze to sweep over the room.

Her heart stilled when she noticed the long shadow stretching across her bed. The shadow of a man. She bolted upright and jerked her gaze over her shoulder.

His left shoulder pressed against the wall, Houston Leigh stood beside the window watching her. The sunlight took a moment to outline a portion of his tall, lean frame before completing its journey into the room.

Amelia threw off the blankets and scrambled out of bed, her knees almost hitting the floor before she jumped upright. She pressed a trembling hand to her chest, the rapid thudding of her heart vibrating beneath her fingers. "Mr. Leigh, it's morning."

"Yes, ma'am," he acknowledged with a slow drawl that did nothing to calm her erratic heart.

"You must think me terribly rude. I only meant to sleep for a moment—"

"Didn't think you were rude at all. Just figured you were tired. Figure now you're probably hungry." He inclined his head slightly in the direction of the table.

"You did this?" she asked as she cautiously neared the table.

He lifted one shoulder in a careless shrug. "Needed to make up for yesterday. Dallas would have my hide if he knew how I treated you yesterday."

"Does he anger easily?"

"He's not a man you want to rile." He settled his hat into place. "Enjoy your meal."

He had picked up the saddlebags, slung them over his shoulder, and walked halfway across the room, his hat pulled low on the left side before Amelia realized he was leaving. "Aren't you going to join me?"

"I've already eaten."

"Then just keep me company." He hesitated, and she knew she should let him leave, but she was incredibly tired of being alone. "Please."

His answer came in the form of a movement toward the table as he removed his hat and draped the saddlebags over the back of a nearby chair.

Amelia rushed to take her seat. He took the chair opposite her, turned it slightly so she had a clear view of his profile, and stared at the hat he held on his lap.

Houston searched the farthest recesses of his mind, but he couldn't locate anything worth commenting on. He thought about telling her that her hair was falling down on the left side, but he was afraid she'd hop up and straighten it, pulling it back into that coil she was wearing the day before. He liked the way it looked now, drooping as it was. He secretly hoped it might work its way free and tumble down her back.

Dallas would, of course, prefer to see every strand pulled back and held in its proper place. The man was a stickler for orderliness, but Houston had always thought a woman's hair should flow around her as freely as the wind blew across the prairie.

He thought about describing Dallas's ranch, but she'd see it soon enough, and he didn't have the skill with words to do the place justice. A discussion of his own place probably wouldn't interest her. It was a pretty piece of land, but it would never bring a man wealth or glory.

"Are you sure you don't want anything?" she asked.

"I'm sure," he replied, cursing his gut for jumping into his throat at the sound of her voice. All he had to do was sit still while she ate and give her no reason to bring up her breakfast. The sight of his face had made him bring up his meals a few times in the beginning, but that was years ago when the wounds were still raw . . . and the guilt still festering.

Amelia tore off a piece of warm bread and lathered it with butter, quietly studying the man sitting across from her. His gaze remained fixed on his hat, his brow furrowed as though he were desperately searching for something just beyond reach.

"How did you and your brothers come by your names?" she asked before she bit into the bread with enthusiasm.

"Our parents lacked imagination. They just named us after wherever it was they were living at the time we were born."

"I suppose you're grateful that they weren't living in Galveston when you were born."

He seemed to contemplate her answer for a moment, as though she'd made her comment in all earnestness. His jaw tensed. "I reckon I would be if I'd ever thought about it."

She had hoped for a smile, a chuckle, a laugh, but Houston Leigh appeared to be a man who did not give into lighthearted banter or teasing. That knowledge saddened her. Everyone needed smiles and laughter to replace the absence of sunshine in a stormy life. She hoped the brothers didn't share this stern outlook on life. "Do you think Dallas will want to carry on the family tradition and name our children after towns in Texas?"

"I'm not sure what names he favors." He shifted in his chair and brought one foot up, resting it on his knee.

Amelia chewed slowly on the bacon and eggs, savoring the flavors, wondering how she could gather all the information about her future husband that she didn't have. Letters could only reveal a man's thoughts. She did not know his smile, the sound of his laughter, or the way emotions might play across his features. She was incredibly curious about every aspect of him and his life. "Dallas mentioned Austin quite often in his letters."

Houston gave a brusque nod. "He's right fond of Austin. You'll like him, too. He's the sort people take to right away."

As he spoke of his younger brother, a trace of warmth flowed through his voice, reminding her of snuggling before a fire on a cold winter's night. She wanted to keep the flames flickering. "I don't remember how old Austin is."

"Sixteen."

"Then he's spared any memories of the war."

"I doubt that."

Amelia set her fork down. "But he would have been so young. Surely he doesn't remember—"

Houston slid his foot off his knee, and it hit the floor with a resounding thud. He shifted in the chair. "I'd rather not talk about the war, if you don't mind."

"No, I don't mind," she said softly, aware that she'd lost the warmth in his voice, in his manner. He clenched his jaw as though he were fighting desperately to remain where he was. She could feel the tension radiating around him, palpable in its intensity. Although more than ten long years had passed, the war still continued to rip through people's lives. "Do you think Dallas will try to break that mustang again when his leg heals?"

He scooted up in the chair, then slid back. "I let it go," he said in a voice so low she wasn't quite certain she heard him correctly.

"I beg your pardon?"

He grimaced slightly. "I set the horse free."

"Why?"

He slowly waved his large hand through the air as though it were a curtain billowing in a spring breeze. "The horse had a heavy, wavy mane and tail. That marks it as tricky and dangerous. Figured Dallas would eventually kill the horse or it would kill him." He sighed. "So I set it free."

"You said he wasn't a man you wanted to rile. Didn't that rile him?"

"He was still laid up in bed. I was long gone by the time he discovered what I'd done."

"So you'll have to deal with his anger once you return to the ranch."

"I'm hoping your presence will distract him, and he'll forget about the horse."

Amelia cleared her throat. Houston shifted his gaze to her, and she lifted an eyebrow. "So, shortly after I meet your brother in person, I'll learn whether or not he values me more than he does a horse?"

Horror swept over his face. "I didn't mean—"

"I know you didn't," Amelia said, smiling as she carefully folded her napkin and placed it on the table. "I've finished eating."

Houston bolted from the chair. "Good. I'll have

someone send up some hot water for a bath. It'll be some time before you'll have that luxury."

He crammed his hat on his head, adjusting it to the lopsided angle to which she'd grown accustomed. He slung his saddlebags over his shoulder and walked to the door in long strides that complemented his height.

"Is Dallas as tall as you?" she asked.

He halted, one hand on the doorknob. "Taller."

He opened the door and hesitated. "I'll be back in about an hour. Then we'll go get the last of the supplies." He slipped into the hallway, closing the door behind him.

Amelia shoved away from the table, walked to the washstand, and glanced in the mirror. She groaned. Her hair had come loose and was sticking out like the raised fur on an angry cat.

Little wonder Houston Leigh had avoided looking at her.

She heaved a deep sigh of longing. A warm bath. The purchase of a few supplies. Then she would begin what she was certain would be the most important journey of her life.

Chapter Three

───·❦·───

Clutching Dallas's letters to her breast, Amelia sat in front of the window and watched as the sun chased the early-morning shadows away from the dusty street. Gathering her courage had never seemed quite so difficult.

Soon Houston would come for her, and she had to be ready to travel toward a dream.

She had read each of Dallas's letters after her bath. He was not a man given to flowery prose, yet she always found beauty within his simple words. During the time they had corresponded, she had come to know the man behind the letters well enough that she had not hesitated to accept his offer of marriage.

She pressed his letters to her lips. Already, she fostered a hint of affection for Dallas Leigh. Surely, love could not be far behind.

The rapping on her door came as softly as the pale sunlight easing through her window.

Taking a shaky breath, she placed the precious letters in her carpetbag, picked up her hat, and walked to the mirror. Ignoring the bobbing bird, she worked a hatpin through the narrow brim. Although it would probably be at least another three weeks before she met her betrothed, she hoped he would recover quickly enough to meet them before the end of the journey.

She anxiously crossed the room, wrapped her trembling fingers around the doorknob, and pulled open the door. Her apprehension receded as she looked at the profile of the man standing in the hallway.

The damp ends of his black hair dragged along the collar of his duster. He smelled of soap, and she realized he'd indulged in a bath as well. She supposed the journey would hold no luxuries for him, either.

"Ready?" he asked in a low voice.

"As ready as I'll ever be, I guess." She stepped into the hallway as he walked into the room and retrieved her bag.

She could think of nothing to say as the click of the closing door echoed along the hallway, effectively drawing to a close one phase of her life. She averted her gaze from the tall man standing beside her. She didn't want him to see the doubts darting in and out like a naughty child searching for mischief: One moment they were gone and the next they were playing havoc with her emotions. She placed her palm over the watch she'd safely stored within a hidden pocket in her skirt. She imagined she could hear its steady ticking as it patiently marked the passing moments until she placed her gift into Dallas Leigh's hand, a hand she was certain was as large and as bronzed as his brother's.

"We'd best get goin'," Houston said.

Breathing deeply, she once again forced her qualms to retreat. "Yes, I suppose we should. Do you have many supplies to purchase?"

"Not many."

In silence, she followed him out of the hotel and onto the boardwalk. His strides weren't as long or as hurried as they'd been the day before. Enjoying the leisurely pace as she walked by his side, Amelia studied the clapboard buildings, the men hunched over as they drove wagons down the street, and the horses carrying riders toward destinations unknown to her. Anticipation thrummed through the warming breeze. Savoring the excitement, she hoarded the images, knowing a time would come when she'd share them with her children, her first impressions of a town that had brought her closer to her destiny.

She was so absorbed in her musings that she nearly bumped into Houston when he came to a dead halt in front of a dress shop.

He glared at the simple plank of wood as though it were a despised enemy. Considering his previous hurry to be on his way to the ranch, she thought his time would be better spent picking up the supplies he needed. She was on the verge of suggesting he move on when he took a deep breath and shoved open the door. Bells tinkled above his head, and he cringed.

"Get inside," he said in a low voice.

Baffled by his choice of stores, Amelia strolled into the small shop ahead of him. When she thought of supplies, she thought of canned goods, cooking utensils, and an assortment of odds and ends that a person would usually purchase at the mercantile or general store. She wondered if he had a wife for whom he wished to purchase some clothing. She knew very little about Houston, but it warmed her to think she might be traveling with a man who would be somewhere he obviously didn't want to be in order to obtain a gift. She imagined his wife would be as dark as he was, small, and quiet. Very quiet.

A buxom woman with bright red hair threw aside the curtains behind the counter and waltzed into the room. "I thought I heard my little bells," she exclaimed in a voice hinting at a French ancestry. Her hands fluttered over the counter. "I am Mimi St. Claire. Proprietor and expert dressmaker."

Amelia watched as Houston clenched and unclenched his hand before reaching up to remove his hat.

"Oh, my," Mimi St. Claire squeaked, pressing her hand above her bosom. She laughed nervously. "You took me unawares, sir. Shadows one moment, none zee next. What can I do for you?"

"She needs to be outfitted," Houston said in a taut voice.

"Outfitted?" Mimi questioned.

Houston gave a brusque nod.

Stunned, Amelia stared at the man. "You don't mean to purchase clothes for *me*, do you?"

"Dallas told me to get you everything you needed before we headed back."

"These are the supplies?"

"Yep."

She wrapped her fingers around his arm and pulled him away from the counter, seeking a small measure of privacy.

"You can't purchase me clothes," she whispered. He stared at her hand as though he couldn't quite figure out how it had come to be on his arm. She snapped her fingers in front of his eye, gaining his attention, and tightened her hold on his arm for emphasis. "You can't purchase me clothes," she repeated.

He shifted his gaze back to her hand. "Dallas is purchasing the clothing."

With a sigh, she released his arm. "He already purchased the tickets for my journey. I don't feel comfortable having him spend more of his hard-earned money on me. What if he changes his mind about marrying me?"

Houston's Adam's apple slid slowly up and down. "He won't change his mind."

She tilted her head slightly. "You don't think so?"

"I'm not a man who lies."

But he was a man easily offended, if the tone in his voice was any indication. One brother who was easily angered, another who was easily offended. She would have to learn to deal with both.

Fingering the collar of her worn bodice, she glanced with longing around the dress shop. "I suppose one—"

"Five."

"I couldn't possibly accept five."

Ignoring her, he directed his attention to Mimi St. Claire, who was leaning over the counter, straining to hear every word. She didn't bother to appear embarrassed at her actions, but simply straightened her back and wrapped a loose strand of red hair around her finger.

"She needs five outfits," Houston said. "Make a couple of them fancy for entertaining. We need them today."

Mimi's eyes widened. "Five? Today?" She patted her chest and smiled brightly. "Sit in zee chair, and I'll show you what I have already sewn."

With a whirl, Mimi disappeared behind the curtains as Houston walked to the corner. Instead of sitting in the chair with the delicate spindly legs that looked as though they could easily snap beneath his weight, he pressed his left shoulder against the wall.

Clasping her hands tightly together, Amelia walked across the small shop. "I can't possibly accept five—"

"Five."

She sighed deeply. "Don't I have a say in this matter?"

He took a long slow nod. "As long as you say five."

She narrowed her eyes, scrutinizing the man standing before her, trying to determine if he was teasing her. His lips curled up not at all, his eye didn't glint with mischief. If anything, he seemed more serious than before.

"Mademoiselle!" Mimi St. Claire stuck her head between the drawn curtains. "Quickly, come in here. We must show zee gentleman zee clothes."

As Amelia passed through the waving curtains, Houston set her bag on the floor and slipped his hand inside his duster pocket. He heard Mimi

St. Claire's deep-throated chuckle. Amelia's gentle laughter quickly followed, reminding him of spring rain, soothing and sweet, the kind of rain that a man simply removed his hat to enjoy as it washed over him.

Her touch had been as soft as her laughter, but he'd felt the determination in her fingers. He'd been surprised when the warmth from her small hand had penetrated the material of his duster and shirt to fan out over his skin.

He strained to hear their voices, but could decipher none of the hushed words. He wondered if Dallas had explained in his letters that Amelia would have no woman with whom she could whisper secrets. Tightening his hold on his hat, he wondered if Amelia knew she was traveling toward godawful loneliness.

She stepped between the curtains, wearing a yellow dress that had ruffles and bows sewn over it. She glanced his way with uncertainty.

Mimi St. Claire came out and waved her hand in a circle. "Turn, turn so he may see all of it."

Amelia pivoted on the balls of her feet. The dress had more ruffles in the back than in the front. Houston imagined if a strong wind blew through, it would carry Amelia Carson and that frilly dress across the plains like the petals of a dandelion.

Dallas would like that dress. He'd like it a lot. Too damn bad he'd broken his leg.

Shaking his head, Houston thought he saw relief fill Amelia's eyes. "You got something that looks like the earth?" he asked.

Mimi St. Claire's face puckered as though she'd just bitten into a lemon. "Zee earth?"

She grabbed Amelia's arm, and they disappeared behind the curtain. When next Amelia emerged, she wore a dark brown dress that perfectly matched the hat with the bird. Houston hated it.

"I didn't say dirt," he grumbled. "Something that looks like the earth. Something like clover."

"Clover?" Mimi asked. "You want green?"

Houston nodded slightly, not really certain what he wanted, just certain he'd know when he saw it.

Mimi rolled her eyes. "Trust men to speak in riddles. Why could he not just say green?"

She pulled a smiling Amelia back behind the curtain. Houston wondered how often Amelia would smile in West Texas, when the sun beat down on her, the dust rose up to choke her, and the nearest neighbor was a day's ride away on a fast horse.

He wished he could ignore her laughter coming from the back room, but he embraced the melodious sound as easily as his fingers stroked the delicate embroidery threads buried deep within his pocket. He no longer had a reason to keep the cloth on his person. He'd identified himself. He could give the embroidered linen back to her or stuff it into his saddlebags. Instead he found himself constantly rubbing the only soft thing in his life.

And staring at the curtain, waiting impatiently to see Amelia again, the sparkle in her eyes, the way her lips curled up as though she found this whole situation amusing.

The curtain billowed out and she slipped

through, wearing a dress the shade of clover. It had no frills, no bows, no lace, no ruffles. Simply made, it hugged her curves as a lover might.

Warily studying him, she turned slowly, keeping her gaze on him until she was forced to snap her head around. "You don't like it either?" she asked.

"I like it just fine," he said as he settled his hat on his head and picked up her bag. "Get it and anything else you want. Take your time. I'm gonna fetch the wagon."

He ignored her crestfallen expression and walked out of the shop, the door rattling behind him. He'd hurt her feelings again, but this time he'd had no choice. If he'd stayed in that room, he would have crossed that wooden floor and trailed his finger along the delicate column of her ivory throat.

Just one finger, just one touch, just one sweet moment . . . but buried deep within his own personal hell, he knew he had no right to claim any sweet moments, especially from the woman pledged to his brother.

Breathing heavily, he came to a staggering stop and dropped his chin to his chest. After years of wanting and waiting, he finally had the opportunity to prove himself. He had only to deliver Amelia Carson safely and *untouched* into Dallas's arms.

He'd never realized how heavy a burden trust was.

AMELIA STARED AT the door, willing the man who'd just stormed through it to return. One moment he seemed interested in her wardrobe, and the next, he was walking out as though he couldn't escape fast enough.

"He does not like zis one either?" Mimi asked, irritation laced through her voice.

"No, he did like this one. It's me he doesn't like."

Mimi threw up a hand in a dramatic gesture. "Nonsense! He adores you."

Amelia walked into the back room. "Actually, I'm a burden to him."

Mimi began unbuttoning the back of the dress. "Oh, little one, I think you must not be wise in zee ways of love. A man sees a woman as a burden only if he thinks he cannot please her."

"All he has to do is escort me to his brother's ranch. How hard can that be?"

"That, little one, depends on zee journey. For you, it will be easy. Your heart belongs to another, yes?"

With the hope that she would indeed give her heart to Dallas shortly after meeting him, Amelia nodded.

"When a heart belongs to no one, zee journey is never easy." With a flourish, Mimi spun around. "Now, let's see what else I have that looks like zee ground!"

An hour later, Amelia breathed a deep sigh of relief and walked out of Mimi's shop wearing her own clothes. She would save the new clothing until they neared the ranch.

"Did you get five outfits?" a deep voice asked.

Amelia spun around. Within the late-morning shadows, Houston leaned against the wall.

"Yes, she just needs you to pay for them, and she'll wrap them up. Although I can't imagine what I could possibly want with so many clothes."

He shoved away from the wall. "Dallas figures other women will come farther west once you get there. He thinks he'll be the king of West Texas." He held her gaze. "You'll be his queen."

"Is he that successful?"

"He's got a good start, he's smart, and he's not a man to let anything stand in his way."

"Are you successful?"

He shook his head. "Nah, I leave the glory of success to Dallas and men like him. I'd just like to watch the sunset in peace."

He tugged on his hat, and Amelia had the feeling something deeper dwelled within his words, something he had no desire to discuss. Although she could not see it, she was certain that he'd just thrown up a wall.

"Take a look around and see if you can think of anything else you need while I purchase the clothes. If not, we'll be leavin'."

He went into Mimi's shop and returned a few minutes later with two large parcels. "Did you think of anything?" he asked.

"No, I feel guilty about all that you've purchased already."

"Don't feel guilty. Dallas won't begrudge the purchase. He's generous to a fault when it comes to those he cares about."

"And you think he'll come to care about me?"

"He already does, Miss Carson. Give you my word on that," he said as he stepped off the boardwalk.

Amelia's apprehensions began melting away. Perhaps the man behind the letters was as she had imagined him. She thought of Houston's comment that she needed clothing for entertaining. One day she would delight the ladies of West Texas with parties and social calls—just as her mother had charmed the women from the neighboring plantations. Perhaps as the wife of a rancher, she would find a semblance of the life she'd known before the war, a life she'd thought would one day be hers.

A life shattered by men in blue and men in tattered gray.

Shuddering, she squeezed her eyes shut and forced the past back into the recesses of her mind. Her future lay before her, clear and untarnished, with a man who had shown her nothing but compassion and respect in his letters.

Amelia came to a halt as Houston placed the packages in the back of a wagon laden with supplies. A brown horse, tethered at the rear, nudged Houston's shoulder. He reached into his duster pocket and brought out an apple. The mare grabbed it and began chomping greedily.

As Houston pulled a tarpaulin over the supplies, securing it in place with ropes, Amelia traced her fingers over an emblem burned into the side of the wagon. An "A" leaned over until its right side touched the left side of a "D."

"What's this?" she asked.

"Dallas's brand. An 'A' and a 'D.' Joined."

Joined. As in a partnership. As in a marriage. "Has he always had this brand?"

"Nope. In the beginning, he just had the 'D.'

He added the 'A' when you accepted his offer of marriage."

Deeply touched, she wished Dallas could have shared this moment when she discovered his gift. "He never mentioned it in his letters."

"Reckon he wanted it to be a surprise."

"A brand is important, isn't it?"

"The choosing of it isn't something a man takes lightly. Neither is the changing of it."

"Is this why you think he cares about me?"

"It's one of the reasons."

"And the other reasons?"

"I reckon they'll be real obvious when we get to the ranch." He tied a final knot in the rope. "Ready?"

More than ready, she nodded. He placed his large hands on her waist. She grabbed his shoulders as he swung her onto the wagon. She sat and arranged her skirt, trying not to think about how the warmth of his hands had soaked through her worn clothing. Dallas's hands would be that warm, his shoulders that steady.

Houston climbed in and settled onto the bench seat beside her. He released the brake and slapped the reins over the backs of the four mules harnessed before them. "Well, Miss Carson, take a last look around because where we're headed there's nothing but open land, cows, and cowboys."

Chapter Four

$\mathcal{I}$t was well past noon before they reached a small stream. As Houston watered and fed the mules and his horse, Amelia sat on a log, using a fork to dig beans out of a can that he had opened for her.

She couldn't hear his words, only his voice, as he talked to the mare. Neither of them had spoken as the wagon had traveled away from Fort Worth. From time to time, she had glanced over her shoulder. He had never once looked back.

He crossed the clearing and hunkered down before her, his right shoulder close to her drawn-up knees. His black duster parted, revealing the gun strapped to his thigh. It served as a gentle reminder that she was headed toward an untamed land.

"My apologies for the simple meal, but I didn't want to take the time for a fire," he said quietly. "We'll have a better meal come evening."

"I'm truly grateful that you thought to bring some canned goods."

Removing his hat, he studied her. "You've eaten worse."

She smiled softly. "As a matter of fact, I have."

"Yep, me, too."

Standing, he settled his hat on his head. "You can wash up by the stream. We'll be leaving soon."

Amelia rose and began to walk toward the water.

"Miss Carson?"

She glanced over her shoulder. His profile was to her again, and he seemed to be studying something in the distance. "Yes, Mr. Leigh?"

"Once, when I stopped by a stream to wash the dust off, I laid my hat beside me. A raccoon carted it away." He ground his jaw back and forth. "If you were to take off your hat while you were washing up, some critter might haul it away."

"I'm so grateful you shared that with me. I'll make certain I guard the hat well."

She thought he grimaced before he turned away. She strolled to the water's edge and knelt beside the stream. The hat, with all its accessories, weighed heavy on her head. She had considered removing the bird or some of the ribbons. She had even considered pretending that she had never received the hat, but she had no talent for telling lies. Dallas would see through her deceit, and she didn't want to risk hurting his feelings after he'd gone to so much trouble.

She dipped her hands into the cool water. She couldn't recall Houston's ever initiating a conversation between them. He politely answered her questions, but for the most part he kept quiet. Yet he had openly shared the story of the raccoon and his hat, although he had appeared uncomfortable reciting his tale as though he had feared offending her. She imagined he had been quite put out not to have his hat, since he seldom removed it.

She caught sight of her reflection wavering in the water, the bird bobbing with her movements. The hat was so incredibly unattractive. She wore it because Dallas had sent it to her, because it was a gift and she had received so few in her life.

She glanced over her shoulder and wondered if Houston wasn't offering her a gift as well: an honorable way to lose the hat without hurting anyone's feelings.

She rose and walked to the wagon where he was tightening the ropes that held the tarpaulin in place over the supplies. "You don't like my hat," she stated in as flat a tone as she could manage.

He visibly stiffened, his hands stilling. "No, ma'am." He removed his hat and met her gaze. "I think it's the most godawful ugly thing I've ever seen."

Amelia released a tiny squeal and covered her mouth.

Regret reshaped his features. "My apologies, Miss Carson. I had no right—"

"No!" She held up a hand to stay his apology and moved her other hand away from her face to reveal her smile. "I think it's awful, too."

"Then why in God's name are you wearing it?" he asked, clearly stunned.

"Because it was a gift from your brother."

He slapped his hat against his duster. "Well, it's not very practical. Your nose is already turning red."

Amelia pressed her fingers to the tip of her nose. She could feel the slight prickling of her skin. She had worn a bonnet to protect her face when she'd worked in the cotton fields following the war. She'd hoped never to have to wear a bonnet again. "I'm not overly fond of bonnets," she said as she gnawed on her lower lip.

"If a raccoon were to carry your hat away, you could borrow the hat I bought for Austin," he offered.

"Do you think he would mind?"

He shrugged. "If he minds, he can keep his old hat. I just bought it because I didn't know what else to get him, and we don't get into town much. He might not even want it."

"I don't want to hurt Dallas's feelings. The hat was a gift—"

"The hat was a way for me to recognize you. You've been recognized."

A twinge of guilt still pricked at her conscience. "Do you think he'll wear the band I embroidered around his hat?"

"No, ma'am. I can guarantee you he won't be wearing it."

"I could just pack the hat away, I suppose."

"Got no room in the wagon for anything else."

She knew that for the lie it was. A little less than half the wagon remained empty. "You really dislike the hat."

"If you pack it away, there's gonna come a day when company's gonna come to call, and he's gonna want you to wear it . . . in front of people who need to respect him. The way I see it, in the long run, you'll be doing him a favor if it goes no farther west than this."

"Are there raccoons around here?"

"Yes, ma'am."

"I think I need to give my face a good scrubbing."

He nodded. "I'll find Austin's hat."

Amelia walked to the stream and knelt. Reaching up, she removed the hat and studied it. Dallas had bought it for her so he could identify her. It had served its purpose. She set it beside her and viciously scrubbed her face, praying he would never discover her deceit. She lifted her skirt and wiped the cool water from her face before casting a sideways glance at the hat. It remained untouched.

She rose to her feet and walked to the wagon. Houston handed her a black broad-brimmed hat.

"Are you sure Austin won't mind?" she asked as she adjusted the positioning of the hat on her head.

"I'm sure." He placed his hands on her waist and lifted her onto the wagon, then settled in beside her.

"I feel guilty," she said as he reached for the reins.

"Don't."

He flicked the reins and the mules began to pull the wagon across the stream. Amelia waited until the wagon had cleared the shallow stream before glancing back. The hat remained where she'd left it.

"Do you really think a raccoon will take it away?" she asked.

"Yes, ma'am. Maybe not today or tomorrow. But someday."

THE FIRE CRACKLED softly, shooting sparks into the night. Despite the vastness of the black sky, an intimacy dwelled within the small camp, an intimacy that hadn't existed in Fort Worth. Amelia wondered if perhaps it existed here because there were only the two of them, alone, surrounded by nothing but the dark shadows of the unknown.

She stole a sideways glance at her traveling companion as he sat on a nearby log and forked beans into his mouth. They had traveled through the afternoon in silence, her thoughts directed toward her hat and the raccoon, his thoughts . . . she had no idea where his thoughts had traveled.

He had set up a tent, tended the animals, and cooked a meal, speaking only when necessary to convey his needs. As he prepared the camp, he had moved with an effortless grace that always kept the right side of his body facing her. She wasn't certain if he sought to protect his scarred face or to protect her from the sight of it. Perhaps it was a little of both.

"Are you married?" she asked quietly.

He jumped as though she'd fired a rifle into the night. His fork clattered onto the tin plate and flipped to the ground. He picked it up, wiped it on the leg of his trousers, and started moving the few remaining beans around on his plate. "Nope."

He jammed the bean-laden fork into his mouth.

She knew his parents had lived in Texas when their children were born. She wondered if they'd lived elsewhere. "Did you grow up in Texas?" she asked, hoping to entice him into discussing his childhood, a childhood that had included Dallas.

"Nope. Lived in Texas when I was boy. Grew up outside of Texas."

She furrowed her brow. "When did you leave Texas?"

"When the war started. When Pa enlisted, he signed me and Dallas up to go with him."

Threads of Dallas's letters wove through her mind. His military life had astounded her, given her cause for pride, but she had thought Dallas was nearly thirty and based on that knowledge, she'd assumed he had enlisted near the end of the war. She wondered if she had misread his letters, misjudged his age. "How old were you?"

"Twelve. Dallas was fourteen."

"You were children," she whispered, remembering so many young faces parading along the dirt road in front of their plantation.

"Pa thought we were old enough. Dallas was commanding his own unit by the time he was sixteen."

The food she'd eaten rolled over in her stomach. "Yes, he gave me a detailed accounting of his accomplishments. I just didn't stop to think how young he would have been when he enlisted. Sometimes, I wonder if it wasn't actually a children's war."

He moved to the fire. "More coffee?"

"No, thank you."

She watched as he poured the black brew into his tin cup before moving back. She had a feeling his movement to the fire was his way of signaling that he wanted to end that particular vein of conversation. Since he had an aversion to talking about the war, she decided to oblige him.

"Could I ask a favor of you?" she asked.

Houston had been waging a battle all evening, fighting to keep his attention focused on the writhing flames dancing in the night instead of on the woman sitting beside him. He didn't think Dallas would appreciate how much pleasure it gave him to watch Amelia, but the lilt of her voice, a soft southern drawl that hinted at no hurry to be anywhere, the hope echoed in her words, was his undoing. Admitting defeat, he shifted slightly, met her gaze, and nodded.

"When your brother and I wrote each other, we didn't describe ourselves, which is why we had to send something for identification. I was wondering if I could tell you what I think he looks like and you tell me if I'm wrong."

"I could just tell you what he looks like."

She shook her head vigorously. "No, I want to see how close I am to imagining him as he truly is."

She sat on a small log, looking like a little girl waiting to be handed a piece of candy. He was willing to give her the whole jar, but in deference to his older brother, Houston merely shrugged. "Go ahead."

She bit her lower lip. "All right. I know he's tall, since you told me that. And I always thought of him as having black hair, like yours. Only it wouldn't be as long. I think his hair might just cover his ears. It wouldn't reach down to his shoulders."

Houston nodded slowly, and her eyes brightened. He imagined the fun Dallas would have keeping those eyes shining. She seemed incredibly easy to please.

She closed her eyes a moment, then popped them open wide. "Blue eyes."

Damn! He hated to disappoint her. He shook his head slowly. "Austin got our ma's blue eyes."

"Are Dallas's brown, like yours?"

"Same color, but he's got two."

She leaned forward, pity filling her eyes, and he wished he'd just kept his mouth shut and not tried to tease her. What the hell did he know about teasing? For some reason, he wanted to hear her laugh again as she had with Mimi St. Claire. And he wanted absolutely none of her pity.

"How old were you when you were wounded?" she asked quietly.

"Fifteen. Thought you wanted to know about Dallas."

Straightening, she gave him a quivering smile, and he knew he'd hurt her feelings again. Damn, he hated when he did that.

"You're right," she admitted. "My interests lie with Dallas." She furrowed her delicate brow. "His nose is straight, not too big, not too small, and it sits right in the middle of his face."

He was on the verge of asking her where else she thought she might find a nose when he noticed the glint in her eyes. She'd already forgiven him for his rudeness, was teasing him. She did it with such ease. He envied her that ability and could do no more than nod.

"He has a strong jaw," she said.

He shook his head slightly, and the sparkle dimmed in her eyes.

"He doesn't have a strong jaw?" she asked.

"Ain't never seen it wrestle a steer to the ground."

The sparkle that lit up her eyes was enough to blind a man. And her smile. Her laughter. Dear God, but a man could start to believe in heaven and angels and an eternity of peace.

She wiped a tear of joy from the corner of her eye. "I meant that his jaw was well-defined, like yours." She reached out and trailed her fingers along his jaw.

He jerked back as though she'd seared his flesh with a red-hot branding iron. He could see the hurt and confusion swimming in her eyes, but he couldn't explain to her about the needs that surged through his body with her simple touch, a touch that belonged exclusively to his brother.

"I'm sorry," she stammered.

He crouched before the fire. "Nothing to apologize for. Tomorrow's gonna be a long day. You'd best get some rest. You can take the lantern into the tent with you. I'll want to leave at dawn."

"Shall I wash the plate in that bucket of hot water?"

"Nope. I heated that up for you. Just leave your plate by the log, and I'll take care of it."

Picking up the lantern and bucket of water, Amelia began walking toward the tent.

"Miss Carson?"

Stopping, Amelia turned around. He stood

beside the fire, the shadows playing over his profile. "Yes, Mr. Leigh."

"Dallas has a mustache."

"A mustache?"

"Yeah, one of those big bushy ones. The sides fall down around his mouth. Heard a woman say once that he was handsome as sin."

"Thank you for sharing that with me. I never imagined him with a mustache. Good night, Mr. Leigh."

"'Night, ma'am."

She walked into the canvas tent, the tarpaulin he'd used to cover the supplies serving as her floor. She set the lantern on the small table and opened her bag. Gingerly, she brought out a stack of letters. She untied the ribbon and removed the letter from the first envelope. Sitting on the edge of the narrow cot, she tried to conjure up an image of Dallas Leigh as she now knew him to be. Brown eyes. Thick mustache.

April 21, 1875

Dear Miss Carson:

I read in your advertisement that you are seeking a husband. If you are still available, I am seeking a wife.

I am in good health, have all my teeth, and consider myself fairly easy on the eyes. I have land, cattle, and a dream to build a cattle empire the likes of which this great state has never seen.

Please write back if you are not yet married,
and I will be pleased to bore you with the details.

Yours,
Dallas Leigh

AN HONORABLE MAN would have looked away.

But Houston Leigh had never been an honorable man.

He lay on his pallet beside the fire, the covers drawn over him, his gaze riveted on the tent.

He hadn't realized until he'd banked the fire and thrown the camp into near darkness that the light from the lantern created shadows inside the tent, shadows visible from the outside.

He could see the woman sitting on the cot reading a letter. Reading with those green eyes of clover that darkened each time she spoke.

She had been reading for some time now. He liked to watch her put one letter away and remove another from the envelope. Her movements were elegant, refined, practiced, as though she often read the letters. He wondered if she was reading the letters Dallas had written her. He wondered exactly what Dallas had told her about his brothers, then he damned himself for caring.

She set the letters on a small table beside the cot, the table that held the lantern. She raised her arms over her head and reached toward the top of the tent.

When she lowered her arms, she began to remove the pins from her hair. He watched as the shadow of her hair tumbled over her shoulders and along her back.

His hands clenched, and he was powerless to look away. She reached into her bag and withdrew her brush. Slowly, she pulled the brush through her hair.

He counted the strokes.

And envied the brush.

And envied his brother, who would have the privilege of watching the woman with no canvas cloth separating them.

A hundred strokes. A hundred long, torturous strokes.

She braided her hair. He thought it a crime to confine something so beautiful. To confine her glorious hair into a braid, to confine a lovely woman to an isolated ranch in West Texas.

Slowly, she peeled away her clothing, every stitch, until nothing remained but the shadow of her flesh. His body reacted to the sight and his hand fisted around the blanket. Sweat beaded his brow, his chest, his throat.

He prayed for a cool breeze to whisper along his flesh and remove some of the heat, but the heat only intensified when she dropped a rag into the bucket and bent over to retrieve it. She tilted her head back, lifted her arms, squeezed the cloth, and let the drops rain over her face, her shoulders . . . her breasts.

Leisurely, she wiped the cloth along her throat, following the trail of droplets coursing down her body.

Houston imagined he could feel the pulse of

her heart, the warmth of her flesh. He imagined it was his hand gliding over her body instead of the cloth, his hand touching her curves, his lips leaving a damp trail over her skin.

Rolling to his side, he brought his knees toward his chest and huddled like a child trying to protect himself from the aching loneliness. A solitary tear slid along his cheek.

He had his horses. He had his solitude. And on nights when the moon was full, he could look across the vast prairie and hear nothing but the lowing of distant cattle, the whisper of the wind, and the promise of tomorrow.

And if there were moments like this one, when he wished for more, he had but to catch a glimpse of his reflection in the still waters of a pond to remember that he deserved less.

So much less.

Chapter Five

Amelia awoke to the scent of strong coffee permeating the air. She had a feeling it would be as thick as molasses on a winter's day. Grimacing slightly, she rolled off the cot. Every muscle, every bone she possessed protested her movements.

Standing, she pressed her fists into the small of her back and stretched backward. She wondered if she would be better off walking part of the day. Sitting in a jostling wagon was hard on the body.

Using the remaining water from last night, she quickly washed her face, then separated the strands of her braid, brushed her hair, and swept it into a coil. She glanced at her clothing, wishing now that she'd taken the time to wash it while they were near a creek. She had no idea if they would have water every night.

She carefully placed all her belongings into her carpetbag, folded the blankets that had covered the cot, and put out the flame in the lantern. It was a childish thing, really, to sleep with a flame burning beside her.

Cautiously, not certain what she would find beyond the tent this morning, she slipped her fingers between the tent opening and peered through the small slit. She could see Houston crouched before a boulder, a razor in his hand. He had set a jagged mirror no larger than her palm on the rock so it rested against the tree. He tilted his head slightly and slid the razor up his throat, scraping away the shaving lather and his morning beard.

Amelia turned away from the opening, and with excitement thrumming through her veins, she snapped open her bag and reached inside. She withdrew her mirror, a large hand mirror that had belonged to her mother.

She rushed out of the tent, grateful that at last she had a way to thank him for all he'd done for her: the tent, the fire, the meals, the warm water. "Mr. Leigh!"

He turned, a furrow creasing his brow.

"You can use my mirror," she said ecstatically as she thrust it toward him.

Waving his hand through the air, he jumped back as though she had offered him a snake.

"God Almighty, get that away from me!"

Amelia hugged the mirror against her chest. "But it's so much larger than yours. I thought it would make shaving easier."

"I don't even know why I bother to shave," he mumbled as he picked up the small mirror and dropped it into a box along with the rest of his shaving gear. "Do whatever it is you need to do to be ready. Coffee and biscuits are by the fire. We'll be leavin' right after breakfast."

Tears filled her eyes as she watched him rush out of the camp as though his life depended on it. She pressed the mirror closer to her chest. She wondered if he used the smaller mirror so he wouldn't have to see all of his face at the same time, if in small pieces, perhaps he could pretend he wasn't disfigured.

He'd only been fifteen when he had been wounded. She tried to imagine how devastating it would have been for a fifteen-year-old boy to awaken from battle to discover that a portion of his face had been ravaged by enemy fire. An older man who had learned not to place much value in appearances might have adjusted, but a young man who had yet to court and marry might have withdrawn from the world.

Every conversation they had shared—with the exception of one—had begun when she had asked a question. She had assumed that he considered her a burden. Now, she wondered if perhaps he simply had no experience at socializing. He always looked as though he was searching for something. Could he possibly be searching for something to say?

She held out her mirror and studied her reflection. She wasn't prone to vanity, but she couldn't imagine avoiding the sight of her face. She thought of him tugging his hat brim down, leaning against walls, and standing in shadows. She had a feeling Houston Leigh carried other scars that were visible only to the heart.

HOUSTON KNELT BESIDE the creek, habit forcing him to stir up the water before he leaned over to fill the canteens. Still waters could throw a man's reflection back at him.

He dropped to his backside, closed the canteens, and rubbed his hands over his face. He owed her another apology. His reaction to her kindness had frightened her. He'd seen it in those eyes of clover that reflected her heart as openly as a book. They had been filled with joy when he'd turned around, and he'd walked away leaving them filled with despair.

He felt as though he'd just squashed a beautiful butterfly for doing little more than innocently landing on his shoulder.

He closed his eye against the memory of last night. He owed her an apology for that as well, even though she had no way of knowing what had transpired by the campfire after she had walked into the tent. How did a man apologize for taking advantage of a situation without causing more harm?

One way or another he needed to make amends. His lustful thoughts had no place on this journey.

He picked up a stick and drew an "A" in the mud. He traced the right side until the groove was deep and water began to seep into it. Then he carved the "D" and stared at his brother's brand, emblazoning the sight in his mind and on his heart.

He knew that the marriage ceremony that would take place when they arrived at the ranch was only a formality. As far as Dallas was concerned, Amelia had become his wife the day he had joined her initial to his. Houston would do well to remember that.

He tossed the muddy stick aside, forced himself to his feet, and wandered back to camp, his apology tagging along like an unwanted puppy.

He stopped dead in his tracks, his practiced words forgotten as he stared at Amelia walking through the camp, her hand covering her left eye. She tripped over a rock, stumbled, caught her balance, glanced down, her eye still covered, and spoke to the rock as though it were some child who had wandered across her path. "Oh, I didn't see you."

She lifted her gaze and continued to roam the small area, her skirt coming dangerously close to the fire.

"What do you think you're doing?" he bellowed.

She spun around. Her cheeks flamed red as she lowered her hand. "I was trying to see the world as you see it."

He hunkered down before the fire and poured the remaining coffee over the low flames. "Believe me, you don't want to see the world as I see it."

With small hesitant steps, she eased closer to the fire, wringing her hands. He knew he should apologize now, but damn if he could remember the words he wanted to use.

"I've noticed that you try to keep . . . your . . . your right side facing me. I thought it was because you were trying to spare me the sight of your scars . . ."

Her words sliced through him like a knife. If he could, he'd spare her his presence altogether. Damn Dallas. All six bullets wouldn't be enough satisfaction.

"I realize now that your vision is hampered," she continued.

"I'm like a horse that wears blinders on one side, so just stay to the right of me," he said gruffly.

"I didn't mean to embarrass you."

"You didn't embarrass me. You just came dang close to setting your skirt on fire."

"Oh." She gnawed on her lower lip. "At least you don't have to squint when you aim a rifle."

His gaze hardened on hers. Sympathy filled those green eyes, along with the tears.

"I was trying to think of a reason why you might be grateful that you lost an eye. I know it's a silly reason, but sometimes when I'm bothered by something if I can find a reason to be grateful—"

Drawing himself up to his full height, he glared down on her. "Do you know what would have made me grateful, Miss Carson?"

She shook her head slightly.

"If I'd lost both eyes."

As DUSK SETTLED in, Amelia scrubbed her blouse viciously in the warm bucket of water Houston had brought her—in silence. He hadn't spoken a full sentence since that morning. He'd grunted, yepped, noped, and for the most part left her alone.

They'd set up camp a little earlier than they did yesterday because he wanted to keep them near water as long as possible. He'd shot a hare for the evening meal. Amelia had wanted to crawl into the dirt and hide when he strode into camp with the hare and his rifle. How could she have said what she did this morning? How could she have thought he'd be grateful for the loss of an eye or the scarring of a face that she was certain would have made women swoon with its rugged beauty?

She knew she could apologize a hundred times, but that wasn't what Houston Leigh wanted . . . or needed. He needed to be accepted as he was, to learn that he didn't have to hug walls or view life through shadows of his own making.

Rising, she slapped her blouse over the side of the wagon, smoothing out the wrinkles so the material could dry through the night. She trailed her fingers over Dallas's brand. She had expected so much more from this trip: laughter, stolen kisses, promises of happiness.

She should leave Houston to mope around in the world he had no desire to share. She should focus her thoughts on Dallas and how she could best make him happy. She wasn't learning much about him from his brother, but perhaps if she read his letters again, she would discover something she'd missed.

She dumped the water out of the bucket, straightened her back with a sigh, and began walking toward the tent and solitude.

A horse's whinny caught her attention. Glancing toward the area where Houston had tethered the mules, she stumbled to a stop.

Houston sat on a log, his left side to her so she was not visible to him. He'd laid a checkerboard on a tree stump. Beside his feet lay his folded duster, his hat on top of it.

He was leaner than she'd expected, and yet

his shoulders fanned out as he planted his elbow on his thigh and cupped his chin in his palm. He had rolled up his sleeves, and she could see the strength in his forearm. Before him, his horse snorted.

"You sure?" Houston asked.

The horse bobbed her head.

"All right," Houston replied and moved a black checker piece across the board. He promptly picked up his own red disk and jumped the black one he'd just moved.

The horse whinnied, dipped her head, and nudged the checkerboard off the tree stump.

"God damn! You're a sorry loser," Houston whispered harshly.

Laughing, Amelia approached the duo. In one seamless movement, Houston grabbed his hat, settled it on his head, sprang to his feet, and spun around.

"Thought you were washin' your clothes," he said from beneath the shadows of his brim.

She took no offense at his actions, but the sadness swept through her. He trusted his horse, but not her. She fought to keep her feelings from showing on her face as she rubbed the horse's shoulder. "I was, but it doesn't take long to wash a blouse." She eyed him speculatively. "I suppose I should have offered to wash your shirt."

"That's not necessary. On a cattle drive, a man gets used to having dirty clothes for a while."

"But we're not on a cattle drive. I'll wash your shirt tomorrow."

He opened his mouth as though to protest, and then snapped it shut.

Amelia pressed her face against the horse's neck. "I never mentioned that I think your horse is beautiful. I thought she was brown, but sometimes when the sun hits her coat just right, she looks red."

"She's a sorrel. Got speed and endurance bred into her, and she's smart as a whip."

She studied the man who was watching the horse with obvious affection. She remembered his description of the horse that had broken Dallas's leg. "You know a lot about horses."

"I'm a mustanger. It's my job to know a horse's temperament. With mustangs, it's usually easy. Their coloring gives them away. A dun with a black mane and tail is hardy, an albino is worthless, a black is a good horse unless he has a wavy tail and mane."

"That's amazing," she said quietly, more impressed with how much he'd spoken rather than what he'd said. "Do you raise them?"

"Startin' to. They used to run wild over Texas, but they're gettin' harder to find so I've taken to breedin' 'em."

She rubbed the horse's muzzle. "What's her name?"

"Sorrel." He lifted a shoulder in a careless shrug. "Reckon I got as much imagination as my parents."

She laughed lightly, delighted with the conversation. Although he still wore his hat, he had relaxed his stance. He appeared to be more at ease with horses than with people. She wondered what would make him comfortable around her, what would have to happen in order for him to leave his hat on the ground. "I play checkers. Probably better than your horse."

He narrowed his eye. "My horse is pretty good."

She tilted her chin. "I'm better."

"You willin' to put that claim to a test?"

She'd thought he would never ask, but decided against showing too much enthusiasm. She didn't want to frighten away the easy companionship that was settling in beneath the shade. She simply waltzed to the log where he'd been sitting and tilted up her face, offering the challenge, "Why not?"

He shot across the short space like a bullet fired from a gun, gathered his playing board and pieces, and set them carefully on the tree stump. He playfully shoved Sorrel aside when the horse nudged his shoulder. "This ain't your game. Get outta here." Then he dropped down, sitting back on his haunches, and the game began.

Amelia had never seen anyone concentrate so hard on a game. Houston balanced himself on the balls of his feet, his elbow resting on his thigh, his chin in his palm, studying each move she made as though each move were equally important.

She remembered playing checkers with her father before the war. Their games went quickly, and usually ended with both of them laughing, neither of them winning. She was beginning to understand why Houston's horse had tipped over the board.

"My father taught me to play checkers," she said. "If I thought I was going to lose, I'd move the pieces when he wasn't looking. He always pretended not to notice."

"You say that like you loved him."

"Of course I loved him. Very much. He was my father. Didn't you love your father?"

"Not particularly."

She sensed from the tightening of his jaw that he might have regretted voicing his feelings.

"Your move," he grumbled.

She promptly removed another one of his pieces from the board and settled in for the long wait as he contemplated his strategy. With his thumb, he tipped his hat off his brow. His attention clearly focused on the game, she was certain he didn't realize that he'd allowed the shadows to slip away from his face. She welcomed the opportunity to view more than his profile. The black patch was larger than many she'd seen. She supposed that he wanted to leave as few scars visible as he could. Her fingers flexed, and just as she had when she had first met him, she felt an overwhelming desire to touch the unsightly scars with compassion. She imagined holding him to her breast, easing the pain that still lingered within his remaining eye.

An unexpected warmth suffused her as though she'd wandered too close to a roaring blaze. She balled her hands into tight fists to stop her fingers from trembling, from reaching toward a face that fascinated her with the history it revealed. Houston's marred features left no doubt that he'd fought in the war. She wondered if Dallas's countenance revealed as much.

"Was Dallas wounded during the war?" she asked.

Houston tugged on the brim of his hat, bringing the shadows home. "Nope."

She chastised herself, wondering if she'd ever remember how quickly talk of the war distanced Houston. Although he sat across from her, she sensed that he was retreating. She wanted desperately to keep him near.

"Does Dallas play?" she asked, grateful to see the stiffness roll out of Houston's shoulders as he leaned forward.

"With all he has goin', I don't imagine he has time."

"Don't the two of you ever play?"

He reached toward a piece, then pulled back his hand without touching or moving the disk. "No."

He scrutinized the board with such intensity that Amelia wished she had planned to lose. With a sigh, he moved a piece forward, placing it so she had no choice but to jump over and claim it. She was certain he intended to forfeit his piece in order to gain two of hers, but she didn't think it would be enough of a sacrifice for him to win. She somehow knew that her winning would also be her loss.

She slipped her fingers beneath the board and quickly tossed it off the stump.

"What the—" He glared at her with obvious displeasure.

Amelia smiled sheepishly. "I thought I might lose."

"You knew darn good and well that you weren't gonna lose."

He reached for the board, and Amelia wrapped her fingers around his arm. He stilled, the muscles beneath her fingers tensing. "It was only a game. You're supposed to have fun when you're playing a game."

"I was havin' fun," he said gruffly.

"You were?"

He nodded, but the muscles beneath her hand didn't relax.

"Then let's play again." She settled into place while he set up the game. She allowed him to have five moves before she dumped the board over.

"Dang it!" he roared.

"You weren't having fun," she said.

"I sure as heck was. I was gonna win that time."

She smiled sweetly. "No, you weren't."

"You're aggravating, you know that?" he said as he collected his board and pieces.

"Does Dallas smile more often than you do?" she asked.

"Everyone smiles more than I do." He laid the board on the stump and put the pieces into place. "Go ahead and move."

Amelia leaned forward and placed her elbow on the stump of the tree, cradling her chin in her palm. "Why don't you smile?"

He averted his gaze, and Amelia studied his perfect profile, imagining how he might have looked if a portion of his face hadn't been torn to shreds when he was a young man. Women would have fallen over themselves to gain his attention. They might have said he was handsome as sin.

He certainly had the temperament of the devil.

"You feel up to riding?" he asked.

His words startled her. The shadows were lengthening. "You want to travel at night?"

He drew his gaze back to hers. "No, I just want to show you somethin' if you feel up to riding. Of course, you'll have to ride on the horse with me."

She glanced at Sorrel and the saddle on the ground. She hadn't ridden in years, not since her father had died. A horse wasn't nearly as wide as the seat of a wagon. She wouldn't be able to avoid the accidental brushing of thighs or elbows. She wouldn't be able to ignore the closeness of Houston's body. Her mouth went dry with the thought, her heart pounding. He wanted to share something with her. No matter how small, friendship was built on sharing. "What are you going to show me?"

"If I could describe it, I wouldn't have to show you."

She rose from the log. "Then I'd like to see it."

A few minutes later, he led Sorrel over to her and lifted her onto the saddle. She clung to the pommel as he slipped a booted foot into the stirrup and threw a leg over the back of the horse.

Reaching around her, he took hold of the reins. "Relax," he ordered. "You'll make the horse nervous."

"I am relaxed," she squeaked, nestled between his thighs, her shoulder bumping against his chest.

"Yeah, and I was having fun playing checkers," he said in a low voice as he prodded the horse forward.

The gently rolling plains stretched out before them. She glanced over her shoulder, but Fort

Worth was beyond her vision, a piece of her past now. Her future lay ahead.

Sorrel plodded up a steep rise. When they reached the crest of the hill, Houston brought the horse to a halt, dismounted, and gazed toward the horizon.

"See where the sun touches the land?" he asked in a reverent voice.

"Yes."

"That's where you'll be living."

Amelia admired the tranquil splendor of the distant site. Lavender and blue hues swept across the sky, reached down, and melted into the green horizon.

"See all the people?" he asked.

"No."

Too late she realized his question required no answer. She glanced down. The dark depths of his eye held a profound sadness, and the purpose of his question struck her hard with its intensity. She looked back at the majestic land, the scattered trees, the vast emptiness.

"Who will you talk to, Miss Carson?" he asked.

"I'll talk with my husband."

"And when he's not there?"

"Our children."

"I don't know what Dallas told you in his letters, but you're heading into a loneliness so deep that it hurts the heart."

"Only if you let it, Mr. Leigh."

Houston didn't know if he'd ever heard words spoken with so much determination or if he'd ever seen anyone look as serene as Amelia did.

The breeze blew wisps of her hair over her face, and her lips curved into a smile.

"I think it's beautiful," she said quietly.

"You have no idea what you're heading toward."

"No, I don't. But I know what I've come from. And I have no desire to return to it." Turning her head slightly, she glanced down at him and gave him a rueful smile. "You were right this morning when you said I didn't want to view the world as you do. You see only the emptiness. I see a place that's waiting to be filled with dreams."

Chapter Six

❧

"Dallas? Dallas, I'm scared."

"Don't be."

But Houston was afraid. The clouds passing across the midnight sky reminded him of ghosts, and he imagined that he could hear their tortured cries in the rushing waters of nearby Chickamauga Creek. He drew the blanket up to his chin, but it didn't stop his shivering.

"Dallas, I'm scared about tomorrow." His harsh whisper echoed around him, more frightening because his pa had told him that Chickamauga meant "river of death" in Cherokee.

Lying on the pallet beside him, Dallas rolled over and mumbled, "I ain't gonna hold you, but you can scoot a little closer to me if you want. Just don't let anybody see you doin' it."

Houston inched over until he could feel the warmth of Dallas's body, but not the solidity of his touch. He didn't want his father to find him sleeping right beside his brother.

"What if I die?" Houston whispered.

"You won't. Just stay by my side. I won't let nothin'
happen to you."

"Swear?"

"Give you my word."

AMELIA AWOKE TO an anguished wail that ripped
through her dream into her heart. With trembling
fingers, she turned up the flame in the lantern.

Her blood pounded at her temples; her breath
came in short gasps. She took a deep breath to
steady herself. In her dream, she and a man she
wanted to believe was Dallas—but who had
looked remarkably like Houston—had been walking through a field of clover. His arm had been
around her, and she had felt safer than she had
felt in years. She didn't think the cry had come
from her.

She slipped off the cot and eased into her night
wrapper, drawing it tightly around her as though
it had the power to ward off her fears.

She tiptoed across the tent, guided her hand
through the tent flap, and peered through the
small opening her narrow fingers created. She
could see Houston hunkered down before the
fire, wearing his duster, his hat drawn low over
his brow as though he had plans to ride out.

She widened the opening in the tent. "I thought
I heard a cry," she said, her voice quivering.

He visibly stiffened. "It was just an animal. Go
back to sleep."

His rough voice didn't ease her doubts. He
reached for the pot of coffee. As he poured the

coffee, he trembled with such intensity that the brew sloshed over the sides of his tin cup.

Amelia pulled her wrapper closer, gathering her courage within its folds. Leaving the tent, she padded across the campsite and knelt beside Houston.

"I said to go back to bed," he said gruffly.

"Do you think we're in danger?"

"No."

He gripped the handle of the pot so tightly that his bones were visible against his skin. Reaching out, Amelia covered his hand, her palm cradling his knuckles. He jerked at her touch, but he didn't attempt to pull away.

She rubbed her hand over his, surprised to find his so cold. Slowly he relaxed, his fingers loosening their grip on the handle. She eased the pot away from him and set it near the fire.

He wrapped his hand around the tin cup. She was amazed that the cup didn't dent with the strength of his grip.

"When I was a child," she said quietly, "I used to have nightmares, and I would pray that I would grow up fast so that the nightmares would go away." She gently placed her hand on his arm, hoping to gain his attention. Ignoring her, he focused his gaze on the fire and clenched his jaw tightly. "When I grew up, I learned that nightmares don't go away. They just become more terrifying because we understand so much more."

She worked the tin cup from his grip, held his hands, and willed him to look at her. He continued to stare into the fire. "Do you want to talk about your dream?"

"Nope."

"You don't have to be embarrassed because you were frightened by a dream."

He broke free of her hold and surged to his feet. "Frightened by a dream? Woman, I'm afraid of life!"

"Do you think you're alone—"

"Yes! Goddamn it! I'm alone!"

Houston regretted his outburst as soon as he saw the stricken expression fall across Amelia's lovely face. She looked as though he'd taken his fist to her. He'd had moments in his life when he'd felt small, but he'd never felt this small or this ashamed. Lord knew, he'd done plenty that he could be ashamed of.

He took a step toward her, his hands moving like a windmill in a slow breeze. He didn't know what to do with them. He didn't want to frighten her, but he was afraid she might grab his hands if he held them still, and he'd end up wrapping his arms around her just so he'd have a tether to hang onto so he'd feel safe. Only a woman shouldn't make a man feel safe. A man was supposed to protect a woman. "Amelia—"

She tilted her head slightly, the wounded expression retreating until she smiled so sweetly that he thought his heart might shatter. Every word he'd ever known rushed out of his head.

"I remember the first time I slept alone," she said softly, her voice drifting on the calm breeze as she shifted her gaze to the fire. "The bed was so large. The night so dark. I thought surely both would devour me. And the sounds. I heard a door creak and a board moan. I felt so incredibly alone." She wrapped her arms around herself and began to rock back and forth. "My father died during the war. And my sisters. Allison and Amanda."

The serenity of her gaze fascinated him. His hands had settled into a stillness as her voice floated toward him. She had a hell of a way of distracting a man. Her remembrances had lulled his memories back into oblivion, his shakes and sweats going along with them. She glanced up at him.

"My mother liked names that began with A. My father's name was Andrew, and I often wondered if that was why she married him."

"That's not a very practical reason for marrying someone," he said.

"Is my reason for marrying your brother practical?"

He stepped closer to the fire, wishing he could attain her composure. She always seemed at peace, relishing each moment as it came. Resting on the balls of his feet, he cautiously bent his knees until his gaze was only slightly higher than hers. "I don't know your reason."

"Because I hate being alone." She closed her eyes. "And because I want to share someone's dream."

"Don't you have your own dream?"

She opened her eyes and smiled mischievously. "A question?"

Lord, he loved the glimmer in her eyes as

though she'd trapped him, and he wasn't alto-gether certain that she hadn't. He lowered his gaze to the fire and watched the orange and red flames writhing in a contorted waltz. "I had no right to ask." But damn, he wanted to know everything about her, about her dreams, her rea-sons for traveling such a great distance to marry his brother.

"I dream of not being hungry. I dream of being warm."

He shifted his gaze to her. The smile had left her face.

"I dream of regaining something of what I lost during the war: a family, a promise that tomor-row will come, and that it will be worth living, savoring, and remembering."

"And you think Dallas will give you all of that?"

Her lips tilted up. "Another question. I'm im-pressed."

He wanted to look away, but her eyes held him captive. At that moment, with those green eyes boring into him, Houston almost had an over-whelming desire to search for his own dreams. "You don't have to answer it."

She scooted closer to him. "I think I do. No, I don't think he will *give* me my dreams, but I think we'll work together to gain them. I've always believed that dreams were meant to be shared. Where's the joy in reaching for something if you have no one to see you capture it?"

He had no idea. He'd stopped reaching long ago.

She laid her hand on his arm. "I don't expect you to answer that."

"That's good because I wouldn't know how."

She laughed, tilted her head back, and looked at the canopy of stars. "Oh, the sky is beautiful tonight. I almost envy you sleeping outside."

"It has its moments." Just as she did. Sweet moments, gentle moments. Moments that filled him with awe.

She smiled softly. "I should stop pestering you and let you go back to sleep."

He unfolded his body as she rose gracefully to her feet and turned away from the fire.

"Oh, look. I can see the shadow of a moth that's flying inside the tent. Isn't it pretty?" The smile eased off her face. "I can see the moth's shadow," she said in a hushed voice, "and everything inside the tent."

Houston stiffened as her gaze streaked to his pallet. With his saddle at one end, it didn't take much imagination to figure out which way he'd been lying or what had been in his line of sight.

Her gaze flew back to the tent, then to the pallet before she snapped accusing eyes his way. "I can see everything. Everything. Have you been watching me each evening?"

Sweet Lord, he wanted to speak but anything he could have uttered would have condemned him. As it turned out, his silence condemned him.

As she drew back her hand, he forced himself to give her an easy target. The blow came, jerking his head to the side.

She stormed into the tent, the flap momentarily billowing and slapping after her. Her shadow reflected as much hurt and anger as he imagined she felt. Then the shadow disappeared into the darkness as she extinguished the flame in the lantern.

Houston felt as though all the light had suddenly gone out of his life. He broke out in a cold sweat as his gaze swept over the camp. He'd told her he was alone, but until this moment he didn't know the true meaning of the word.

She'd shut him out of her life with a single breath. She'd ask no more questions of him, of that he was certain. He should have been relieved. Instead, he thought he might keel over and die. With trepidation, he neared the tent. "Miss Carson?"

A thick heavy silence was her reply. For some reason, he thought he'd feel a sight better if he could hear her sobbing or throwing things around.

"Miss Carson, you need to step outside and slap me again. The side you hit is mostly dead. You need to hit the other side of my face so I can feel it like I should."

He could hear nothing but the heavy pounding of his heart. He could see nothing but a vast emptiness filling the coming days. Dear God, what words could atone for what he'd done?

"Miss Carson, I know what I did was wrong. It was shameful, and I regretted it even as I did it, but dear Lord, woman, I swear to God, I've never seen a sweeter shadow than yours . . . and that's all I saw. Just your shadow."

"Without clothes! Washing up! Enjoying a few moments of freedom!"

Sweet Lord, yes, and he'd enjoyed her moments

of freedom most of all, but he didn't think she'd appreciate hearing that at this moment.

"Miss Carson, if I could undo what I'd done, I would. But I can't. If you just knew how beautiful—"

"I don't want to hear it, Mr. Leigh. Just leave me alone."

"You have every right to be upset—" He heard a sob. He'd been wrong. Hearing a noise was worse than hearing the silence.

"Miss Carson, I'd do anything on God's green earth to make this up to you. I'd pluck out my eye—"

A light flared inside the tent, and the flap flew open. She stood before him, her eyes rimmed in red, and he could see the faintest trail of tears along her cheeks. In all his life, he'd never loathed himself more.

She sniffed. "Do you mean it? Would you do anything?"

He glanced at her hands, expecting to see the knife she no doubt planned to use to remove his remaining eye. But her hands held nothing but the cool night air.

He swallowed hard. "Yes, ma'am. Anything."

She folded her arms beneath her breasts and swept out of the tent like a queen granting her least favorite subject an audience. She held her chin high with a dignity unlike any he'd ever seen. Dallas had been right to refer to her as the Queen of the Prairie.

She spun about and looked down her nose at him—as much as she was able, considering the top of her head didn't reach the height of his shoulder.

"You may sleep in the tent tonight."

Although her words had come softly, she'd spoken them with the force of a hissing snake. His gut clenched. He wasn't exactly sure where she was headed with this train of thought, and he wasn't certain that he wanted to know, but she appeared to be waiting on him to respond.

"Excuse me?"

"You may sleep in the tent," she repeated slowly as though he hadn't a lick of sense, and he was beginning to think that he might not have any sense at all. "Undress. Wash up. Do whatever it is men do before they go to sleep." She dropped to the log, placed her elbows on her thighs, cupped her chin, and smiled sweetly. "And I'll watch."

"Are you out of your mind?" he roared.

"You said you'd do anything. Well, Mr. Leigh, you have just heard my idea of anything."

He glared at the tent. The goddamn moth was still flying around. If he stepped into that tent, his first order of business would be to murder that pesky critter. He glanced at the woman sitting on the log. "No, ma'am, I can't do it."

"Why not? What's good for the goose is good for the gander."

"It ain't the same at all. I'll know you're watching."

She came off the log like vengeance sweeping through hell. "And you think my *not* knowing made what you did acceptable?"

No, it didn't make it acceptable at all. "What if I gave you a real pretty apology with some fancy words—"

"No."

"If I don't do this, you're gonna stay mad, aren't you?"

"Yes."

Good Lord, based on the delivery of that one simple word, she'd stay angry until they reached the ranch . . . and maybe beyond that. He'd be traveling through hell when he was just getting used to being near heaven.

His stomach was knotted so tightly that he didn't know if he could even walk into the tent. But it was the tear shimmering in the corner of her eye that decided him. The firelight caught it, and he could see himself as she must see him: a man who had shattered her trust.

Without another word, he flung back the tent flap and stormed inside, allowing the flap to fall behind him, encasing him in the golden haze that filled the tent.

He could smell her sweetness surrounding him. He couldn't identify the scent. It wasn't horses, or leather, or sweat. It was soft, reminding him of something so far back in his memory that he didn't know if he could pull it forward. His mother, perhaps, leaning over him, brushing the hair off his brow, telling him not to be afraid.

"You can't just stand there, Mr. Leigh. You have to wash up!"

Her voice penetrated his memories, reminding him more of his father than his mother. "Don't just stand there, boy! When the battle starts, you march into the thick of it."

And he'd marched, while everything inside him had screamed for him to run.

He took a step toward the small bucket and glanced at the water. With no steam rising up, it looked cold, but he'd taken cold baths before.

"Mr. Leigh!"

"All right!" Damn impatient woman. He tore his hat off his head and tossed it onto the rumpled covers of the bed where she'd been sleeping before he'd cried out like a baby. He was tempted to place his palm on the bed and see if it still carried her warmth, but she was watching him now, watching him as he'd watched her. Damn his eye for remaining open when it should have been closed.

Rolling his shoulders, he worked his way out of his duster and laid it beside his hat. He sat on the edge of the cot and discreetly placed his hand near her pillow. His fingers lightly brushed the area, searching for her warmth and finding only the cold.

She wouldn't be giving off any warmth until he'd done what she asked. *Anything*, he'd said. In the future, he wouldn't use *that* word around her.

He jerked off his boots. Unbuttoning his shirt, he stood, pulled it over his head, and dropped it on his duster.

He turned, presenting the silhouette of his backside to the front of the tent. Praying that she wasn't circling the tent, he began to unbutton his trousers.

Amelia watched, mesmerized. The shadows were distorted, not nearly as clear as she'd imagined, but that didn't change the fact that he'd wronged her. Considering the slowness with which he was removing his clothing, she assumed he was beginning to understand that.

With a quickness she wasn't expecting, he dropped his trousers. She buried her face in her hands. Dallas would no doubt send her back to Georgia if he found out what she'd required of his brother. It didn't matter that she couldn't actually see his flesh or the rigid contours that probably ran along his body.

He was standing inside her tent, buck naked. Whatever had she been thinking to require such a thing of him? She had wanted him to experience the humiliation that she'd felt when she'd discovered that he'd been watching her.

Only now mortification swamped her. The warmth flamed her cheeks as her mind brought up images of Houston washing himself. She couldn't bring herself to look, but in her mind's eye, she could see the glistening drops of water trailing down his throat, over his chest, along his stomach, traveling down . . .

She doubled over and pressed her face against her knees, but she couldn't block out the images. She had always been a dreamer, but no decent woman would conjure up the fantasy swirling inside her head.

Had he been content to stare at her silhouette or had he imagined the drops of water—

"I learned my lesson."

Amelia screeched and shot off the log, but not before she caught sight of a knee resting above a hairy calf. She hadn't heard him kneel beside her, but she was listening now, listening hard for his approach as she stood near the edge of the shadows, within the ring of light that the fire created. "I said you were to sleep in the tent," she reminded the man behind her, grateful she couldn't see him.

"I don't think you're really interested in watching me sleep. I gave you your show. Now, get inside the tent and get some sleep. We'll be leaving at dawn."

"That wasn't the bargain."

She heard his knee pop and assumed he'd risen to his feet. She was tempted to step beyond the light, to disappear into the night, but she feared the darkness while she was only wary of the man.

"I'm used to sleeping outside. I'm not sure you'll know what to do if you wake up with a snake coiled on your chest."

"A snake?" Without thinking, she spun around and found the breath knocked out of her. He stood stiffly beside the fire, his clothes bunched before him offering him some protection from her wandering gaze.

The firelight played over his flesh like a lover's caress. He had additional scars on his left shoulder, healed flesh that trailed down his chest toward his stomach and finally blended into oblivion. Old wounds the water may have kissed on its journey.

He shifted his stance, and his muscles rippled with the slight movement. He appeared much stronger than she'd imagined. She lowered her gaze as his hands tightened their hold on his clothing. She could see the veins and muscles in his arms straining with the force of his grip.

"Git inside the tent," he growled in a low, warning voice, "or you're gonna see a lot more than my shadow."

With a quick nod, Amelia scurried into the tent.

Houston fought to hold back his laughter. The woman was precious. Bold as brass one minute, ordering him into her tent; timid as a mouse the next, with wide eyes and a blush that just begged a man to touch her cheek.

Dropping to his pallet, he worked his way back into his clothes. Inside his cabin, he did sleep without a stitch of clothing, but not out here where a man *could* wake up with a snake curled over him.

He hefted his saddle to the other end of his pallet and stretched out, his gaze focused on the mules instead of the tent. He should have done it this way the first night.

He chuckled low, remembering the relief he'd experienced when he'd peered out the tent and seen Amelia crouching on the log, her face hidden. He wondered at what point she'd covered her eyes. Maybe he could have spared himself the cold wash-up. He'd done it so quickly that his body had barely noticed the touch of the cloth. He supposed out of fairness, he should have let the cloth caress his body the way she did when she washed. He should have slowly removed every speck of dust and every remnant of dried sweat until he could have come out of that tent smelling like she did: clean, pure, and tempting.

How could a woman be both pure and tempting? A decent woman shouldn't wash herself the way Amelia did. A decent woman shouldn't travel halfway across the country to marry a man she knew only through letters. Maybe Amelia Carson wasn't a decent woman. Maybe—

"Mr. Leigh?"

Her soft, gentle voice brushed over him like the finest of linen rubbing against his coarse body, sending his thoughts to perdition where they belonged.

Rolling over, he came up on his elbow and met her troubled gaze as she knelt beside his pallet, her hands folded primly in her lap. "Amelia, don't you think after what we learned about each other tonight that we can call each other by our first names?"

Even in the night shadows, he could see the flush in her cheeks as she lowered her gaze to her clenched hands.

"That's what I wanted to explain. I didn't watch for very long so I just . . . I just didn't want you to think I was wanton."

He didn't know what possessed him to slip his finger beneath her chin and lift her gaze back to his. He could feel the slight quiver beneath her soft skin and hated himself because his weakness—and not hers—had brought them to this moment.

"I don't think that."

Her green eyes held a depth of sadness. "Dallas might feel differently if he were to find out about tonight."

"He won't hear it from me."

He ached for his fingers to spread out across her face, his palm to cup her cheek, his thumb to graze her softness, his hand to draw her heart-shaped mouth to his. In all his life, he'd kissed only one woman—a whore whose breath had carried the stench of all the men who had come before him.

He had a feeling that the first time Dallas kissed Amelia, he'd taste nothing but her sweetness . . . as he should. Dallas had earned the right to nibble on those tempting lips because he'd dared to offer her a portion of his dream.

Houston drew his hand away before his fingers stopped listening to his head and started listening to his erratic heart.

"You'd best go back to bed now," he said in a rough voice he hardly recognized as his own.

"I don't like to be inside the darkness, but if I keep the lantern burning, I'll create shadows."

"I won't be lookin'."

"Promise?"

He deserved that hesitancy, that lack of trust. Dallas had told him once that if a man went back on his word one time, his reputation as a man of honor became little more than dust. He'd never known Dallas to break a promise. The strength of his word had laid the foundation for his empire. "I give you my word."

She pushed to her feet. "Sleep well."

Nodding, he settled back against his saddle, resisting the urge to watch her walk into the tent, knowing if he did, he might never find the strength to look away.

Chapter Seven

$\mathcal{M}$orning brought with it the glaring sun and harsh reality. Amelia had avoided Houston's gaze as she had eaten her breakfast. When he had begun packing their belongings into the wagon, she'd come to the stream seeking solace.

It had been one thing to meet Houston's gaze by the campfire, with more shadows than light, but when no shadows separated them . . . she couldn't meet his gaze, knowing what he had seen, what she had seen.

She had issued her challenge last night much as she had often dared her sisters—much as they had dared her—to step beyond the rigid guidelines their parents had set for them. But as imaginative as the dares had been, they had been children's dares, designed to make hearts race and giggles erupt, designed to strengthen a bond.

Last night her heart had raced, but she'd felt no desire to giggle, to laugh, or to smile. No bond existed between her and Houston that could be strengthened.

She stared at the small stream and listened to the gurgling water. She felt soiled, inside more than out. She wished Dallas had come for her. She wished they would reach the ranch today. She wished she'd never seen the firelight skim over Houston's bronzed skin.

She dropped to her backside, removed her shoes and stockings, and wiggled her toes in the cold water. It wasn't enough to wash away the memories of last night, to make her forget how for one insane moment she had envied the firelight.

Lifting her skirt higher, she waded into the stream until the brown water lapped at her calves. Brown like Houston's gaze, Dallas's eyes. Brown like fertile soil.

"Amelia?"

Refusing to acknowledge Houston's presence by turning around, she glared at the trees lining the opposite bank. Anger swelled anew, anger at herself because she liked the way her name sounded coming from his lips, with his deep timbre wrapped around the sounds. She hoped Dallas's voice would carry the same resonance.

"You got any plans to look at me or talk to me today?" he asked.

"Perhaps at nightfall. It's easier with the shadows around us."

"Then I reckon we'll wait here till nightfall."

She clenched her hands. "I thought if I did to you what you had done to me, I would find what you took from me. But trust isn't gained back that easily." She pivoted in the water and tilted her face up slightly.

He wasn't wearing his hat. No shadows kept his gaze from hers. Within the dark depths, she read sorrow, shame, and a profound apology that almost made her weep. "I'm sorry," she whispered hoarsely.

"No need to apologize. It was all my doing. I have a habit of taking the easy road. It was easier to watch than it was to turn away." He settled his hat on his head. "The wagon's loaded. We can leave whenever you're ready."

"Just a few—Oh!" The sharp pain came suddenly, without warning. She stumbled back, falling into the cold water.

Houston thrashed through the gentle current, lifted her into his arms, and carried her out of the stream. "What happened?"

"My leg. Something bit me. A fish or something."

Gingerly he set her on the grassy bank and knelt beside her.

"Close your eyes," he demanded tersely as he tore the hat from his head. "God damn it! Close your eyes!"

He had only sworn at her once—last night—and normally she would have obeyed anyone who yelled at her with such urgency. But she couldn't bring herself to move, to act, to do anything but stare at the two puncture marks in her calf and the blood trailing toward her ankle.

"What happened?" she asked.

"Snake," he replied as he wrapped a strip of leather around her calf before unsheathing the knife he carried at his side. The early-morning sunlight glinted off the steel.

"It's gonna hurt. I'm sorry," he said quietly as he sliced the blade across her calf. She clenched her teeth and balled her hands into fists, wishing she could reassure him, but afraid if she opened her mouth to speak, she'd scream.

He dropped the knife. Wrapping his warm hands around her calf, he lowered his mouth to the wound. His jaws worked feverishly as he sucked and spit. Sucked and spit. Over and over.

She touched her finger to the black patch dangling from her calf and shifted her gaze. No strip of leather indented his brow as he worked. His thick black hair fell over his face, and she had a strong urge to brush it back.

"Am I going to die?" she asked quietly.

He jerked his head up, apparently forgetting or unaware that he wasn't shielding his face from her gaze. Nothing remained of his left eye or cheek. His tangled flesh was stretched taut in places, ridged and heavily scarred in others, as though his ravaged face hadn't quite known how to repair itself. She wanted to weep for the pain he must have endured, for the wounded child he had once been.

"No," he said with conviction. "No, you're not gonna die."

He scooped her into his arms as though she were little more than a bouquet of flowers, freshly picked. She pressed her face against his chest as he carried her in long strides back to the camp. She could hear the pounding of his heart, so hard, so fast that she was certain he was in pain. He set her down near the cold ashes of their campfire.

"I'm still bleeding."

"That's all right. Let your leg bleed for a while. I'm going to set the tent back up."

"Why?" she asked, the panic knotting her stomach.

Gently, he cradled her cheek. She felt the slight trembling in his fingers and placed her hand over his. His Adam's apple slowly slid up and down.

"You're gonna get sick," he said, his voice ragged. "Real sick."

"I didn't see a snake," she said, hopefully.

"He left his mark. Probably a water moccasin, maybe a rattler that close to shore."

He withdrew his fingers, and a coldness seeped through her. A shudder racked her body.

He tore off his duster and gently slipped it over her shoulders, tucking it in around her. He pulled his shirt over his head and wadded it up. "Here, lie down."

She curled up on the ground. "I'm tired," she said, her tongue feeling thick. "Didn't sleep well last night."

"You'll sleep today. I'll be back for you."

Before she could reply, he raced to the wagon and began searching through its contents, an urgency to his movements. Her eyelids grew heavy, but she forced them to remain open as she watched him set up the tent beneath the shade of a tree.

His back was lean, tanned, and she wondered if he often worked without a shirt. His muscles reminded her of a stallion's, sleek but powerful, bunching with an easy grace as he worked.

She closed her eyes and the dizziness assaulted

her as the blackness swirled around her. Jerking her eyes open, she fought to ignore the throbbing pain in her calf and concentrated instead on the plainness of the patch that usually covered the harshest of Houston's scars. Perhaps she would decorate it with tiny flowers before she gave it back to him.

As she reached for it, to examine it more closely, so did long brown fingers. She watched as Houston removed the strip of leather from her leg and tied it around his head, the patch falling into place to cover his loss.

He wrapped a strip of cloth around her wound. Then he lifted her into his arms and carried her into the tent, gingerly setting her on the cot.

"Do you think you can get out of your wet clothes or do you need me to help?" he asked.

She glanced at her nightgown waiting on her pillow. She nodded lethargically, her tongue struggling to form the words. "I . . . can."

"Good. I'll be back in a few minutes."

He disappeared before she could say more. Sluggishly, she worked her way out of her clothes, leaving them heaped on the floor. She slipped on her nightgown before curling up on her side and drifting off to sleep, trusting her life to Houston's keeping.

HOUSTON SCOOPED THE mud out of the bowl and patted it over the swollen flesh on Amelia's calf, hoping the coolness would reduce the swelling. Damn, he didn't want to have to cut out part of her muscle. He knew the venom could kill the flesh, the muscle, and in rare instances, the victim.

The thought of her dying caused a hard, painful knot to settle deep in his chest. He was certain she had more questions she wanted to ask, discoveries she wanted to make.

He wanted her to see a sunset from the porch of his cabin, with the far off horizon a distant haze. He wanted to learn to answer her questions with patience.

He wanted to watch her daughter grow up.

For some ungodly reason, he thought she'd give Dallas a little girl instead of the son he craved. He imagined a little girl with Amelia's golden hair, her green eyes, and her tiny tipped-up nose, running over Dallas's ranch, wrapping cowhands around her tiny finger. He hoped sometime she'd visit with her Uncle Houston. He'd give her a gentle mare to ride and share his secret place with her where the wildflowers bloomed, the water misted, and the sky was always blue.

And he'd love her. If she was half as sweet as her mother, he'd love her.

He shifted his gaze to Amelia's face. Dear God, but she was pale. He brushed his mud-caked fingers over his trousers until they felt clean, then he gently wiped away the dewy sweat beading above her upper lip.

He wished he'd been able to spare her the sight of his face uncovered. He'd told her to close her eyes, but she hadn't obeyed him, and he hadn't had time to press the issue.

If Dallas had told her to close her eyes, she'd have closed them. His voice carried the mark of authority. If the man said, "Jump!", every other man within earshot would ask, "How high?"

Hell, Houston hadn't been able to make those two ragamuffins at the train depot follow his order to leave him alone. Maybe that was the reason he enjoyed working with horses so much. They listened to him.

Amelia's eyes fluttered open, her green gaze vacant. Damn, he wished the snake had chosen him.

Her lips lifted slightly, and a small spark glinted in her eyes. "No shadow show tonight."

He swallowed hard, wondering how she could tease him when she was feeling so poorly. "You get to feeling better, and I'll give you one," he promised, knowing he'd give her anything, do anything if she just wouldn't die on him.

Her smile withered away like flowers pulled from the earth and left too long without water. Reaching out, she pressed her palm against his left shoulder, her warmth seeping through his flannel shirt. "Did you get this wound at the same time?"

"Yes. I'm sorry you had to see my face—"

She moved her hand up to palm his left jaw. The scars were fewer there, and he could feel the gentleness of her touch.

"The scars suit you," she said quietly.

Yeah, the scars suited him. A man should be as ugly on the outside as he was on the inside.

Self-consciously he wrapped his fingers around her hand and placed it on the cot. She tucked it beneath her chin and drew her legs up as she lay on her side, vulnerable as the day she was born. He brought a blanket up to her shoulders, but it could only protect her from the chill of the evening, not the harshness of life. Offering comfort was as foreign to him as giving an apology. He desperately searched the recesses of his mind for some memory to help him.

An image came to him, so powerful that his hands shook. A time when he'd had nothing but pain, fear, and the overwhelming desire to die. Another memory teased the back of his mind. Small hands, a nurse's hands, rubbing his back, making the pain tolerable with her sweetness. Like most of the young wounded soldiers, he'd entertained the idea of marrying her . . . until he'd caught sight of his reflection in a mirror.

He placed his hand against the small of Amelia's back and felt her stiffen beneath his fingertips. "I won't hurt you," he reassured her. "Just gonna help you forget."

Awkwardly, he rubbed his splayed fingers over her back. She had such a small back. He wondered if she'd have the strength to bear Dallas the son he wanted . . . or the daughter Houston thought she would have.

He stroked her shoulders, stopping just short of the nape of her neck. Touching her flesh, absorbing her warmth appealed to him, appealed to him as it shouldn't. He had no right to feel her skin beneath his fingers, even if he was only offering comfort.

"My mother used to rub my back when I was sick," she said quietly, and his fingers faltered.

His thoughts were anything but motherly. "I just thought it might help."

"It does."

His hand continued its slow sojourn over her

slender back. Touching her in a less than intimate manner warranted a bit of reverence that could best be appreciated with silence: like watching the rising of a full yellow moon or hearing a wolf calling out to his mate.

"Would you mind reading one of Dallas's letters to me? I always find comfort in his words. They're in my bag." Her mouth curved up. "But I suppose you know that."

He preferred stroking her back to reading, but his desires didn't seem nearly as important as hers. Opening her bag, he removed the bundle of letters. His fingers felt clumsy as they untied the delicate ribbon that held the letters together.

"Take one from the middle," she said. "Any one."

He took the one that looked the most worn, figuring it would be her favorite. He removed the letter from the envelope. "You sure you want me to read it?"

She nodded. He turned up the flame in the lantern and angled the letter so the faint light could home in on his brother's words. He cleared his throat.

April 6, 1876

My dear Miss Carson,

The wind blew through this afternoon, turning the wheel on my windmill for the first time. The wheel groaned and complained as some men are wont to do, but eventually, it worked hard enough to bring up the water. I enjoyed listening to its steady clack. Hopefully, many a night it will serenade my family to sleep.

Loneliness does not exist for me when I am surrounded by the vast expanse of land and the endless possibilities. I think you would find much here to ease your loneliness—the land, the howling wind, the braying of cattle, the sun, the moon, the stars. When I ride out at night alone, I find companionship in all that surrounds me. I tell you this because I do not want you to think that loneliness is responsible for the following words.

I believe a wife and sons would enrich my life beyond measure. And I would do all in my power to enrich theirs.

After a year of corresponding, I am convinced you and I are well suited, and I would be honored to have you as my wife. I shall anxiously await your reply.

Yours,
Dallas Leigh

"I said yes," Amelia stated softly.

Houston set the letters aside, picked up the cloth, and wiped her brow. "Yep. Dallas was grinning like a fool for a week after he got your letter."

Her laughter washed over him as gentle as a spring rain. He couldn't recall ever making someone laugh . . . or causing them happiness. A measure of disquiet swept through him. He didn't want her depending on him for laughter, happiness, or comfort because eventually she'd learn the truth about him: He wasn't a man that a person could depend on.

He knew Dallas had experienced qualms about sending him to fetch his future wife, but he'd had no choice. He wanted to believe Dallas had sent him because he trusted him and had gained a measure of respect for him, but he knew the truth: Dallas had no one else to send.

Her laughter drifted into silence, and she placed her hand on his arm. "You really can be quite charming." Her cheeks flushed, and he wasn't altogether certain it was from the fever. "Dallas will be a good husband, won't he?"

"The best." He dropped the cloth in the bowl of water. "I'll get you some water to drink."

He started to rise. She reached out, wrapping her fingers around his hand. "Thank you for saving my life."

He didn't have the heart to tell her the worst was still to come.

AMELIA PRAYED FOR death when she thought she was going to live, prayed to live when she thought she was going to die. She prayed while she heaved up her breakfast. She prayed when she had nothing left to heave but her body insisted on trying anyway. She prayed when she was shaking from cold and prayed while she was burning with fever.

She prayed Houston wouldn't leave her. It was the only prayer answered to her satisfaction. He stayed with her throughout her ordeal, lying constantly.

He'd tell her the worst was over when it wasn't

so she wouldn't give up. He'd tell her the chills were a good sign, then he'd say the fever was good. Using a cool cloth, he'd wipe the sweat from her brow, cheeks, and throat, all the while saying she would be all right in his deep voice.

She decided that she loved that voice, even when it was lying. It had a soothing, calming quality about it. She imagined the horses responded well to it. She wanted to live long enough to watch him train a horse, her horse, the horse he'd promised her when she'd felt certain she would die.

She watched him now as he gently washed the mud from her calf. His brow didn't furrow as deeply at the sight of the discolored and slightly swollen flesh as it had when he had examined it before. She wondered if anyone had cared for him this tenderly when he had been injured. She couldn't imagine with all the war casualties that anyone would have found time for a fifteen-year-old boy so badly wounded. She was surprised he'd come through his ordeal.

But he had survived, and she was determined not to let a little snake claim her life.

"Did your father take care of you when you were hurt?" she asked.

He visibly stiffened. He so hated talking about the war, and yet it was such a part of his past and Dallas's. How could she understand the men she would live with if she didn't understand their history?

"Our pa was dead by then. Dallas saw after me.

"Dallas seems to have a habit of taking care of people."

"He has a knack for it. He'd have taken better care of you than I have."

"I can't imagine how he could have," she said as she placed her hand over his. His eye was red rimmed, his face haggard. "You need to sleep," she said.

"I will as soon as your fever breaks."

"When will that be?"

"Soon."

Soon could be any moment, any day. Soon could be when death came.

"Tell me something nice," she said. "Something nice about the place where we're going."

He touched the damp cloth to her throat. "Flowers. You'll see beautiful flowers come spring: blue, red, yellow. Not as pretty as what you sew, but pretty just the same."

"What else?"

"There's nothing to block your view of the sunset. You can just watch it sweep across the land, making you feel so small."

"I am small."

He lifted a corner of his mouth. "Yeah, you are small."

Smiling softly, she touched the corner of his mouth. "A smile. I thought I'd die without ever seeing you smile."

"You're not gonna die."

She lifted a brow. "Dallas will have your hide if I do."

Leaning low, he brushed a strand of hair from her cheek. "Damn right, he will."

"Can't let that happen," she said as she drifted off to sleep.

HE HAD THE longest eyelashes she'd ever seen. She'd never noticed before, but as he slept with his face pressed to the cot near her hip, she could clearly see the length and thickness of his lashes. His hair—black as a midnight sky with no stars—curled over his ear, rested against his chin. He needed to shave.

Staring at his profile, she no longer tried to imagine how he might have looked if he'd never been wounded, but she found herself mourning what he might have had. A life that included a wife and children. A smile that would have warmed many a woman's heart. A laugh that would have rung out strong and true.

She'd never heard him laugh, had only seen a ghost of a smile. He wasn't hers to care about, but she did care. She wanted to hear him laugh. She wanted him to smile without feeling self-conscious. He had fought to give her back her life. Giving him a smile was a small payment.

She combed her fingers through the thick strands of his hair. It was coarser than hers, as though the wind and sun had battled against it.

He awakened with a jolt. "Your fever broke."

She smiled softly. "I know. You were sleeping."

He sat up and stretched his shoulders back. "How do you feel?"

"Tired."

"You'll be weak for a couple of days."

"Have you ever been bitten by a snake?"

"Nope, but it happens now and then to men on the trail."

"Do you take care of the men then?"

"Nope. The cook usually does the doctoring. Think you could eat a little something?"

"I'll try. Are we going to travel today?"

"Nah, we'll let you rest for a couple of days."

"Won't Dallas worry if we're not there on time?"

"I don't think he'll start to worry unless we're not there within a month."

HOUSTON CARRIED HER outside during the day to enjoy the sun and carried her back into the tent at night to sleep. He'd taken to sleeping on his pallet, his saddle placed so he was watching the tent. Under the circumstances, he didn't think she'd mind. She wasn't giving any shadow shows.

On the morning of the third day after her fever broke, he awoke, his gaze fixed on the tent. With the early light of dawn filtering through the leaves and dancing over the canvas, he couldn't see any shadows or movements within the tent, but he could envision Amelia clearly, lying on the cot, sleeping soundly. In the past two days, she'd slept more than she'd been awake.

He thought they'd be able to travel today. He supposed he should get up and wake her, but he liked the thought of letting her sleep, letting her wake up on her own, stretching, washing her face, brushing her hair. He would be able to see none of the movements, but knowing they would take place almost made him smile.

She was sweet, so incredibly sweet.

He threw off the blanket, scrambled to his knees, rested his hands on his thighs, and continued to look at the tent. He'd make her some coffee before he woke her. Thicken it with sugar just the way she liked it. He'd warm up some water for her.

He turned and froze. She was sitting on a log, her hands pressed between her knees.

"Good morning," she said softly.

"You're awake," he croaked, grimacing for telling her something she obviously knew.

She smiled, and he lost the ability to draw air into his lungs.

"I wanted to see a Texas sunrise. It was beautiful."

He sank to his backside, fighting off the urge to tell her that she was more beautiful than any sunrise he'd ever seen. Her braided hair was draped over one shoulder, her face pink from an early-morning scrubbing, her green eyes bright with appreciation. He thought he'd never again be able to look at the sun easing over the horizon without thinking of her, just so, enjoying the start of a new day. To him, a day was just something to be gotten through.

"I guess when you think you're going to die, you start to appreciate things a little more. What was the first thing you wanted to see after you were wounded?" she asked.

"My ma." He grabbed his hat and settled it into place. He'd never told anyone that. He'd wanted his ma so badly that he'd felt like a baby.

"But she was too far away to come to you."

Her eyes held so much understanding that he couldn't stop himself from dredging up the memories. "Yeah, she was too far away, and she had Austin to care for, so even if she'd known I'd been hurt, she wouldn't have been able to come."

"You didn't tell her you were hurt?"

He shook his head. "Dallas said knowing would just make her worry. After the war ended, we headed home. When we got there, it was so quiet. You could feel in your bones that something wasn't right . . ."

His voice trailed off into the dawn.

"What wasn't right?" she asked, gently prodding him to continue.

Houston shifted his backside over the hard ground. Physical comfort eluded him as easily as peace of mind. He'd never discussed that day with anyone, not even Dallas. Sometimes, he felt a strong need to discuss it with Austin, to see if he remembered, but if Austin held no memories of that time, he didn't want to give him any. "We found our ma in her bed. She'd been dead for some time. I was glad then that Dallas hadn't written her about me, that we hadn't give her more cause to worry."

"Do you know how your mother died?" she asked.

"Figured she'd taken the fever. Our pa wasn't one to make friends so no one checked at the farm while we were gone. We don't know how Austin managed to survive. He was like a wild animal when we found him."

"Those are the memories you think Austin has of the war?"

"I've got no idea what memories he has. If he doesn't have any, I don't want to give him mine."

"So you never talk about it."

"Nope." He stood and rubbed his hands along his thighs. "If you're feeling strong enough, we'll head out this morning."

She smiled then, a smile that made his heart ache, a smile that made him wish that, in his youth, he'd traveled a different path.

Chapter Eight

As the wagon rumbled over the uneven ground, Amelia clung tenaciously to the seat. She was regaining her strength with each passing day, and with each passing mile, she grew closer to Houston.

She knew she *shouldn't* have these feelings. She knew she *couldn't* have these feelings. She had signed a contract stating she would travel west to marry Dallas. She didn't think he was a man prone to breaking contracts or dismissing them. She had been wallowing in the depths of despair, her world closing in on her, her options dwindling when she'd received his letter of hope. She owed him for lifting her out of the mire into which the war had dropped her, for altering her destiny.

She read his letters each night before she went to sleep, trying to hold an image of the man within her heart, but it was Houston she heard whimper in the hours past midnight, it was Houston she would sneak out of the tent to watch sleeping.

He never seemed truly at rest. As he slept, beads

of sweat would coat his face and neck. He would begin to breathe hard as though he were running a great distance.

She told him she awoke early to appreciate the sunrise, but the truth was she enjoyed those moments before dawn when the sun's feathery fingers would touch his face and his breathing would calm as though in sleep he recognized that he'd survived another night.

Amelia spotted the small log cabin near dusk. Her heart tripped over itself when she saw the few cattle grazing in the fields beyond. "Are we already at Dallas's ranch?" she asked.

"Nope. Just stopping to look in on some of Dallas's neighbors."

"So we're close."

"Nope. Out here, anyone you pass along the way is considered a neighbor." He pulled the wagon to a halt between the house and a weathered barn.

A tall gangly man holding a rifle stepped out of the house. He cupped a hand over his brow and squinted against the setting sun. "Houston, that you?"

"Yep, Dallas told me to stop by." Houston climbed off the wagon and held his arms up to Amelia.

She scooted over the bench as the man ambled over.

"You got you a woman there?" the man asked.

Houston wrapped his hands around her waist and lifted her to the ground. "Yep. Miss Carson is betrothed to Dallas. He busted his leg. Sent me to fetch her."

A wide grin split the man's face. "Well, I'll be. She a heart-and-hand woman?"

"Yep."

"Dallas sure got himself a pretty one, didn't he?"

"Reckon he did," Houston said quietly. "Miss Carson, this here's John Denton."

Smiling, Amelia brushed her hand over her dusty skirt and toyed with the brim of Austin's hat. At the moment she imagined she looked anything but pretty.

"Beth, we got company!" John hollered.

A young, dark-haired woman rushed onto the porch, wiping her hands on her apron. A little girl, with a rag doll draped over her arm, clutched the woman's skirt and peered around her. "Land sake's, company. John, don't just stand there. Invite them in for supper."

Amelia glanced at Houston. He gave her a brusque nod. "I'll see to the animals' needs, then I'll join you."

John trailed after Houston as he led the mules to a trough. Amelia strolled to the house.

The woman's smile grew brighter. "I'm Beth." She rested her hand on the child's dark head. "This is Sarah. She's four years old and into everything."

Amelia knelt before the child. She had her father's blue eyes, her mother's dark hair. "Hello, Sarah. I'm Amelia."

Sarah held out her doll. "This is Mary Margaret."

Amelia touched the doll's cloth arm. "She's very pretty, just like you."

Sarah pressed her face against her mother's skirt and giggled.

"You'll have to forgive her shyness. We don't get much company out here."

Amelia rose to her feet. "I guess that's something I'm going to have to get used to."

"I never expected Houston to take a wife."

"Actually, I'm going to marry Dallas."

Beth's eyes widened. "Dallas? Have you met him?"

Amelia shook her head. Beth slapped her hand over her breast. "Handsome as sin." She eyed Amelia speculatively. "Are you a heart-and-hand woman?"

"I just heard Houston say I was, so I guess I am, although I'm not sure what that is."

Beth slipped her arm through Amelia's and led her into the house. "A mail-order bride. Cowboys call us heart-and-hand women because most place their orders from *The Heart and Hand*. That's where John found me. Our little house might not look like much, but what I have here is a hundred times better than what I had before."

The furniture looked as though it had all been carefully crafted. The fire crackled in the hearth. The room smelled of freshly baked bread and cinnamon.

Beth reached into a cabinet and brought out wooden bowls, setting them at the square oak table. She picked up Sarah and plopped her into a chair that was taller than the others. "John made all the furniture."

"It's lovely."

"He works hard, trying to keep me happy. I imagine Dallas will do the same for you."

"I only know Dallas through correspondence.

I was hoping to learn more about him as we traveled, but Houston isn't very talkative."

Beth looked at her, complete understanding reflected in her eyes. "Oh, Amelia, none of the men out here are. They won't ask you for the time of day. They figure if you want to share that information, you'll take out your pocket watch and tell them."

"Why do you think they are like that?"

Beth brought a pot from the hearth and began to ladle stew into the bowls. "I think it's because a lot of the men came here after the war to start over. Or they had a past they weren't particularly proud of. A lot of them change their names, or just go by their first names. No one questions them. That's why they come out here. If they want to be alone, they're left alone."

"And if they don't want to be alone?"

Beth smiled. "Then they order themselves a bride." She placed the pot on the table and returned to the hearth, bringing back a black pan that held something that reminded Amelia of a yellow cake.

"Corn dodgers and stew," Beth explained. "It's not fancy, but it's filling and out here the men need something that fills up their bellies." She looked past Amelia and pointed a finger. "Keep that dust out there where it belongs!"

John and Houston stomped their feet on the porch for a minute before walking in and taking their seats. Amelia sat beside Sarah, across from Houston, who had angled his chair so he sat with the scarred side of his face away from the table.

When Beth took her chair, everyone bowed their heads.

"Dear Lord," John began, "thank you for bringing company to take the burden of talking off me for a day or so. Amen."

Grinning, he looked up at Beth. She wagged a finger at him. "You were listening at the door."

"No, missus, but I've been married to you long enough to know poor Miss Carson here is gonna get her ear chewed off afore the evening's over."

"Please, call me Amelia."

He blushed before digging into his stew.

Beth placed her hand over Amelia's and squeezed. "You'll have to forgive me," she said. "As much as I've come to love John, I miss a woman's voice from time to time."

Amelia cast a furtive glance Houston's way. He watched her in seeming innocence, but she wondered if Dallas had indeed told him to stop by here or if he was just trying to bring home his point regarding the absence of company in this part of Texas.

"I think you're delightful," Amelia said with all sincerity. "And I know what it is to long for a gentle voice."

Amelia received a good dose of what Houston endured each evening as Beth fired off questions, one after another. She wanted to know about life back East, the journey on the train, and how fashions had changed. She talked about everything but the weather. John commented from time to time, but Houston held his silence on all matters.

When John's bowl was empty, he leaned back

in his chair and asked a question only Houston could answer. "How many head of cattle does Dallas have now?"

Houston glanced up from his stew as though he hadn't noticed that the majority of the previous conversation had not included him. He had asked no questions, prompted no replies, and caused no soft chuckles. "Around two thousand."

John released a low whistle. "Have him send word if he needs some help getting 'em to market. I could bring Beth to the ranch and she and Amelia here could visit."

"I'll let him know."

"John, why don't you drag out the bundle board? We'll let Amelia and Houston sleep in the bed tonight. You and I can sleep in the loft."

Amelia's heart slammed against her ribs. She thought the intimacy surrounding her and Houston as they sat beside a campfire would pale in comparison to the intimacy that would surround them if they slept in the same room, the same bed, beneath the same covers.

John cleared his throat. "I'm not sure that would be proper, Beth. Usually, we pull the bundle board out when the two people are engaged."

"Don't be silly. Dallas trusts Houston, or he wouldn't have sent him to get Amelia. And she must trust him, or she wouldn't be traveling with him. Nothing will happen in that bedroom that couldn't happen on the trail."

John shrugged. "I reckon you got a point there."

"I appreciate the kindness, but I'll sleep in the barn," Houston said.

"Nonsense," Beth said, slapping her hand on the table for emphasis. "When was the last time you slept in a bed?"

Houston looked as though he'd been trapped which Amelia realized he had been. He couldn't even claim to have slept in a bed while they were in Fort Worth.

"A while, but I'm used to sleeping on the ground."

"Then tonight you will sleep in a bed, and we'll prepare you each a bath. A good hot meal, a hot bath, and a soft bed. I would have sold my soul for those when I was traveling out here. It warms my heart to be able to offer them to you."

Amelia met Houston's gaze, and she knew he wanted an honorable way out of the situation, knew she should help him find one. But he had made one sacrifice after another for her on this trip. Surely Dallas would find no fault with her for making this one sacrifice for Houston.

"I truly appreciate your generosity, Beth," she said quietly. "I would love to have a hot bath."

Beth slapped her hand on the table in front of her daughter. "Sarah, stop staring. It's not polite."

Amelia glanced down at the little girl. She bowed her head, but Amelia could see that her gaze was still trained on Houston.

Houston shoved his bowl back. "It was a fine meal, ma'am. If you'll excuse me, I need to check on the mules." He scraped the chair across the floor, stood, and headed out the door.

Beth sighed. "That's such a shame he had to get wounded like that, but I imagine Dallas sleeps better at night."

"What do you mean?" Amelia asked.

"It's not unusual for a mail-order bride to meet someone along the way and never make it to the man who sent for her. Imagine Dallas figured that wouldn't happen if he made Houston come after you. You're not going to fall in love with him."

HOUSTON CROSSED HIS forearms over the fence railing. Sorrel snorted and nudged his elbow.

"No apples." He scratched behind the horse's ear. Most cowboys wouldn't be caught dead riding a she-horse, but Houston had discovered he could approach a herd of wild mustangs with more success when he rode a mare. Although wary of a strange horse, a stallion was more likely to accept a female into his domain. He'd viciously fight another stallion. "You'd best get some sleep, old friend. I sure as hell won't get any tonight."

The horse nudged Houston's elbow again and when no apple was forthcoming, she trotted away, leaving Houston to enjoy the solitude he craved.

He knew it wasn't uncommon for people to offer their bed to visitors, even when the travelers weren't married. The lack of towns and hotels had resulted in a code of hospitality across the plains that Houston couldn't help but admire. Still, he wasn't certain that Dallas would appreciate his neighbors' generosity. He could only hope that his brother would understand that Beth couldn't have spoken truer words: Nothing was going to happen in that bed. Nothing at all. Hell, he probably wouldn't even be able to sleep.

Houston felt someone watching him, the gaze more of a tickle than a stare. He glanced down. Big blue eyes looked up at him. Incredibly innocent. He wished he could give the little girl a smile, but he knew no matter how hard he tried that the left side of his face wouldn't cooperate, and he'd end up giving her something distorted and uglier than what she was looking at now, something that might frighten her.

"I got a hurt," she said. She lifted her skirt until her white bloomers came into view along with her scraped knee. "My ma kissed it and made it better." She released her skirt and pointed her finger. "You got a hurt."

"Yeah, reckon I do." Right in the center of his heart.

She scrunched up her face. "I can kiss it and make it better."

Something inside his chest grew so tight that he thought he might not be able to breathe. She crooked her little finger and wiggled it at him. "Come here."

Holding on to the railing for support, he bent his knees, squatting until he was as close to her height as he could get. Her eyes grew large and serious. She puckered her tiny lips, bobbed her head forward, then ran off. The brush of her mouth against his cheek had been as faint as the first breath of dawn. Deep inside, he smiled.

Standing a few feet away and slightly behind his left side, Amelia knew that his hampered vision prevented him from seeing her. She also realized with awe that he was smiling. Not on the outside where it would show, but within a secret place where he harbored his fears and his doubts, where she imagined a fifteen-year-old boy mourned the loss of his youth.

She knew that she was wrong to watch him without his knowledge, but she wanted to understand him as much as she needed to understand Dallas. With Dallas, she would have an advantage. She was certain he would talk with her and ask her questions. His brother would hold his hurts, his longings, his dreams close to his heart where no one could share them.

She turned and walked back to the house, where her bath waited. She hadn't seen Houston's smile, but it hovered around him, like a whispered sigh, sweet and unexpected.

HOUSTON SANK INTO the steaming hot water and released a slow, appreciative breath. Beth had draped blankets over the back porch railing to give him a measure of privacy. He could feel the cool night air moving in. In the distance, he could see orange and lavender sweeping across the sky.

A man couldn't ask for much more than that.

He closed his eye. Amelia had been in the water before him. Although Beth had added more hot water to the tub after Amelia got out, if he concentrated hard enough, he imagined he could smell her sweet scent. Her scent had to be that of a flower, but it wasn't any flower he knew. He imagined her tiny feet resting against the bottom of the wooden tub where his were now. He imagined the lye soap skimming over her body, touching her before it touched him. It seemed such an intimate image, to have the same water, soap, and air caressing both their bodies.

His mouth went as dry as the West Texas breeze. He was sitting in a tub of water, dying of thirst. He opened his eye. The cake of soap slipped out of his hands, spiraled through the air, hit the porch, and skidded toward the dirt.

Amelia bent down and picked it up.

"What are you doing out here?" he croaked.

She straightened and leaned against the porch railing, her gaze holding his. "I've never seen you enjoy anything."

"I was enjoying the bath."

"I know." She smiled so sweetly that he wondered if his thoughts had been visible. He held out his hand. "I need the soap and some privacy."

She handed him the soap and held up a cup brimming with shaving lather. "The beard doesn't suit you."

He rubbed his hand over his rough jaw. "I'll shave it, then."

"I'd be happy to shave it for you."

"I can do it."

She gnawed on her lower lip. "I'm very experienced at shaving a man's face. I shaved Mr. Bryant every morning."

Amelia watched the expressions flitting over his face, and she knew that he wanted to ask, but as always, with rare exception, he held his silence.

She walked forward and knelt beside the tub, her courage faltering as he plunged his hands under the murky water, splashing her with his frantic efforts.

"Woman, I'm not wearing any clothes!"

She'd seen him without clothes, but she saw no reason to remind him of that fact. He'd argue that the circumstances had been different, and she'd have no choice but to agree. Although she had no intentions of dropping her gaze below his bare shoulders, she jerked a blanket off the porch railing and draped it over the tub. "I can't see anything but your face and shoulders now. I'd like very much to shave you. It's such a small thing, a way to thank you for caring for me while I was sick."

He glanced around the porch.

"Beth and Sarah have already gone to bed. John's closing the barn."

Watching his throat muscles work, she would have sworn he was terrified. "I won't hurt you," she assured him, smiling softly. "I just want to help you forget."

"You're using my words," he grumbled.

"They're easy to remember. You don't say very many."

"You're aggravating, you know that?"

She smiled warmly at his disgruntled expression and began to swish the brush in the cup, hoping to put them both at ease before night fell, and they found themselves together in the same bed.

"My father owned a plantation before the war." She had his undivided attention as she brushed the lather over his face and along his throat. "I had two sisters. No brothers. I was the youngest. Papa's favorite. I was quite pudgy and he used to call me his little pumpkin."

He furrowed his brow. "Can't imagine you pudgy."

"War changes people."

His brow relaxed. "Yeah, I reckon it does."

She set the lather cup down and slipped the razor out of her pocket, giving him time to ask a question, but no question came.

Placing her finger beneath his chin, she tilted his head back. "I told you that Papa died. It was just before the war ended. Mama said he took the fever, but I think he just grieved for the South he loved, the South that was disappearing. My sisters died shortly after he did. Then it was just Mama and me."

She took a moment to enjoy the sound of the razor scraping over his unmarred jaw. "Mr. Bryant came from the North and paid the taxes on the plantation. He let me and Mama stay on to serve him. We moved to the slave quarters."

His jaw dropped. She pushed it back up. "You need to keep still so I don't cut you."

"He shouldn't have done that."

She shrugged. "I'm just grateful he didn't make us sleep in the fields or turn us out completely. When he planted cotton, we picked it."

"Me and Dallas used to pick cotton when we were young."

She sat back on her heels. "You did?"

He nodded. "I didn't mind it so much, but Dallas hated it. Swore when he got old enough, he'd find himself a job that didn't involve plowing fields or picking crops. Reckon that's why he likes cattle."

She stood and walked to the other side.

"I can finish shaving," he said, reaching for the razor.

She batted his hand away. "I can do it." Carefully, she began to shave the area below the patch, to work her way around his scars. "Anyway, eventually, Mr. Bryant let Mama work in the house. When she died, I took over her chores. I tended to his needs when he got too feeble to take care of himself. He was such a proud man. In the end, I grew rather fond of him, even though he was a Yankee."

She angled her head to study Houston's face. "Shall I leave the whiskers above your lip so you can grow a mustache?"

"If you want. A man with a face like mine doesn't put much stock in how he looks."

But he did care, she realized, thinking back to the day she'd met him. He'd been clean shaven then. The morning they were to leave, he'd bathed and shaved. And he'd brought along his shaving equipment and a tiny mirror so he could keep up his appearance as they traveled. If he had wanted a mustache, he would have grown one without her suggesting it. She pursed her lips and narrowed her eyes. "No, I think a mustache would hide your mouth, and you have such a nice-looking mouth."

In the fading light, she could see the blush creep over his face. Gingerly, she shaved over his lip. A shiver shimmied up her spine when his breath fanned her knuckles.

She wiped the remnants of lather away and trailed her fingers along his smooth jaw, across his chin, and up his cheek until her palm cradled the side of his face, her fingertips resting lightly against the patch. It pleased her that he didn't grab her wrist and pull her hand away. "Does it still hurt?"

She watched as he swallowed. "Sometimes . . . when a Norther blows through, it'll ache."

Her gaze drifted back to his lips. They looked incredibly soft and out of place on a face as rugged as his. She lifted her eyes and discovered that he was studying her mouth as well. Self-consciously, she licked her lips.

His gaze slowly roamed over her features until they settled on her eyes. "It'll be dark soon. You'd best get inside. All manner of animals come out at night."

Withdrawing her hand from his cheek, she rose. "I set some towels by the fire to warm. The breeze can be quite chilling when you're wet. I'll get them for you."

As calmly as she could, her stomach quivering, she strolled away, knowing that she shouldn't have enjoyed shaving Houston as much as she had, knowing that she shouldn't wonder if his lips were as soft and warm as they appeared. She made a silent vow that on the morning following her wedding, she'd shave Dallas.

AMELIA SAT ON the edge of the bed, waiting for her sleeping companion. She'd put on a clean blouse and skirt that she'd brought from Georgia. She couldn't quite bring herself to sleep in her nightgown. She heard a soft tapping and rose to her feet. "Come in."

The door opened, and Houston peered into the room. "You ready for me to come inside?"

She nodded. With one long stride, he was in the room, looking as uncomfortable as she felt.

"You want the door closed?" he asked.

She nodded again, not certain her voice had come into the room with her.

He set his saddlebags near the door and glanced around the room, looking at everything but Amelia and the bed. Finally, he released a long, slow breath and met her gaze. "I figure we got two choices here. I can either sneak out the window and sneak back in at dawn, or I can sleep on the floor."

"Or you can sleep in the bed."

His gaze darted over to the bed.

"I think it would hurt Beth's feelings if she somehow discovered that you hadn't slept in the bed."

"Yeah, well, right now I'm more concerned with your feelings."

"Are you?"

He swept his gaze over to her. "Yes."

"Well, right now, I'm tired and would love to sleep in a bed. If we keep our clothes on, with the bundle board between us, I see no problem with us sharing the bed."

A corner of his mouth crooked up. "You don't think I could crawl over that?"

She angled her chin. "I don't think you *would* crawl over it."

He met her challenge gracefully. "All right. Which side do you want?"

"I'll take this side next to the table."

He walked across the room and sat on the side of the bed nearest the window. The ropes supporting the mattress creaked beneath his weight. "Can I take off my boots?"

"And your hat and your coat."

Amelia took a last glance around the room. Beth's clothes hung in a wardrobe with no doors. Her wardrobe contained fewer clothes than Amelia's new wardrobe, but Beth possessed something Amelia didn't.

"Oh, isn't this beautiful?" she asked in a quiet voice of reverence as she crossed the room and touched her fingers to the finely detailed white lace covering the silk gown.

"White's not very practical," Houston said. "It'd be showing all the dirt before the morning was half over."

"A woman would only wear it once."

"Seems like a waste of money then."

"I suppose, but I guess you're paying for all the memories it would hold."

"Memories?"

"Yes," she replied, glancing over her shoulder at the man sitting on the bed, wondering briefly if men held onto memories as women did. "A woman would wear it on her wedding day."

He furrowed his brow. "What are you gonna wear when you marry Dallas?"

She shrugged and walked to the bed. "Something that we purchased in Fort Worth, I imagine."

"You should have told me you needed something special."

She sat on the bed with her back to him and removed her shoes. "I don't need something special." She quickly slipped beneath the covers and rolled to her side, her back against the bundle board.

The bed shifted as he stretched out on the other side of the board.

"Do you mind if I keep the lamp burning?" she asked.

"Don't mind at all."

"Will it keep you awake?"

"No. I always sleep with a light burning."

Amelia rolled to her back. "You do?"

"Yep. The light from a campfire or the lamp beside my bed."

The gruffness of his voice stated more clearly than his words that it had cost him dearly to admit that, to reveal a part of himself that she imagined no one else knew. She hugged herself, hoarding the information he'd shared with her. "Is Dallas's house like this one?"

"Nope."

"What does it look like?"

He took a long moment to answer. "It's big."

"Is it pretty?"

"Dallas thinks so."

"But you don't think so."

He heaved a deep sigh. "I don't think you can really appreciate it until you've seen it."

"Do you live there?"

"No, I got my own place about an hour's ride away."

"Is it big?" she asked.

"No. It's smaller than this place. Just one room, but it suits me."

Amelia drew the covers up to her chin and watched the shadows play over the wall as the flame inside the lamp quivered. She could well imagine Houston in a one-room house, tending his horses during the day and watching the stars at night.

"Good night," she said softly, rolling over to her side.

"Amelia?"

"Yes?"

"If you hear that animal cry out like you did some time back . . just ignore it."

She had suspected all along that it was his cry she had heard, but the sound hadn't been that of an animal; rather the wail of someone who was lost.

"Sometimes, I cry out at night, too," she said softly.

He didn't reply. She didn't really expect him to. She allowed the silence to ease in around her. She closed her eyes. The light from the lantern danced across her eyelids, comforting her with its presence. The bed shifted.

"Amelia?"

Rolling over, she came up on her elbow, only to find Houston had done the same. Their gazes locked, his only slightly higher than hers. She stilled, her breath held. She watched his Adam's apple slowly slide up and down.

"I . . . uh . . . I wanted to thank you for the shave. I've never felt anything so fine in my whole life."

"It was my pleasure. I . . . I'm going to shave

Dallas after we're married," she felt compelled to add.

He gave a brusque nod. "He'll like that. 'Night."

"Good night." She snuggled beneath the covers, trying to forget the feel of Houston's jaw cradled within her palm. Once she had tried to imagine what his smile might look like. Now she wondered how his mouth would look poised for a kiss.

She squeezed her eyes shut. She had done nothing wrong. She'd simply shaved her fiancé's brother as a way to repay him for his kindness . . . but her reasoning did little to ease her guilt.

Chapter Nine

As dawn eased over the horizon, Amelia hugged Beth tightly.

"We'll try and come in the spring, during round-up," Beth promised.

"I'll look forward to it," Amelia assured her just before she allowed Houston to hoist her onto the wagon. She tightened the ribbons on the bonnet Beth had given her. As the wagon began to roll forward, she turned and waved at the family left behind.

John slipped his arm around his wife. Amelia smiled. Soon she would have a husband to do the same with her. If only he would love her as much as John loved Beth.

Amelia faced forward. "Wasn't it nice of Beth to give me a bonnet?"

Houston kept his opinion on that to himself. All he could see was the tip of her nose and as cute as it was, it wasn't enough. He knew the bonnet would protect her from the sun and wind, would keep her face soft, her skin pale. But it didn't mean he had to like it.

"Will we be meeting any other neighbors?" Amelia asked.

"Not that I know of."

"How much longer until we're at the ranch?"

"A good fifteen days." Or a bad fifteen days, depending on how he looked at it. He'd drop her off at Dallas's door and head on to his own small place, where he ate alone, slept alone, and dreamed alone.

If he dared to dream. He'd been right in the beginning. Having a woman around made a man long for things he shouldn't. He'd stayed up all night listening to her even breathing, watching her snuggle beneath the blankets, and wishing that damn bundle board hadn't been there so she could have snuggled against him.

His stomach tightened as he thought of Dallas's holding this woman through the night, protecting her from whatever it was that made her sleep with a light burning.

A light seldom kept his own demons at bay. He sure as hell couldn't keep hers away.

THEY TRAVELED FOUR days, the land growing flatter, the trees scarcer. Amelia imagined in summer, when the sun baked the earth, that men worshipped the shade they found beneath the few trees scattered about. As Houston had promised, nothing blocked her view of the sunset.

As dusk settled in, she glanced at the scattered trees, the brush, and the withering grass blowing in the breeze, rippling across the land like the sea washing over the shore.

"What can I do to help?" she asked as she followed Houston from the wagon, his arms loaded with supplies while hers remained empty.

"You can gather up some prairie coal."

"Prairie coal?"

A corner of his mouth tipped up. "Cow dung."

"What are you going to do with it?"

"When there's no wood, we burn cow dung."

She wrinkled her nose. "Isn't that rather unpleasant?"

"You get used to it." The corner of his mouth lifted a little higher. "But I'll gather it up. Why don't you look in the wagon and decide which can I should open for tonight's meal?"

She angled her chin. "You've done everything since we left Fort Worth. I can handle prairie coal." She walked back to the wagon, picked up her reticule, and pulled out a white linen handkerchief with tatted edges.

She marched to the first brown lump she could see peering through the tall prairie grasses. Carefully, she placed her handkerchief over the object and gingerly lifted it off the ground, making certain her fingers never actually touched anything other than the linen.

Holding the coal—she much preferred to think of it as coal rather than dung—as far away from her as possible, holding her breath as well, she walked back into the camp. "Where do you want the fire?"

Working to stretch the tent into place, Houston glanced over his shoulder and a shaft of warmth pierced his heart. He'd never thought of Amelia as prim and proper, but she sure as hell looked prim and proper with some lacy thing hanging over cow dung. "Right there ought to do just fine."

She started to bend down.

"No, no," he amended. "A little closer to the tent might be better."

She straightened and walked toward him. "Here?" she asked.

"Yep."

She placed the dung on the ground and began shaking out her linen.

"On second thought, that might be too close. A strong wind comes through here and the tent would go up in flames."

"Where do you want it, then?" she asked, her lips pursed.

He wondered what the hell he thought he was doing. He'd often seen cowboys pull pranks on each other, but he hadn't been on the giving or the receiving end of a prank in years, and he had forgotten how it was done so everyone ended up laughing.

He wanted to hear her laugh, but playing with manure sure as hell wasn't the way to accomplish that goal. Irritated with his stupidity, he released his hold on the tent, and it fell into a heap. He picked up the cow dung and tossed it a foot or so away. "Right there ought to do it."

A look of horror crossed her face. "You touched it."

"It makes the chore go quicker."

She visibly shuddered. "Should I set it on fire or do you want to?"

"We're gonna need a few more. Since my hands are dirty, I'll gather them. You check the cans."

This time Amelia didn't protest. She scurried back to the wagon and studied their supplies. Nothing appealed to her.

A shiver raced down her spine, and she shuddered with the realization of how quiet everything had suddenly become. Silent and still, like a funeral. Even the mules and Sorrel seemed to sense it as they lifted their noses and turned their ears back.

She glanced at the sky. It was growing darker, but not from the approaching night. Blocking out the late afternoon sun, black clouds rolled in as though pushed by the mighty hand of a giant.

Without warning, the wind rose, sweeping up the dirt, whipping it around her, and startling her with its ferocity. A fat raindrop splattered on her nose.

She heard a harsh curse and spun around. Houston was fighting the wind to get her tent into place and having very little luck. She wondered if he would stay in the tent with her if it rained.

She heard a crack of thunder. A sheet of lightning flashed, igniting the sky so brightly she would have sworn she was standing in the center of it. Houston flung the tent to the ground and strode toward her, seemingly a man with a purpose.

A wide arrow of white lightning streaked to the ground. Sorrel whinnied and dropped her head between her knees. The sky reverberated with rolling thunder as another streak of lightning burst through the darkening sky. Houston reached her.

"Climb inside the wagon," he ordered as he began to unbuckle his gunbelt.

Amelia backed up a step. "I don't mind getting wet."

"It's not the rain I'm worried about," he said as he laid his gun on the floorboards. "It's the lightning. Now, get inside." Kneeling, he removed his spurs and tossed them into the wagon.

"Are you going to get in the wagon?"

"No, I need to get all the metal off the animals." As though tired of waiting on her, he quickly came to his feet, grabbed her waist, and hoisted her into the back as though she was nothing more than a sack of flour.

The wind wailed, thunder roared, and lightning flashed across the sky.

"Get down, damn it! I don't have much time!"

It was the desperation in his voice that convinced her. She lay on her side and wrapped her arms around her drawn-up knees as he brought the tarpaulin over her. Darkness enclosed her, encircled her, and taunted her with the memories of another time when she'd been huddled in a wooden box.

The rain began to pelt the tarpaulin, a steady staccato beat, like the distant sound of long-ago gunfire, the pounding of a thousand hooves . . . or so it had seemed at the time.

The terrifying darkness trapped her inside its windowless cocoon, blacker than night with no stars, no moon. She was a little girl again, eight years old. Too small. Too frightened. And the enemy was coming.

Amelia grew hot. Breathing became difficult . . . just as before. The memories rose up and howled louder than the wind that rushed past the wagon.

She could hear her mother's frightened voice. "Hurry, Amelia. Hurry!"

"No, Mama! No!"

Her mother's fingers dug into the delicate flesh of her arm as Amelia tried to dig her heels into the wooden floor. Her mother jerked her so hard that she thought surely her arm would come off her body. "Come on, child. Your papa will protect you. You'll be safe with him."

"No, Mama! No!"

The room loomed closer and closer. The shadowed room. The flames from the candles flickered, and the ghosts danced along the wall.

"Hurry, Amelia. Papa will save you."

"No, Mama! No, please! Papa can't save me. Papa's dead!"

Amelia couldn't breathe. She was suffocating, drowning in the memories. She yanked on the ribbons and jerked the bonnet off her head. Still she couldn't draw air into her lungs. Desperately she tore at the tarpaulin.

Houston was working to get the harness off the mules when he saw Amelia scramble out of the wagon and begin running toward . . . nothing but a distant horizon. He was familiar enough with lightning storms to know the damage they could do on the flat open plains. With a harsh curse, he bolted after her.

She stumbled, her knees hitting the ground.

She scrambled back to her feet and continued to run, her arms waving around her as though she were warding off the very demons of hell.

His legs were longer, churning faster than hers. He caught her, totally unprepared for the stark terror in her eyes when he swung her around. She flailed her arms, hitting his face, his shoulders, his chest.

"Don't put me back in there! Please, don't put me back in there! I'll die! I swear to God, I'll die if you put me back in there!"

He wrapped his arms around her, drawing her against his chest. "I won't," he promised, his breathing labored, his heart pounding so hard he was certain she could feel it. "I won't."

She slumped against him. Still holding her, he brought his duster around her and eased them both to the ground. She trembled violently.

"It's all right," he cooed as though she were a horse he wanted to tame. "It's all right." He began to rock gently back and forth while the mild rain splattered his back and dripped slowly from his hat. Lightning flashed around them, so brilliant, so close that he thought it might blind him. He pulled the right side of his hat down and ducked his head, hoping to give her more shelter. A short distance away, lightning struck the ground, igniting a fire that the rain quickly drenched. Smoldering smoke trailed along the ground.

"If it hits us, we'll die, won't we?" she asked in a quiet calm voice, a voice too calm, too quiet.

"Probably."

"Do you think it'll hurt?"

"No," he replied, tightening his hold. "We'll just see a flash of bright light, and everything will go black."

She tilted her face. "You don't have to wait here with me."

"You'll get wet."

She smiled, an endearing crooked grin, and right then, he didn't care if the lightning did strike him. Dying with her in his arms couldn't be worse than living a life alone.

His backside was drenched, mud coated his trousers, rivulets of water ran into his boots, and water dripped off the brim of his hat onto his shoulders. His muscles ached from the un-natural way he held his body, trying to shield her from the storm. He brushed his knuckles over her tear-streaked face and lowered his mouth until it rested beside her ear. "Tell me," he said simply.

The crack of thunder filled the air. The smile eased off her face, and a great sadness filled her eyes. He wished he had the power to remove the sadness from her life—forever.

The rain lessened, falling softly, its patter a somber melody to accompany her words.

"I told you that my father died during the war. The day we were to bury him . . ." She swallowed and turned her gaze toward the darkening sky. "Some men came. I don't know if they were sol-diers or deserters. They wore blue uniforms, but no one seemed in charge. My mother was terri-fied, so she hid me."

A tremor traveled the length of her slight body. He remembered that she'd told him that she didn't like being inside the darkness. Not in the dark, not afraid of the dark. But inside the darkness. Dread crept through him. "Where did she hide you?"

"With my father." She looked at him then, tears welling in her eyes. "Inside his coffin. It was so dark. I was afraid that no one would find me. That they would bury me with him. I cried until I fell asleep."

"You said at the hotel that you'd slept with worse."

She nodded, her voice growing ragged. "He was so cold. When I woke up, Mama was holding me, but she was different. I don't know what they did to her. Her face and her throat were bruised. Her dress was torn. I always thought that she should have been crying, but she wasn't. She just stared, but not at anything I could see. It was like she was staring inside herself, like her mind, her heart had gone away, and only her body remained to hold me."

The bile rose in his throat. "Your sisters?"

She pressed her face harder against his shoulder until he thought she might crack his bones. She moved her head back and forth, and the warmth of her tears soaked through the flannel of his shirt. "They were staring, too," she rasped. "Staring at the sky. They were lying side by side, holding hands . . . and there wasn't much left of their clothes. It was so ugly." She dug her fingers into his sides.

"Don't think about it," he ordered. He hated the war. It had brought out the best in men like his brother, the worst in men like him, and turned the rest into animals.

She sobbed. "I didn't want to look at my sisters, but I did. I didn't want to see the blood, but I did. So much of it. I think I know what those men did—"

"They weren't men. Animals, maybe, but not men. Men don't harm the innocent." He cupped her cheek and pressed her face against his chest. "They didn't hurt you?"

"Not my body, but my heart. I wanted to leave the plantation then, but I was only eight. And Mama was in no condition to travel. So we stayed and survived as best we could."

She tilted her head back, her eyes as dark as the storm clouds. "That's when I began searching for things, small things, for which I could be grateful. It didn't matter how trivial, how silly. I just needed something each day to make me go on to the next day."

He knew that feeling. Damn, he knew that feeling all too well.

"When Mama died, I placed my ad to travel west and become a wife. I had to leave, to get away from the land that had soaked up my sisters' blood, away from the memories. I need new memories to replace those that haunt me when darkness closes in."

The thunder echoed around them, the lightning shimmered through the air, and the rain began to fall again, harder than before. She nestled up against his shoulder.

Houston removed his hat, giving the rain the freedom to wash over them, to wipe the tears from her face, and to ease the hurt in her heart.

The deluge prevented him from hearing her

voice, but the shape of her lips revealed the words "Thank you."

He could only nod and pray that when the storm ended, he would find the strength to let her go.

Chapter Ten

$\mathcal{H}$ouston stared at the roiling brown river and cursed last night's storm. It lingered on the air, threatening to return, leaving gray clouds hovering low and a strong brisk wind toying with the prairie grasses. If the storm returned, it had the power to make the river impassable for days, leaving Houston's options damn limited as far as he was concerned.

They could wait until the water receded and hope the storm moved on with no others coming to take its place. But they were already behind schedule. As it was now, they wouldn't arrive when Dallas was expecting them. He didn't think Dallas could afford to send his men out on a wild-goose chase, so instead, his brother would be pacing on his bad leg, staring toward the rising sun, and working himself into a slow simmering temper.

Or Houston could haul Amelia and the wagon across the river, and hope the good fortune he'd lost somewhere along the way would catch up with him. Not one thing had delayed him in reaching Fort Worth. Nothing should have delayed him in returning to the ranch.

He prodded Sorrel forward. The horse moved cautiously through the swirling water, but she didn't hesitate. Houston trusted the animal's instincts. If the horse had balked, he wouldn't have pressed her on.

The cold water lapped at Houston's calves. Crossing rivers had never been his favorite part of trailing cattle or moving from one spot to the next.

They reached the middle of the river. The small waves slapped at Sorrel's sides, but the river itself wasn't as deep as Houston had expected it to be. He glanced over his shoulder. Amelia sat in the wagon, worry etched along her delicate features.

Despite the cold water, her concern warmed him. She would soon become his sister by marriage, but he seemed unable to steer his feelings toward brotherly concern. They ran deeper, so much deeper. He pulled the reins to the right, guiding the horse back to the bank from which they'd come.

"What do you think?" Amelia asked as they cleared the water.

"I think it's safe, but I want to take you over on the horse. Then I'll come back for the wagon."

"Why are wooden crosses lining the bank?" she asked.

He glanced toward the crude markers, made from tree limbs. "It's not unusual to lose a man when you're crossing a river, herding cows. Horse gets spooked, cows get spooked. Man goes under, can't swim, the cows stop him from coming back up."

"I suppose, then, that I should be grateful we're not herding cows."

"Yep. Reckon you should be."

She gnawed her bottom lip. "Do you swim?"

"Yep."

Relief quickly flickered in her eyes, trust soon replacing it. Dallas's trust had been heavy enough to bear, hers seemed incredibly heavier.

He positioned his horse and held out his hand, anticipating the warmth of her fingers within his grasp. She slipped elegantly onto the back of the horse and wrapped her arms around him.

"The water's cold," he said as the horse skidded down the bank and splashed into the river.

Releasing a small gasp when the water rose up to their calves, she tightened her hold on him. "How many more rivers do we have to cross?" she asked.

"Not many, but this is the widest and deepest. It would have been better if we'd been able to cross before the storm."

Sorrel momentarily lost her footing. Houston's heart leapt into his throat, nearly suffocating him with the thought of Amelia's falling from her precarious perch behind him, but she clung tenaciously to him while he held fast to the saddle horn, calming the horse with the pressure of his thighs, his sure hand on the reins.

He knew the moment the horse regained her footing. He urged Sorrel forward, breathing an unsteady sigh of relief as the water grew shallow. Sorrel struggled up the muddy tree-lined bank.

Reaching behind him, Houston helped Amelia slide off the horse. He shrugged out of his duster and draped it over her shoulders. "Why don't you see if you can find some dry wood so we can warm up before we head out?"

With concern clearly reflected in her eyes, she rested her hand on his thigh. He would have sworn her touch latched onto his heart.

"Please be careful," she said quietly.

He gave her what he hoped was a smile. He couldn't remember the last time his face had broken into a real smile. The muscles felt tight, unaccustomed to the movement. He hoped he didn't look ridiculous. "Got no choice in the matter. Dallas would have my hide if I left you out here all alone."

She gave him a smile, a beautiful smile that made her green eyes sparkle and chased away the worried frown. The sight of it tightened something in his chest.

He prodded Sorrel back across the river. Once on the other side, he tied a rope to the saddle horn, his intent to lead Sorrel back across the river. He left the other end unsecured, simply threading it through his fingers along with the reins. He didn't want the horse tethered to the wagon if something should happen. Every now and then, a strong rush of water had pushed against them as they'd crossed back over.

His more practical side told him to wait . . . but the side that housed his heart urged him to take the wagon across and get Amelia to the ranch as soon as possible.

He looked across the river. She stood on the far

bank, watching him, not gathering wood as he'd told her. For some reason he couldn't explain, it alarmed him and warmed him to see her watching, waiting for him.

He indulged himself for a moment and envisioned her standing within the doorway of his cabin, wearing that green dress they'd purchased in Fort Worth, her loose hair brushed to a golden sheen, the scent of fresh-baked bread wafting behind her . . .

He shook off the image. She'd be standing on Dallas's veranda. Houston Leigh would be nothing more to her than a brother by marriage, which was as it should be. Women like Amelia belonged to men like Dallas. And Dallas had branded her as his long before Houston even knew her name.

With a slap of the reins and a coarse yell, he sent the mules moving slowly toward the river's edge. The wagon teetered as it rolled over the uneven, muddy ground.

Houston whacked the reins over the mules' backsides and yelled louder, urging the animals forward into the rushing water. The four mules moved sluggishly, dragging the wagon slowly across the river. Floating brushwood rushed rapidly downstream, spinning and dipping.

The wagon jerked to a stop. Houston slapped the reins and hollered. The mules strained against the harness, strained against the water. Houston was on the verge of jumping into the water in order to work the wheels free when the wagon lurched forward, a loud crack filled the air, and all hell broke loose.

A mule brayed, and the other mules no longer worked as a team. It flashed through Houston's mind that something—possibly a snake—had spooked them.

Then nothing but panic roared through his mind as the wagon began to lean with the force of the current. He released the rope holding Sorrel and prayed the horse had the good sense to cross to the other side of the river. Then he prayed Amelia would have the good sense to ride the horse west.

A log traveling rapidly with the current rammed into the wagon. The mules screeched. Houston was losing control, losing control of the team, losing control of the wagon. He jumped into the river with the thought of gaining control by grabbing the lead mule, but the current was stronger, the river bottom slicker than he'd anticipated. His foot slid out from under him and he went under.

Amelia watched in horror as Houston disappeared beneath the raging current. When he surfaced, he plowed through the water until he reached the back of the wagon. He wrapped a hand around a wheel, then bent, his other hand disappearing under the water, and she wondered if he thought he could lift the wagon, free it, and push it across the surging water.

Then the wagon groaned and tilted further until it looked as though it might topple onto him. She balled her hands around his duster, silently urging him to leave the wagon, to escape the river. As though he heard her pleas, he began to fight the current. She barely had time to release her breath before she realized he wasn't heading toward shore, that his destination was the mules. Helplessly she watched as he struggled to release the mules. An eternity seemed to pass before one mule began to wander toward the shore where she stood.

Amelia's heart leapt into her throat when she spotted another log traveling quickly with the current. She screamed out a warning at the same moment that one of the remaining mules sidestepped and shoved its shoulder against Houston. He stumbled backward. The log rammed into the base of his skull. Once again, the current dragged him down.

Amelia threw off his duster and jumped into the river.

White light exploded in Houston's head before the brown water sucked him under. He heard Amelia's scream, and dear God, help him, he thought he saw her leap into the river.

He forced back the pain, forced back the welcome oblivion, and resurfaced to see her splashing in the water, screaming his name.

With long, swift strokes born of desperation, he swam toward her, fighting the current, fighting the fear. If she lost her footing as he had, she'd go under the murky waters . . . and find herself surrounded by the darkness that terrified her. No sunlight would filter through the churning river to guide her back to the surface. He wanted her to see another sunrise, to know again the feathery touch of dawn.

As he neared, he could see the fear darkening her eyes. Gaining his footing, he snaked out his arm, wrapping it around her waist and drawing her trembling body against his. The mud sucked at his boots as he hauled her to the bank of the river and collapsed in the muck, her body falling alongside his, her breathing labored, his own chest aching as he fought to draw in air. With the blinding stars dancing across his vision, he rose up on an elbow and glared at the quivering woman lying beside him. Her lips were incredibly blue in a face that was amazingly white. He pressed his wet body over hers, trying to warm her.

She laid her palm against his bristled cheek. "You're safe," she whispered.

"What the hell did you think you were doing?" he growled, his heart pounding wildly in his chest.

"I was going to save you."

He threaded his fingers through her tangled hair. She'd lost her bonnet. She was damn lucky she hadn't lost her life. "You little fool," he rasped in a voice rift with emotion. "You brave little fool."

His mouth swooped down to cover hers. Her cold, quivering lips parted slightly, and he thrust his tongue through the welcome opening like a man desperately searching for treasure.

And treasure he found.

He gentled the kiss because she wasn't a whore whose body he wanted to use to gratify his lust. She was a woman whose warmth he wanted to relish as it seeped through his body, touching his heart as none had before her. He wanted to feel the gentle swell of her curves as they pressed against the hard planes of his body. He wanted—

for just one moment—to be young again and innocent. To have no knowledge of betrayal.

Her mouth was warm and sweet, so incredibly sweet. And small, just like the rest of her. She tasted so damn good. He savored her flavor the way a man might enjoy a glass of fine whiskey, leisurely, allowing the liquor to fill his mouth before releasing the brew, allowing it to burn his throat.

He touched his tongue to hers and heard her small sigh. She scraped her fingers up the side of his face and wove them through his hair. He'd lost his hat as well, and for the first time since he'd been wounded, he welcomed the absence of the shadows.

She smelled of the river, but still he caught the slight scent that was hers and hers alone. He longed to give his mouth the freedom to warm all of her, to kiss every inch of her.

She stopped trembling from the cold, and he could feel the intoxicating warmth as their bodies pressed together. Another tremor passed through her body, a tremor that had nothing to do with the cold. He deepened the kiss, his hands bracketing her face, turning it so he could better the angle and touch her mouth with the intimacy of a long-time lover.

Kiss her as he'd never kissed another. Kiss her as he had no right.

Drawing away, he gazed at her. Her eyes were dark with passion, her lips no longer blue, but red, a deep red, swollen from his kiss.

"I shouldn't have done that," he said in a low voice.

Hurt plunged into the depths of her eyes. Gingerly, he removed his fingers from her tangled hair. "I'll get a fire going."

He struggled to his feet and staggered to the place where she'd left his duster. He snatched it up, returned to her side, and spread it over her as she lay there staring at him. A coldness seeped through his flesh and wrapped around his heart. He went in search of something—anything— with which he could build a fire.

Amelia sat up and slipped into the duster, drawing it tightly around her. It carried his scent of horses and leather.

She touched her fingers to her trembling lips. She had always imagined that Dallas Leigh would be the first to kiss her. But she had never imagined the kiss would be like the one she had just received, would make her feel so warm, so scared, so safe. All the feelings jumbling around inside her made no sense.

She watched as Houston built a fire nearby. She waited until he'd brought the fire to life, just as he'd brought feelings to life within her.

She rose to her feet, walked to the fire, and knelt beside him. "I suppose I shouldn't have kissed you back."

"No, you shouldn't have," he said, tersely, never taking his eyes away from the smoldering fire. "But I figure you were probably just scared and not thinking."

"Were you scared?"

Houston felt his stomach clench. By God, he was terrified, more now than he had been when he'd seen her rushing into the river. That kiss had him shaking clear down to his boots.

He'd expected her to be sweet. He hadn't expected her to be everything he'd ever dreamed of when he was younger and deserved dreams.

Damn Dallas! Damn him to hell for wanting women in addition to cattle, land, and wealth. Damn him for wanting this woman, for earning the right to have her.

Houston shoved himself to his feet. "I need to round up the mules. You stay here and dry off."

His long strides couldn't take him far enough, fast enough. Her flowery scent followed him like a shadow. The lingering taste of her lips taunted him, made him hungry for more. He could still feel the soft swells of her breasts shifting beneath his chest. His fingers ached to hold them, shape them, and caress them with a tenderness he'd never known existed.

He released a shudder as he skidded down the muddy bank. He needed a sporting woman. He'd gone too long without spending himself on a woman. That was the reason he found this journey so damn difficult, the reason he wanted to hold Amelia close. He just needed to purge his longings. Maria would help him. She always did. She would douse all the flames, and in total darkness, he'd take her without passion, without love, without hope. And in the darkness, she couldn't see the ugliness that made him the man he was.

He didn't want Amelia to see the ugliness, either, but she would. Sooner or later, she would.

WHEN NIGHT FELL, Amelia eased as close to the fire as she dared and wrapped the horse's blanket around herself. The wind came up off the river, damp and frigid. She shuddered.

"Cold?"

She lifted her gaze to the man sitting on the other side of the fire. He'd found the horse and three of the mules. She had a feeling that he'd found the fourth mule as well. She'd heard a gunshot, but he hadn't brought any food back to their small camp. Tomorrow, they would comb the banks of the river to see what they could recover.

"A little," she said, hating the way her teeth clicked together as she spoke. She hadn't been able to regain any warmth since he'd ended the kiss.

Watching him, if she didn't know better, she would have thought he was having an argument with someone. His brow furrowed deeply, his jaw clenched, and with his finger, he drew something in the dirt. Then like a man who had lost the battle, he shoved to his feet and walked around to her side of the fire.

Curiosity getting the better of her, she scrambled to her knees so she could see what he'd written. The light from the flames danced over Dallas's brand.

Houston sat beside her, and she met his gaze. "Why did you draw that?"

"As a reminder that he has a claim on you." He stretched out on the ground and opened his duster. "Come here."

She hesitated, her heart pounding. As an unmarried woman betrothed to his brother, she knew she should suffer through the cold, shouldn't welcome the warmth his body could provide. She closed her hand around the watch, her gift to Dallas that was still hidden in her pocket, and lay next to Houston.

He wrapped his duster and one arm around her, crooking his other arm. "Here, use my arm as a pillow," he said quietly.

She scooted back, nestling her backside against his stomach and laying her head on his arm.

"Better?" he asked.

"Warmer." She studied his curled hand, the long, tanned fingers. She knew the strength those fingers held, had felt it this afternoon as he'd braced her face and lowered his mouth to hers. The pads and palms of his fingers were callused, and she resisted the urge to place her hand over his, to press palm to palm, fingertip to fingertip.

"What will we do tomorrow?" she asked.

"See what we can salvage. Use the mules as pack animals."

"I guess we should have waited to cross the river."

"Yeah."

She heard his sigh more than his word. "Why didn't we?"

Silence fell heavy between them. Amelia rolled over within his arms and felt him stiffen. "Why didn't we wait?"

"Because we'd already lost too much time," he stated flatly.

"Why did you kiss me?"

"Because I'm a fool."

She touched her fingers to his lips. He grabbed her wrist and pulled her hand back.

"Don't do that," he said gruffly.

"We shouldn't have crossed the river. You shouldn't have kissed me. Yet, you did both. Why?"

"Because it's been too damn long since I've been with a woman. Don't read any feelings into what happened this afternoon. I'm a man and I've got needs. Needs any woman would fill. Right now, you're the only woman within two hundred miles."

"So it's not me specifically. It's only because I'm a woman."

"That's right," he said curtly.

"And why did I kiss you back?"

"I reckon women have needs, too."

"And any man would do? That makes me no better than a whore."

He released her wrist. "That's not what I meant."

"I know," she said softly. "You think it's the circumstances and not the people that made us turn to each other this afternoon."

"That's right. You won't be turning to me once we get to the ranch. Once you're with Dallas. Now go to sleep."

She rolled over, giving him her back. She watched the flames in the low fire flicker, just as her thoughts flickered. Was he right? Had she kissed him just because he was there? Because she'd been terrified? "Houston?"

She had been quiet for so long that Houston had been certain she'd fallen asleep. He'd never before heard his name come from her lips as anything but a scream. His heart tightened, and he fought against pulling her closer. "What?"

"What sort of man is Dallas?"

A better man than me. He swallowed, searching for the words that would do his brother justice, true words that would ease her doubts. "He's the kind of man who casts a long shadow . . . a shadow that reaches out to touch everyone and everything. Years from now, people who never knew him will remember him."

She rolled over, pressing her face against his shoulder. "And my shadow will be short. I worry that the man I imagined in the letters doesn't really exist. He seems almost perfect."

"All I can tell you is that I couldn't ask for a finer brother, and I don't imagine you could ask for a finer husband."

"What if he's disappointed when he meets me?"

Tenderness filled him at her insecurity. "He won't be disappointed. I can give you my word on that." Reaching over her, he tucked his duster around her. "Now you'd best get to sleep. Tomorrow's gonna be another long day."

"I'm so grateful you were with me today," she said quietly as she closed her eyes.

Houston couldn't remember if anyone had ever before been grateful for his presence. His mother, he supposed. Certainly not his father.

Unlike Dallas, Houston had never measured up to his father's expectations. He had never been strong enough, smart enough, or fast enough.

"Swear to God, I ought to dress you in girl's clothing!" his father had bellowed the day he had discovered Houston holding a rag doll in the mercantile.

The doll had looked so lonely sprawled over the counter, where a little girl had left her while she browsed the assortment of candies. And so soft. He'd just wanted to see if she was as soft as she looked.

She had been. Her embroidered face had carried a permanent smile, a smile that had made Houston grin crookedly at her.

He realized now that the smile more than the doll had probably set his father off. Or maybe it had been both. Either way, his actions hadn't been of a manly nature. When they'd returned home, his father had taken a switch to Houston's backside. A switch he'd made Houston find.

When the punishment ended, Houston had pulled his trousers up with as much dignity as he could muster. When he had turned, and his father had seen the silent tears coursing down his cheeks, he'd struck Houston's face. The switch had cut into his tender young flesh, leaving a scar that ran the length of his cheek.

He'd hated the scar, often wished it was gone. His mother had warned him to be wary of what he wished for.

When he was fifteen, his wish had come true. Yankee artillery fire had blown the scar off his face, leaving a place for thicker scars to form. He hadn't made a wish since.

But he found himself wishing now. Wishing that the arm holding Amelia hadn't grown as numb as the left side of his face. He could no longer feel the warmth of her body, the sureness of her weight. His one chance to hold a decent woman within his arms through the night, and his arm had fallen asleep.

He thought about adjusting his position, but he didn't want to wake her. His free hand hovered over her face, and like a moonbeam kissing the waters of a lake, he brushed her hair away from her cheek. So soft. So incredibly soft. Like the rag doll he'd held so long ago.

Only she wasn't a doll. She was a woman, flesh and blood, a woman whom Dallas had entrusted into his keeping.

A woman with eyes the green of clover, hair the shade of an autumn moon.

And courage as boundless as the West Texas plains.

Chapter Eleven

Everything. Everything was gone.

Amelia stared at the brown flowing river and wondered why they even bothered to look. Her letters from Dallas were gone. A miniature of her mother. She had brought everything that had ever meant anything to her—and now everything was gone.

Everything except the pocket watch she'd purchased for Dallas.

She fought back the tears welling in her eyes. She'd lost everything once before, and somehow she'd managed to survive. She would survive again.

She lifted her chin in defiance, daring the fates to toy with her. Out of the corner of her eye, she saw the sunlight glint through the mud. Lifting her skirts, she walked cautiously to the water's edge.

Her mirror, the mirror her mother had given her, caught and reflected the sunlight. Reaching down, she pulled it from the mud and washed it gently in the water. A sweet memory from the distant past.

She dried the mirror on her skirt, then held it up to gaze at her reflection. She was a mess. Her hair tangled, a bruise on her sun-tinged cheek, a button missing from her bodice. She stared harder at the mirror. In the background, a green cloud billowed in the breeze. She gazed over her shoulder and looked down the stream.

She trudged along the water's edge until she reached the green dress, the bodice wrapped tightly around the spindly branches of a bush, the skirt flapping in the wind. Amelia gathered the skirt close, buried her face in the smooth fabric, and let the tears fall.

And that was how Houston found her. Sitting in the mud with the water lapping at her feet, her knees drawn up, her face hidden by the abundance of green silk.

He wished he could have spared her this journey, could have just plucked her up and put her in Dallas's house without asking her to endure heartache, storms, and raging rivers.

He imagined sitting on the porch years from now with his nieces and nephews circled around him, telling them about the journey he'd made with their mother. A woman of courage, he'd call her.

And he hoped that no one would hear in his voice or see reflected in his gaze that he'd fallen in love with her.

He skidded down the muddy bank and caught

his balance, stopping himself before he plunged into the river. He trudged through the mud and knelt beside her. "Amelia?"

She lifted her tear-streaked face. "This was the first dress I'd had in over ten years that didn't belong to someone else first. I was going to save it for the day I married Dallas." She crushed the skirt to her chest. "It's all caught up on the branches."

He knew well the feeling of wearing someone else's hand-me-downs. He had worn Dallas's discarded clothing until the war. The first piece of clothing he had worn that had been his and his alone had been the gray jacket his mother had sewn him so he could ride off with pride alongside his father and older brother.

Only he hadn't felt pride . . . only fear, a cold dread that had slithered through his bowels. A terror as unsettling as the one surrounding him now. He wanted this woman safe, safe within his brother's arms, where Houston couldn't touch her, where he couldn't drag her down into the hell that was his life.

He removed his knife. "I'll cut the branches, and you can take your time working the dress free. Maybe you can repair the damage."

He moved around her and began hacking at the limbs.

"I found my mother's mirror," she said quietly. She touched his brim. "You found your hat."

"Yep. Other than that, I haven't had much luck. The water's too strong. The current's too fast."

"Are we going to go back to John and Beth's?"

"Didn't see that they had much to spare. Think

we'd just end up losing time and gaining very little."

"Then what will we do?"

He cut through the last branch and sheathed his knife. "We'll survive. We've still got everything I'd packed on Sorrel. It's not much, but it's enough. I've traveled with less."

She bundled up the green silk and rose. Houston shoved himself to his feet, removed his hat, and extended it toward her. "You'll need to wear this."

Her eyes widened. "But that's your hat."

"I know, but I can't find Austin's hat or your bonnet, and the sun will turn your pretty skin into leather. It can't hurt mine much." He grimaced as a tear trailed along her cheek. "Don't start crying on me."

"But I know what your hat means to you."

He almost told her that she meant more, but reined in the words that he had no right to voice aloud. "Then take good care of it because I'll want it back when we get to the ranch."

THE COLD WINDS whipped through the intimate camp. Amelia pulled the blanket more closely around her, tugged Houston's hat down so the brim protected her neck, and scooted closer to the fire. They had traveled most of the day, she on Sorrel, Houston straddled across a mule. They had Sorrel's blankets and the nearby brush to ward off the winds.

"Do you think it will snow?" she asked.

He glanced up. "No. Imagine in a day or so, it'll be warm again."

"This isn't winter?"

He shook his head. She returned her gaze to the fire. She wished she had Dallas's letters. After all the times she'd read them, she should have had every word memorized, but she couldn't remember anything he'd written.

All she could remember was the way Houston's kiss had made her toes curl, the firmness of his body folded around hers last night, and the warmth of his breath fanning her cheek.

Would Dallas tuck her body protectively beneath his as they slept after they were married? Would he gently comb her hair back when he thought she was sleeping? Would he make her body grow as hot as the flames licking at the logs?

She rose to her feet, walked around the fire, and knelt beside Houston. "I've been thinking."

"Yeah, I figured that."

His words surprised her, although she supposed he was coming to know her as well as she was coming to know him. "How did you know?"

"You get this deep dent in the middle of your forehead."

"What else do you know about me?"

"That you're about to start asking me questions."

"Not exactly." She scooted a little closer to him. "You said you had needs—"

"I shouldn't have said that."

"Don't you have needs?"

"Yeah, I got needs, but I shouldn't tell a lady about them."

"Why not?"

"I just shouldn't, that's all."

She gnawed on her lip. "So I shouldn't tell you I have needs, either?"

"No, you shouldn't."

Bringing the blanket more closely around her, she stared into the fire. She tried to imagine Dallas as she had envisioned him all those months, without a mustache and with blue eyes. She concentrated on the image she now had of him: brown eyes, a mustache. A woman's dream. A dream she couldn't yet touch . . . "I do have needs," she said quietly. She turned her head slightly and thought he looked terrified. "I was thinking about what you said . . . that any woman would do. I'm wondering if it's the same for me. If any man would satisfy what I'm feeling right now."

"What exactly are you feeling?"

"That I want to be kissed. If you want to be kissed, and any woman would do, why not kiss me? Then both our needs would go away, and maybe we could both go to sleep instead of sitting here staring at the fire."

"I'd rather stare at the fire."

Pain shot through her as though he'd just sent a herd of his horses stampeding over her heart. His words shouldn't have hurt. He wasn't the man she was going to marry—

"Don't do that," he ordered. "Don't get those tears in your eyes."

She gave him her back, fighting the sorrow, the anger, and the hurt. "It's not fair. Until we crossed that river, I'd never been kissed." Surging to her feet, she turned on him like a wolf trapped in the wilderness. "It wasn't fair to give me these needs and then leave me to deal with them on my own. I've never felt like this . . . like I'll die if you don't kiss me."

She whipped around and marched into the darkness away from the fire, immediately regretting her foolishness, but having too much pride to return to the warmth and the light. Surely, Dallas would want to kiss her and satisfy her needs anytime she wanted.

A large hand cradled her shoulder. "I'm sorry," she whispered. "I made a fool of myself. I can't remember what Dallas wrote in his letters. I feel lost . . . just like all our belongings. And afraid. And—"

"He said he wasn't lonely." Gently, Houston turned her and nudged his hat up off her brow. The firelight crept over his shoulder and caressed the patch and scars while leaving his eye and unmarred cheek cast in darkness. Once, she would have wasted the moment trying to imagine him as he might have looked if he'd fought no battle. Now, she simply accepted the rugged features that war had carved into his face.

"He said a wife and sons would enrich his life." He glided his hand from her shoulder up to her cheek and tilted her face. "He asked you to become his wife."

"And I said yes, but surely a simple kiss . . ." Her voice trailed into silence as he rubbed his thumb over her lower lip. Since the war, she had always feared the dark, and it seemed as though it had swallowed them both as he lowered his mouth to hers.

Leaning against him, she twined her arms

around his neck, wanting him closer, relishing his warmth as it seeped into her.

He groaned deeply, and she felt the rumble of his chest against her breasts. He plowed his hand into her hair as his mouth plundered hers, his tongue probing, seeking, causing her toes to curl.

He slipped an arm beneath her knees and lifted her against his chest. She kissed his neck, his throat, his jaw as he carried her to the fire. She clutched his shirt as he laid her on the ground and fanned out the sides of his duster before stretching his body over hers and settling his mouth against hers.

She could hear the howling of the wind, the far-off cry of a wolf, and the beating of her own heart keeping pace with his. Needs swelled up within her, needs she'd never known existed. The hard, even lines of his body melded against her soft curves. Over the worn fabric of her bodice, he palmed her breast, kneading her flesh tenderly. She couldn't hold back the whimper that rose in her throat or the desire that exploded like fireworks on the Fourth of July. She arched her back, wanting, needing him closer than he was.

He dipped his head and trailed kisses along the column of her throat.

"It's not working," she rasped.

"I know." Lifting his head, he gazed down on her, brushing the stray strands of hair away from her cheeks.

"You knew it wouldn't work, that what I was proposing was silly—"

"Not silly." A wealth of tenderness filled his gaze. "Definitely not silly."

"I need more."

He brought her hand to his lips and placed a kiss in the heart of her palm. "It's not mine to give you."

"Will Dallas give me what I need?"

"And more. He'll give you the very best. Sporting women don't even charge him for the pleasure of his company."

"Do they charge you?"

"Double." He nibbled on her lips. "Remember that. You'll be getting the best when you marry Dallas. No need to settle for less before then."

He shifted his body and wrapped the duster around her. Then he reached for the blanket, draped it over her, and tucked her in close beside him. "Go to sleep now."

But she couldn't sleep. Unfulfilled desires ravaged her body. She watched the firelight play across his features, golden shadows, amber hues. His body held a tenseness that rivaled hers. How did he expect her to sleep when her toes were still curled, her skin tingled from his touch, and her breast ached for the feel of his palm? "It would have been better if Dallas had come for me."

"Yep."

She turned into him. "Rub my back like you did when I was sick."

He splayed his fingers over her back and began the lonely sojourn.

"What I feel when you kiss me—"

"It's lust, just lust," he interjected.

"That's why you said any woman would do."

"Yep."

She snuggled against him and concentrated on the motion of his hand, the small circles, the occasional sweeps. She imagined she was lying within Dallas's arms, wanting his warmth, his touch, and his even breathing surrounding her.

But when she drifted off to sleep, she dreamed of Houston.

AMELIA AWOKE TO the sound of thunder and groaned. "Not another storm."

"Not a storm, a stampede," Houston said, an urgency to his voice as he rolled away from her. "Get up."

She rose to her feet, the full moon playing hide-and-seek with the shadows. He grabbed her hand and tugged her toward a tree. "What are you doing?" she asked.

"Need to get you off the ground. Grab that branch," he ordered as he swung her upward.

She did as he instructed and scrambled into the tree. "Aren't you coming?" she yelled as the thunder grew louder.

She didn't know if he heard her as he raced to the mules and freed them from their hobbles. Then he released his horse and started running back toward the tree.

Terror swept through her heart as the tree began to shake and the air reverberated around her. "Hurry!"

He lunged toward the tree, grabbed a branch, and swung to safety just as the herd reached the outskirts of their small camp.

Amelia tightened her hold on the tree limb as

the horses rushed under her. The moon sheathed their backs in pale light, outlining their muscles as they bunched and stretched with their movements. Their manes whipped through the breeze. Their galloping hooves pounded the earth and stamped out the campfire. Their frantic neighs filled the night.

Amelia watched, mesmerized by their beauty, their singular purpose. The last horse shone the brightest, the color of the moon. It came to a staggering stop, raised on its hindquarters, threw its head back, and neighed defiantly before continuing on, following the herd.

When the thundering hooves fell into an eerie silence, Houston slid down the tree. He held up a hand and waited, as though testing the night. Amelia could sense the tenseness in his stance. Slowly, he reached for her. "Come on."

She eased down, and he wrapped his hands around her waist. She could feel the trembling in his fingers, feel her own body shaking. She collapsed against him and listened to the pounding of his heart.

"That was incredible," she said on an escaping breath.

"Yeah, it was," he said quietly as he led her back to the remains of their campfire.

She sat on the ground and watched as he worked to bring the fire back to life. "That last horse . . . I've never seen a horse the color of the moon," she said in awe.

"Palomino. That shade of coloring is called palomino."

"She was beautiful."

"He."

She scooted toward Houston. "He? How could you tell?"

"The pride in the way he held himself. And the fact that he was last. That was his band of mares."

"I always expected the stallion to be the fastest. He couldn't even keep up with the others."

Houston chuckled low. "He's fast. He was putting himself between the mares and danger. The first horse that came through would have been his favored mare. She's the fastest, strongest, probably the smartest of his brood."

As the fire began to crackle, he gazed into the darkness where the retreating mustangs had disappeared. She sensed a wistfulness about him, as though he wished he could have galloped along beside them.

The mules and Sorrel had moved out of harm's way. As they meandered back to camp, Houston secured them for the night. He was quiet, contemplative when he rejoined her by the fire, lay down beside her, and took her into his arms.

"What are you thinking about?" she asked.

His hold on her tightened. "The beauty of those mustangs."

"Who do you think they belong to?"

"The land. Right now, they just belong to the land. They're wild and they're free."

"Are you going to capture them?"

"Nah, I need to get you to Dallas." His voice reflected mourning, loss.

"Will you come back for them?"

"Might. Wild mustangs usually stay in the same area for a while."

"And if they move on before you get back here?"

He shrugged as much as he was able with her in his arms. "There'll be others."

She lifted up on an elbow and met his gaze. "You told me once that the wild ones are becoming rare, that's why you're breeding them. If I wasn't here, would you take the time to capture them?"

"If you weren't here, I wouldn't be here. I never would have left my place, never would have seen them, never would have known they existed . . . so I never would have had them anyway."

She smiled and touched his rough jaw. "But I am here, and you do know they exist. When you left the ranch for Fort Worth, did anything slow you down?"

He furrowed his brow. "No."

"And yet going back, we've had one mishap—"

He chuckled low. "Mishap?"

"All right. We've had one catastrophe after another. Maybe these horses are your destiny, are the reason this journey has been so difficult. They'll give you fine horses to raise. How can you leave without at least trying to capture them?"

She thought he might have shoved her aside if she wasn't wrapped so snugly within his duster.

"We've lost too much time already." He pressed her face into his shoulder. "Go to sleep."

"Then I'm grateful for every incident that slowed us down. Just seeing those magnificent horses was worth it. Don't you agree?"

Silence was his answer. She wondered if he'd wanted other things in his life, but had put his desires aside in favor of someone else's. A horse's whinny broke through the silence. Beneath her cheek, Houston's heart thudded rapidly.

"Do you think that's him?" she whispered.

"Yep."

"And you're going to let him go?"

"Amelia?" She heard the frustration in his voice. "It's not like I'll ride out and rope him and be done with it. Capturing mustangs the way I do is slow goin'."

She came back up on her elbow. "How do you capture them?"

He sighed deeply. "I become one of them."

A warm smile crept over her face. "I'd love to see that."

"Well, you're not gonna. I need to get you to Dallas. Now go to sleep."

She snuggled back against him. "What color did you say he was?"

"Palomino."

"And the first horse that ran through, his favorite mare was the same color, wasn't she?"

"Yep."

"And their manes looked silver in the moonlight."

"They were silver."

"They ran so incredibly fast. Have you ever seen horses run that fast?"

He held his silence.

"I like the way he threw his head back—"

"You're aggravating, you know that? I'm trying to forget I ever saw them, and you won't stop talkin' about them."

"If you don't capture them while we're here,

you might lose them forever." She rose back onto her elbow and cradled his unshaven cheek in her hand. "Sometimes, we only get one chance to realize our dreams."

He threaded his fingers through her hair, holding her face immobile. "I don't deserve dreams," he growled through gritted teeth.

"Everyone deserves a dream. Dallas wants a son. Our staying here a couple of more days won't stop him from obtaining what he desires. Your dream is to raise horses. Don't let Dallas's dream overshadow yours. Yours is just as important. Those horses could be part of it." She placed her hand over his. He turned his palm, intertwined his fingers with hers, and brought the back of her hand to his lips.

"You don't know what you're asking," he said, his voice taut.

She heard the palomino stallion whinny in the far distance. "I'm pledged to your brother, but that doesn't mean I've closed my heart to other dreams. If I'm with you when you capture the horses, then I'll become part of your dream as well. And years from now, someone will ride a magnificent palomino horse because we dared to reach for the dream . . . and we'll be remembered."

Chapter Twelve

Houston had never considered his desire to raise horses as a dream, but he supposed that it was. He always found a measure of peace when he worked with the mustangs, perhaps because he knew what it was to have one's spirit broken, to be beaten down, and to be left feeling worthless. As a result, he worked damn hard not to break the horse's spirit.

Some horses, like the black mustang Dallas had tried to break, simply couldn't be broken. They were too proud or just too ornery, much as his older brother was. He figured his father had recognized that stubborn trait in Dallas and realized that he couldn't be broken so he'd never tried to bend him to his will. He'd accepted him as he was.

Houston, though, had been another matter. He'd have gladly given his life if just once his father had looked at him with pride reflected in his eyes, but then he had to admit that he'd probably never given his father cause to feel pride toward him.

He glanced around the small boxed canyon. The mustangs could drink at the pond nestled in the corner and rest after the chase until he was ready to take them out. He wouldn't have enough rope to take them all, but he'd take the best. The stallion, his favored mare, and any others he thought would be worth his time. The remaining horses he'd let run free.

Wiping his brow, he watched the woman who wanted to be part of his dream, her fingers nimbly uncoiling a thick rope so he could wrap the individual strands around the tree limbs he had gathered. He didn't dare tell her that she was already in his dreams, those he had at night while he held her in his arms, those that would never become reality.

He would never wake up with her in his bed. He wouldn't grow old holding her hand. He would never see her eyes darken with passion. He would never tell her that he loved her.

He could only hope that Dallas's dreams would extend beyond wanting a son once he met Amelia. That he would cherish her as Houston wanted to.

He didn't think Dallas could avoid falling in love with Amelia. Her grit would appeal to his brother. Houston had dragged her through three weeks of hell, and she hadn't complained once. She'd make Dallas one hell of a wife.

Bending, he began to crisscross the sturdy limbs one over the other until they resembled a lengthy checkerboard. When Amelia finished her task, he would tie the branches tightly together at every juncture where they met to form a "T." The opening to the canyon was small enough that his makeshift gate would cover it. He'd secure one side of the gate to one side of the opening in such a way that Amelia could easily swing it across to block off the canyon once he'd brought the horses here.

He was probably insane to try and capture the horses with the few provisions he had and a woman at his side. Austin had been with him before when he'd captured wild mustangs, staying on the perimeter while Houston infiltrated the herd. He wouldn't have that luxury this time. He wouldn't leave Amelia to fend for herself, although he imagined she was capable of it, but time was running out. He'd only have her to himself for a little while longer . . . and then he wouldn't have her at all.

DAWN ARRIVED. AMELIA had slept little, the prospect of watching the horses race into the enclosure filling her with excitement.

Houston had doused the fire as soon as they'd finished eating breakfast. She watched him now as he readied the camp for his departure, her anticipation mounting. He placed a rope halter he'd fashioned on Sorrel. He dropped to the ground and removed his boots and socks before pulling his shirt over his head and tossing it on top of his duster.

He turned to face her, and she balled her hands into fists to prevent them from reaching out to touch the hardened contours of his body. "How long do you think you'll be gone?"

"Not long. Today, I just need to find them."

He walked across the small expanse separating them and took her hand. "We need to talk."

Her breath caught. At that moment, she needed a kiss. Lord, she needed a kiss. She fought to keep her gaze locked onto his, her hands from trailing along the scars on his shoulder and chest. She licked her lips.

"I want you to come with me, but I need you to understand what I'm asking. I'm leaving everything here but my revolver, my trousers, and a canteen. I want the mustangs to get used to my smell; the less I have, the less they have to get used to. I'll stay with them until they trust me enough to follow me. I'll sneak away at night to get food and water. I'll bed down where they do. If they take it into their heads to stampede . . . I'll do all I can to protect you, but it might not be enough." He released her hand and started to pace. "Hell, this was a stupid idea. I can't leave you and I can't take you with me. I don't know what I was thinking. I wasn't thinking. If Dallas knew what I was thinking, he'd have my hide."

"I want to go."

He stopped pacing and stared at her. "This ain't no buggy ride."

She wrapped her arms around herself to keep the excitement from carrying her to the clouds. "We're going to ride with the herd? Become part of the herd? This is something I'll share with my grandchildren." She dropped to the ground and began to remove her shoes. He knelt beside her, placed her foot in his lap, and worked her shoe off.

"If something happens—"

"Nothing is going to happen." She hopped up and carefully placed her shoes alongside his boots; the action couldn't have felt more intimate if she'd done it in a bedroom that only the two of them shared. She whipped off his hat.

"Keep the hat on," he ordered.

She spun around. He had already mounted Sorrel. "We're not likely to find much shade."

She settled his hat back in place, grateful that he hadn't wanted her to leave it behind. She would have hated for a raccoon to cart it away.

"Climb on that rock," he said.

He eased the horse over and held out his hand. She slipped her hand into his, using his arm for support as she threw a leg over the horse's back and scrambled into place. She wrapped her arms around Houston's bare chest and pressed her face against his broad back.

The world seemed more beautiful than it had the day before; the leaves were just beginning to turn golden and a briskness to the air promised cooler weather would return. They rode in silence for several hours, Houston studying the ground and the terrain. She could have easily drifted off to sleep with him as her pillow. She wondered if Dallas's back would be this broad, this smooth, this warm.

Houston tensed beneath her cheek and drew the horse to a halt. "There they are."

Leaning to the side, she peered around him. The mustangs grazed in the open.

Houston prodded Sorrel forward. Amelia was certain the pounding of her heart would drive the horses away. They neared the herd. The stallion lifted his head, eyed them warily, released a shrieking neigh, and took off at a gallop. The mares rapidly caught up and passed him, his silver mane blowing in the wind, his tail lifted in the air.

Amelia wanted to weep. "They ran away."

Houston rounded his leg over his horse's head and slid to the ground. Reaching up, he placed his hands on her waist and brought her to the ground. "Expected them to, the first time. That's why I said I wouldn't be long today."

"Why didn't you chase after them?"

"They would have just run harder. This is their range; they'll come back. When they do, we'll be waiting."

"How long before they accept us?"

"Hard to say."

He slipped his arm around her, and in a gesture that seemed as natural as breathing, she leaned against him, waiting for the promise of his dream to return.

FOR SEVERAL DAYS, they found the herd, walked into its midst, and watched the horses scamper away, but each day the mustangs didn't run quite as far or quite as fast. On the fourth day, they didn't run.

Houston felt Amelia's arms tighten around him as he guided Sorrel into the middle of the herd. The palomino stallion eyed them warily, slowly approached, and sniffed Sorrel, sniffed Houston's leg. Houston thought he could feel Amelia holding her breath against his back. How he wished he could have turned around to watch her. He imagined her green eyes bright, her lips curved into a smile.

When the stallion had determined they were no threat, he shook his head, sending his long silver mane rippling over his neck, and sauntered away as though to say, "Do as you please."

Houston did just that. He wove his horse through the herd, studying each horse, judging its merit. He would capture them all, but he would keep only the best. He didn't have enough rope to tether them all on a lead.

The one thing he missed throughout the day was Amelia's questions. She held her silence, and he longed to hear her voice. He had a feeling his place was going to seem so much quieter for his having known her.

AMELIA LOST TRACK of the days as they traveled with the mustangs. Their range covered a considerable distance, but she wouldn't have minded if they'd galloped forever toward the dawn. She loved the feel of the horse beneath her, the man before her when the herd sensed danger and ran. She loved the night sounds when the mustangs settled in around them. Houston would draw her close, and she'd sleep in his arms. Sometimes, they'd talk quietly about the horses, which ones they preferred. Or they would talk about the moments during the day when they hadn't spoken, but each had sensed the other's thoughts revolving around the same conclusions.

She knew before he told her that he preferred the stallion's lead mare over the others. She knew he would use her as the foundation of his own herd. She knew he would take care in breaking her.

And she knew in the hours before dawn when he quietly led Sorrel away from the herd and took her to the small box canyon that she'd fallen in love with him.

"I don't understand why I can't stay with you."

Cupping his hands, he brought the water from the small pond to his lips and gulped. "Because I'm gonna ride them hard, and I need someone to close the gate behind us once I lead them in here."

"What if they don't follow you?"

He stood and dried his hands on his trousers. "Then I'll have to chase them down and rope the ones we want. We've lost enough time as it is."

She wrapped her arms around herself. "I don't understand how you can view the past few days as losing anything. It was the most incredible experience of my life."

He ran his finger along her chin. "I didn't mean it that way, but you have someone waiting for you. I need to get you to him."

He strode to his horse and mounted. "Stay behind the brush until you hear me holler. Then start closing the gate. I'll get over to help you as soon as I can."

She sat on a boulder and waited. She watched the sun ease over the horizon and felt the loneliness sweep through her. Could a person love more than once in a lifetime, love more than one person this deeply, this strongly?

Dallas had answered her advertisement; she

had given him her word that she would marry him. She had an obligation to fulfill, but she imagined years from now her children would circle her feet, and she'd tell them how she'd helped their uncle capture the beginning of his dream.

She heard the pounding hooves, felt the ground vibrate. She scampered behind the brush and waited. The herd came into view, thundering over the plains, their heads thrown back, their tails raised, their sleek muscles bunching and stretching as they rushed toward their destination.

Trailing behind, guiding them, keeping them on course rode Houston, low over his horse's back, the wind whipping his hair, the sweat glistening over his body. She thought if she lived to be a hundred, she'd never see anything more magnificent.

Breathing heavily, their coats shiny with exertion, the mustangs galloped into the small canyon, heading for the pond. She heard Houston call her name as he roared past.

She moved the brush aside and began pushing the gate of limbs and rope. Then he was beside her, shoving it into place as the horses milled within the canyon. He fastened it, grabbed her about the waist, and hauled her to the side. "Don't know if it'll hold them," he said as he released her.

The stallion was the first to notice that they were trapped. He reared up and rushed toward the gate of tree branches but stopped short of ramming against it. He trotted back and forth. Amelia could almost feel his anger.

"I have a feeling he's a horse you don't want to rile," she said.

"Yep." Houston dug through their belongings, located his shirt, and drew it over his head. "I could geld him. He wouldn't be so spirited then."

Amelia was appalled. "You won't, will you?"

"Nope. He wouldn't be much good to me then." He walked to the gate and held out his hand. The stallion snorted and trotted into the late-morning shadows.

"What now?" she asked.

"We'll give them a day to calm down, then we'll pick the ones we want and head out."

AMELIA BEGAN TO relish the approaching darkness, the coming of night. Houston never voiced his thoughts or feelings, but she thought he welcomed the night as much as she did.

They spoke seldom during the day, but at night, after they'd eaten, after he'd banked the fire and drawn her into his arms, they'd talk quietly about the past, the present, but never the future.

She came to know more about the man she was to marry in those quiet moments. Houston was more comfortable relating tales of his brother than tales of himself, but she loved best the moments when his story carried a portion of his life.

She learned that Dallas was the favored son, although Houston never came out and admitted it. From the warmth in his voice when he spoke of his mother, she knew that Houston had adored the woman who had fought to bring him into the world.

She hoarded the stories he told her like a miser might hoard gold, sifting through his words, searching for all the keys that unlocked the mysteries that were his.

Houston lost track of the number of days that they traveled, but every night when he gathered Amelia in his arms to sleep, he fought a battle with his conscience, trying to justify what he'd done. He could have taken her to the ranch and returned for the mustangs. He *should* have taken her to the ranch.

But dammit, he'd wanted her with him, to share the capture, to know the horses as he knew them, to be able to lay claim to a corner of his dream.

When he turned her over to Dallas, she'd begin to live her own dream, and he had no place in it.

He drew his mule to a halt. Amelia's mount stopped, along with the mustangs he had in tow. They'd settled on eight. One was a puny thing that he didn't think would ever amount to much, but the woman beside him was afraid it wouldn't survive on its own when they released the horses without the stallion and his favored mare to guide them. So he'd kept the gentle creature, knowing full well his world wasn't made for gentle things.

The shadows were lengthening but they had plenty of daylight left, too much daylight left. He veered his mount to the left, trusting everyone else to follow.

IN AWE, AMELIA stared at the small spring. Three waterfalls, each no taller than a man, cascaded over the moss-covered rocks and through the brush, melting into the wide pond. The horses lapped at the clear water.

Beside her, Houston hunkered down, stirred up the water near the edge of the bank and dipped his palm beneath the surface. "It's colder than I expected it to be."

His voice reflected disappointment, and he glanced up at her. "Thought you might like a swim . . . but it's too cold."

She knelt beside him and flitted her fingers through the water. "When I was little, I used to run and hide when my mother told Dulce to get my bath ready. I thought it would be wonderful to never have to take a bath, to get as dirty as I wanted, and have no one care." She tugged on her bodice. "I have never felt so filthy in my whole life. I'm surprised you get as close to me as you do."

"I'm not too sweet smelling myself."

"I think the horses smell better than we do."

He nodded slowly. She lowered her hand into the water. "It's not too cold once you get used to it." Her gaze circled the pond. "Do you think there are snakes here?"

"I've never seen one, but let me scout around."

As he studied the perimeter of the pond, she removed her shoes, her fingers shaking with the thought of a snake digging his fangs into her again. She took a deep, calming breath, determined not to let her fears guide her life.

"Think you'll be safe. I'm gonna gather up some wood, then I'll get a fire goin'. You can wade in. Holler if you see anything."

He walked away. She didn't care how cold the water was. They'd been traveling for days with little more than shallow streams that wouldn't get her big toe wet. She wanted a warm bath in a big wooden tub, but she'd settle for this cold spring.

She'd placed his hat on a boulder and stripped down to her undergarments before she thought to glance over her shoulder. Houston was sitting back on his haunches before a pile of wood, staring at her. He scuttled around until he presented her with his back.

After all they'd been through, removing her clothes in front of him had seemed natural. She waded into the water and screeched.

Houston surged to his feet and raced across the clearing. Laughing, Amelia held up her hands. "No, it's just cold."

He skidded to a halt. "Don't go hollerin' like that. You made my heart stop beating."

Tensing, holding her breath, she sank beneath the water. She came up laughing and sputtering. "It's not so bad once you get used to it. Come join me."

He looked as though she'd just plowed her fist into his stomach. She glanced down. The white linen clung to her body, outlining her curves, shading the different facets of her body. She eased into the water, welcoming its chill. "Come join me," she repeated softly.

"Good Lord, woman, are you outta your mind?"

"Maybe I am, traveling across the country to marry a man I barely know. Traveling across Texas with a man I didn't know. You could have taken advantage of me and you didn't. I don't think you will now." She tilted her head to the side. "It feels nice to get the dust off."

Houston knew his body needed a cooling off . . . bad. He tossed his duster onto the ground and pulled his shirt over his head. He dropped down to remove his boots and socks. If his body didn't like the sight of her so much, he'd remove his trousers. As it was, he waded in, cringing as the cold seeped through his remaining clothing. "How long before I get used to it?" he said gruffly.

She laughed. Lord, he loved her laugh. He loved the sparkle in her eyes, the way her lips curved up.

She splashed water at him. He couldn't afford to play with her, afraid he'd wrap his arms around that slick body of hers, pull her against him, and never let go. Instead, he settled on the sandy bottom and leaned back on his elbows, allowing the cold water to lap around him, fighting a losing battle, trying not to notice how her white cotton was melting against her flesh.

She dropped her head back, her throat an arched column of ivory. He'd like to lay a dozen kisses from the tip of her chin to the base of her throat.

"Sometimes, I wish this journey would never end," she said, wistfully. She lowered her gaze and met his. "But it will, won't it?"

"Yeah, it will."

She slid through the water until she neared him. "And all I'll have are the memories of the time we shared," she said softly.

The molten heat flowed through him with her nearness. He was surprised the water surrounding him didn't steam. "We probably ought to get out now," he suggested as he started to rise.

She placed her hand on his bare shoulder, and he dropped back into the water. "Amelia—"

"I didn't mean to embarrass you," she said.

"You didn't embarrass me. It's just that every now and then we start heading down roads we shouldn't, and I just figured you were fixin' to get on one of those roads."

"Because I've enjoyed the time I've been with you?"

He nodded.

"That first day I met you, I expected this to be the longest trip of my life. I never thought I'd find myself hoarding moments with you as though they were gold." She pressed her finger to his lips before he could protest. "Do you know which moment was my favorite?"

He shook his head, held by the glow of her gaze.

"After we crossed the river on Sorrel, before you returned to the other side for the wagon . . . and you smiled."

He grimaced. "Woman, you must be part-near blind. If it looked anything close to what it felt like, it should have given you nightmares."

"I could pull out my mirror—"

"Nope." He sank deeper beneath the water. "I don't like mirrors."

"You're not scarred that badly."

"It's got nothing to do with my scars." And he'd be damned if he'd explain himself. Not this evening, not when their time together was drawing to a close.

She sighed heavily. "I'll admit that the left side didn't go up as high as the right side, but I still liked your smile." She touched her fingertip to the corner of his mouth. "Smile for me again."

He pressed his lips together.

She placed her thumbs on either side of his mouth and tugged up. He jerked back. "I can't smile if I'm thinkin' about it."

"Then don't think about it."

She scooted back, skimmed her hand over the top of the pond, and sprayed him.

"Don't do that," he ordered.

She smiled mischievously. "Why?" She splashed water on him again.

"Because I said, that's why."

"Oh, I'm scared," she teased as she spattered water at him again.

"You're gonna be, if you don't stop," he threatened.

She laughed then, laughed loud and clear, the melodious sound echoing around the falls. He'd probably never know what overcame him, but he lunged for her, grabbed her waist, and carried her under the water.

When he brought her back up, her arms and legs were wrapped around him. She tossed the hair out of her eyes and laughed. "I'm still not scared."

He couldn't help himself. He added his laughter to hers as it floated on the breeze. Deep and strong. The sound shook him, and he fell silent.

Amelia touched his cheek. "You've never laughed," she stated simply.

"Not as a man. Not that I can recall."

Tears welled in her eyes. "I find that incredibly sad."

He moved her aside and pushed himself to his feet. "Time to get out and get warm."

But he could still hear his laughter reverberating between the falls, and it was all he could do not to weep himself.

WRAPPED IN A blanket, Amelia huddled beside the crackling fire in her damp bodice and skirt. Her drenched undergarments were stretched over a rock to dry.

Night hovered around her. A million stars twinkled overhead. She could hear the waterfalls, the occasional splash of a fish, frogs croaking, and the silence of her traveling companion as he gazed into the fire, his brow furrowed. She wondered where his thoughts traveled tonight.

Based on the depths of his creases, she had a feeling he was traveling back toward a war that had catapulted him into adulthood, stolen a portion of his sight, his smiles, and his laughter.

"A penny for your thoughts," she said quietly.

He glanced at her. "They're not worth that much."

"They are to me."

A corner of his mouth crooked up, and the warmth raced through her. She'd given him that, small as it was, a halfhearted attempted at a smile that she hoped would one day brighten his life.

"Even when you aren't asking questions, you're asking questions," he said.

"You don't like questions."

"Don't mind the questions. It's answerin' 'em that I'm not fond of."

She eased closer to him. He'd long ago stopped shielding her from the sight of his face. She couldn't imagine him looking more perfect than he did at that moment. Nor could she imagine him asking her a question of his own free will. "Play a game with me."

"The checkerboard is at the bottom of the river."

"I know a game that doesn't require a board. A simple game, really. I used to play it with my sisters. The rules are easy. You decide if you want to truthfully answer a question or take a dare. I'll ask the questions or issue the dare." She smiled sweetly. "The question will be something you wouldn't want to answer; the dare something that frightens you."

Horror swept over his face. "You call that a game?"

She slapped his shoulder. "It's fun. We always ended up laughing. Do you want to answer a question or take a dare?"

"Neither. I'm goin' to sleep."

She placed her hand on his thigh, effectively halting his movements. "Humor me. I'll go first. Ask me a question."

"Why are you so partial to questions?"

"Oh, that's an easy one. It's the best way to find out information. Now do you want to answer a question or take a dare?"

He looked as though she'd just set his favorite horses free. "That wasn't hardly fair."

She fought the urge to squeal with the realization that he would indeed play. "You have to choose your questions carefully."

He narrowed his gaze. "I'll take a question."

"It'll probably be something you don't want to answer."

"I don't want to answer any of them."

"All right." She shifted her backside, planted her elbow on her thigh, her chin in her palm, and studied the scowling man, wondering what she could ask that would present a challenge but not scare him off. "When you cry out in your sleep, are you dreaming about the war?"

"A dream is something you want. No, I don't dream about the war." He looked toward the fire. "But it's there in my head when I sleep." He shifted his gaze back to her. "This sure ain't like any game I ever played."

"When was the last time you played a game . . . not counting checkers?"

"How many questions do you get?"

She smiled. "You're right. Your turn. I'll take a question."

"Anything?"

"Anything."

Houston stretched out beside her and traced a finger in the dirt. He could ask her anything, and she'd answer it. Maybe she would have all along, but asking questions was as foreign to him as giving an apology had once been. He didn't want to parrot her, but he couldn't think of anything to ask. "Sometimes, you whimper in your sleep. What are you thinking about then?"

"My sisters . . . as they were the last time I saw them."

"I should have figured that."

"I don't dream about them as much since the storm, since I told you about them. And more often when I do dream about them, I see them as they were before the war . . . when we played games like this. It still hurts to think about them, but it's a different sort of hurt. A good hurt."

"That doesn't make any sense. What exactly is a good hurt?"

She held up a finger. "One question. Tell me the truth or take a dare."

"A dare, I reckon. I've answered enough questions."

She eased alongside him. "Kiss me as though I had no contract binding me to another."

"You don't want that."

"Afraid?"

Hell, yes, he was afraid. Afraid he'd forget that she was bound to his brother. Afraid he wouldn't find the strength to keep riding west in the morning. Afraid she'd touch the part of him that longed for softness until he couldn't ignore it. "Unbraid your hair," he rasped.

She sat up and draped the long braid over one shoulder. Nimbly her fingers worked the strands free. The firelight sent its red glow over her golden tresses, each strand seeming to have a life of its own as it curled over her shoulder, circled the curve of her breast, trailed down to her waist.

It was her game, her rules. He'd always been afraid not to follow the rules or to stray from the path. She ran her tongue over her lips, the innocent woman he knew turning into a temptress. Raised on an elbow, he threaded his fingers through her hair and pulled her mouth down to his.

She released a sound, more of a mewl than a whimper, her lips parting slightly in invitation. He didn't have to be asked twice.

Rolling her over, he slipped his tongue into her mouth and relished the feel of heaven.

Amelia ignored the hard ground below her, and welcomed the firm man above her. His fevered kiss curled her toes as she rubbed her foot along his calf. Groaning, he slipped his knee between her thighs, and she arched up against him.

He tore his mouth from hers, his breathing labored as he laid his bristly cheek against hers. "Don't do that."

"Why?"

"Just don't," he rasped as he brought his mouth back to hers.

She thought his hot mouth might devour her, and she didn't care. She had embraced Dallas's dreams, but now she wanted more. She wanted love; she wanted to feel the sunrise in a kiss, the glow of a full moon in a touch, the warmth of the fire in a caress.

His questing mouth gentled, but his fingers tightened their hold.

"God, I want to touch you," he said in a husky voice as he trailed his mouth along the column of her throat.

"Then do."

He chuckled low. "Woman, you don't know what you're saying."

"But I know what I need. I need you to touch me."

Houston surged to his feet, stormed to the spring, and leaned against a rock. "You don't know anything. If I touch you the way I want, I'll destroy every dream you came here to find."

"We could build new dreams together."

He shook his head, refusing to acknowledge the hope in her voice. "You came here to start a new life. Dallas can give you that."

She sat up. "You could give me that."

"It's not my place. Dallas asked you, damn it. He built you a huge house and changed his brand. He can give you everything that I can't, everything you deserve . . . everything I'd want you to have. I can only give you rags, loneliness, and nightmares."

AMELIA BUNDLED UP her damp clothes and stuffed them into a saddlebag. Dawn had been clear and should have filled her with joy, not despair. She had lain within Houston's arms, but he had somehow distanced himself from her. She wasn't even certain he'd slept.

He shook out the blanket, laid it over the fire, then quickly flicked it back. Black smoke spiraled into the air. He repeated his actions.

"What are you doing?" she asked.

"Letting Dallas know we're here."

Amelia's heart slammed against her ribs. "We're that close?"

He rose from his crouched position, crossed the small expanse of space separating them, and touched his rough palm to her cheek, holding her gaze. "We're that close."

"Last night was good-bye?"

"It was supposed to be. I couldn't think of the right words to use. You deserve prettier words than I can give you."

Reaching around her, he grabbed the canteens, walked to the spring, and began filling them.

As though she were ensconced in a dream, Amelia walked to the spring and knelt on his left side, her way of showing him that she didn't care if he was scarred, if he was imperfect. "I love you."

He continued his task as though she'd said nothing at all. Perhaps it was best. If he had acknowledged her feelings, she might have found it harder to honor the contract she'd signed.

"Houston?" She placed her hand on his arm.

He twisted around, meeting her gaze, his expression somber. She extended his hat toward him. "You'll want this back."

He took her offering, but didn't settle it onto his head. "Yeah, I reckon I will."

With a feather-light touch, she trailed her fingers around his patch. He went as still as stone. If he wouldn't accept her declaration of love, she'd give him something easier to accept, another version of the truth.

"When I began this journey, I cared for Dallas," she said quietly. "I still do. Only I've come to care for you more."

"That's because you've been with me for a while. Once you've spent some time with Dallas, your feelings will change back to what they were."

"And if they don't?"

"I'll take you back to Georgia."

She shook her head vigorously. "I don't want to go back to Georgia."

"Then give Dallas a chance."

"Do you care for me at all?"

He touched his knuckles to her cheek. "More than I have any right to."

Chapter Thirteen

Houston saw the cloud of gray dust billowing in the distance, the riders shimmering against the afternoon sun. If he weren't on Dallas's land, he might have felt a measure of panic, but he was certain Dallas would have had his men out patrolling the area where he expected them to ride in. Besides, he recognized the black wide-brimmed hat that was his brother's trademark, ordered special from the Stetson factory in Philadelphia. He didn't know of any other man in the area with a hat brim that wide.

He drew the mule to an ungainly stop. He wished he'd had time to tame one of the mustangs, but his method of taming a horse was slower than his method of capturing them. He didn't relish meeting his brother with a mule beneath him. He nearly snorted at the odd timing of his pride. His pride. His father had first beat it out of him. Then the war had buried it in an unmarked grave.

Amelia brought Sorrel to a graceful halt. Houston couldn't stop himself from engaging in a moment of self-indulgence, of watching her from beneath the shadows of his hat. She was one hell of a horsewoman as far as he was concerned, an even finer lady. She'd do Dallas proud.

"Why are we stopping?" she asked.

Reaching over, Houston unwrapped the canteen from her saddlehorn and handed it to her. "Riders."

She cupped her hand over her furrowed brow and gazed into the distance. He thought of a hundred things he should say to her at this moment before she left his side, never to return.

But he held his silence because it was easier, so much easier. Or at least it should have been easier. For the first time in his life taking the easy way seemed damn hard.

He watched the column of her throat lengthen as she tilted her head back and drank deeply from the canteen. Several strands of her hair had worked their way free of her braid and the prairie breeze whipped them around her face. Her dress was soiled, her feet bare, her face kissed by the sun.

He thought she'd never looked more beautiful.

She handed the canteen back to him, worry etched within her eyes.

"The man riding in the front, the one wearing the black hat, is Dallas," he said.

She nervously combed her hair back. "I look a mess."

"You look beautiful."

He swung his gaze away from her, and Amelia wondered what it was she had briefly seen reflected in his face. Regret? Loneliness? He wore each one closely woven together, like a layered second skin.

The land surrounding her was vast, as vast as her future, her dreams. The man with whom she'd agreed to share both rode toward her. She wrung her hands together, her trepidation increasing. "I didn't expect to meet him with an audience."

"It's just his trail hands. Imagine he had them out lookin' for us."

The pounding of hooves intensified as the riders neared, a tide of dust rolling behind them. Then a deafening silence roared around Amelia as the men brought their horses to a staggering halt, as though they'd slammed against a brick wall. The horses snorted and whinnied, prancing before her. The men simply stared, slack jawed.

The man who had been in the lead removed his hat, and Amelia was struck hard by his handsome features. His black hair was cut shorter than Houston's, trimmed evenly, and indented where his hat had pressed against it. His thick black mustache draped around full lips that she longed to see shaped into a smile. His brown eyes scrutinized her as they slowly traveled from the top of her head to the tip of her tiniest toe. She fought the urge to squirm in her saddle, wishing she'd at least gone to the trouble to work her feet into her shoes.

Slowly, each of the six men surrounding him removed their hats as though in a trance, their mouths gaping open, their solemn gazes riveted on her. Only the young man who had ridden beside Dallas seemed comfortable with the sight that greeted them, his grin broad, his eyes the mesmerizing blue of the hottest flames writhing within a fire.

Dallas dismounted and, with a pronounced limp, walked toward Sorrel, his gaze never leaving Amelia. He grabbed the reins when the horse shied away, and Amelia sensed that his one movement left no doubt in the horse's mind who had just become his master.

"Miss Carson, it's a pleasure to have you here," he said, his voice rich with confidence, his stance bold as though he knew no one and nothing could topple him from the mountain of success he'd climbed.

He was all that she'd expected. He wore self-assurance the way Houston wore his duster. She touched her braid. "A raccoon ran off with my hat."

Dallas blinked hard and stared at her. Houston cleared his throat, and Amelia wished a dust storm would rise up and sweep her across the plains. After all these many months, she finally had the opportunity to speak with him in person, and she'd said something that might make him think she'd left her wits back in Georgia.

"I told you to put a rattlesnake on that hat instead of a bird. Raccoon wouldn't have touched a rattlesnake."

Dallas snapped his head around and glared so intensely at the young smiling man that she was surprised he didn't topple out of his saddle. "Was she talking to you?"

The young man's smile grew. "Nah, but I was listenin'."

Dallas's eyes narrowed. "Miss Carson, that youngster is my brother, Austin. I'll introduce you to my men in time."

Amelia smiled warmly at the young man. "It's a pleasure to meet you," she said.

Austin ducked his head, blushing clear up to the roots of his scraggly black hair. Amelia's cheeks grew warm. From the corner of her eye, she saw a muscle in Houston's jaw strain as he fought to hold back what she was certain would be a smile if he gave it freedom. He had told her the truth about Austin: He was the sort people took to right away. Even while sitting in a saddle, he was more relaxed than either of his brothers.

His dark brown gaze uncompromising, his jaw tight, and his stance foreboding, Dallas turned his attention to Houston. "You're over three weeks late, with no wagon, no supplies. Reckon you got some explaining to do."

Houston shifted his body and pulled the brim on his hat low. "Reckon I do," he said simply.

"We'll discuss it up at the house," Dallas said before he limped to his horse and pulled himself into the saddle. He urged his horse forward until it sidled up against Sorrel. "Miss Carson, will you do me the honor of riding at the front with me?"

She glanced over at Houston. He gave a brusque nod. She hadn't expected to say good-bye to him like this—without saying good-bye at all. She thought of a hundred things she should say, wanted to say. She held her silence, forced a smile, met her future husband's gaze, and nodded because at that very moment her throat was knotted with emotions. As Dallas guided her horse through the waiting men, she felt as though she was leaving something precious behind her.

Houston had expected his farewell to Amelia to consist of more than a quick nod, but at that moment he couldn't have spoken to her if his life had depended on it. He watched Dallas lead her away from him, lead her toward her rightful place at his side. He told himself it was for the best, but he hadn't hurt this badly since Yankee mortar fire had torn into him.

Austin urged his horse toward Houston. "You got some new ponies."

Houston cleared his throat. "Yep." His voice sounded as though he'd just swallowed a handful of dust. He cleared his throat again before prodding the mule forward to ride behind the awestruck procession.

Austin kicked his horse into a short canter and caught up before slowing down to keep pace. "She's pretty, ain't she?" Austin asked.

"Yep."

"Think Dallas is pleased?"

Houston glanced over at Austin, his young face incredibly earnest. "If he ain't pleased, then he's a fool."

Austin's face split into a wide grin. "I ain't never known him to be a fool."

Houston heard Amelia's light laughter, followed quickly by Dallas's deeper chuckle. She needed a man who'd laugh with her. She'd find that in Dallas.

"She's got a pretty laugh," Austin said.

"Yep."

"Dallas was fit to be tied waiting on you to get here."

"Figured he would be."

"He ain't gonna like it at all that you took time to capture some horses."

Houston sighed deeply. "Didn't think he would."

"He said that he was gonna shoot you for lettin' that black stallion go."

Houston gave his brother a sideways glance. "Now, how'd he know it was me that let the stallion go?"

Austin shrugged. "Just guessed, I reckon. Is she gonna be my ma?"

"Hell, no, she's not gonna be your ma."

Austin looked like a puppy that had just been kicked. "It ain't fair to grow up without a ma. I was hoping Amelia might just sort of pretend she was my ma."

"She's Miss Carson to you, and she's gonna be too busy being a wife to Dallas to be pretending much of anything."

"Not until that circuit preacher gets back here, and Dallas is probably gonna shoot you on account of that, too."

Houston snapped his gaze over to his brother. "The preacher's not here?"

"Nope. He got here about three weeks ago, waited a whole week, then said he needed to get about searching for lost souls."

Houston tightened his hold on the mule's short cropped mane. Without a preacher, no marriage would take place. Until Amelia was safely tucked away as Dallas's wife, Houston wouldn't feel safe from his heart's longings.

He wondered why he thought a little piece of paper could snuff out the flames of desire building within him. He wondered how much longer he had to wait before he had to endure the hell of watching Amelia become another man's wife.

"TWO MONTHS!" DALLAS barked as he dropped into the leather chair behind his desk. He looked at Houston, grimaced slightly, turned the chair, and stared out the distant window. "It'll be at least two months before the circuit preacher gets back here."

Houston shifted in his chair on the other side of the desk, grateful Amelia was in a room upstairs taking a bath. He was accustomed to Dallas grimacing whenever he was in a fit of temper and looked Houston's way. When he wasn't in a fit of temper, he remembered that he couldn't stomach the sight of his brother. Houston knew the reason Dallas preferred not to look at him. It was a testament of Dallas's love and strength of character that he'd never thrown the reason into Houston's face.

"I got her here as fast as I could."

Dallas leaned back in his chair and raised a dark brow. "You just happened to find a bunch of horses tied together on a rope?"

"Wild horses are gettin' scarce. I thought—"

"I don't need horses. I need a son!"

"So send somebody to fetch the preacher back," Austin suggested as he hitched up a hip and sat on the edge of the desk.

Dallas glared at him. "Was I talking to you?"

Austin's face split into a wide grin. "Nah, but I was listenin'."

"Why don't you go listen somewhere else?" Dallas asked.

" 'Cuz I wanna know what happened to the wagon."

Dallas thrummed his fingers on the desk. His jaw clenched. "What did happen to the wagon?"

"Lost it when I tried to cross a swollen river."

"Why in the hell did you do that?" Dallas roared.

"Because we'd already lost some time, and I thought you'd be worrying."

"He was worryin' all right. Just like an old woman—"

Dallas slammed his hand on the desk and came out of his chair. Austin slid off the desk and took a step back, the grin easing off his face, his gaze never leaving his brother's.

"Children are to be seen and not heard," Dallas said in a low deep voice.

"I ain't a child," Austin said, his chin quivering, his voice anything but deep. He balled his fists at his side. Houston could see that he was trying to decide if this was the moment when he should stand his ground . . . or if he should save his hide and run.

"As long as you live under my roof, eat the food from my table . . ."

Houston resisted the urge to cover his ears as Dallas continued his tirade much as their father had before him. Houston could remember those very words directed his way. He'd been eight, sitting in a patch of clover, tying the little flowers together, making his mother a necklace. He'd made the mistake of slipping the chain of flowers over his head to see if it was big enough. His father had torn the flowers off, scattering them on the wind before he'd told Houston how he should behave in the ways of a man. Houston had felt smaller than the ants crawling beneath the clover.

"He didn't mean any harm," Houston said quietly.

Dallas stopped his tirade midsentence and shook his head. "What did you say?"

"I said that Austin didn't mean any harm. You're angry at me, not him. So take your anger out on me, not him."

"It's my fault," a soft voice said from the doorway.

Houston bolted out of the chair, nearly knocking it over.

Amelia walked into the room wearing a scoop-necked peasant blouse and skirt like the women wore in Mexico, her feet bare, her hair loose. She looked like an angel, only Houston knew differently. He could see the anger reflected in her eyes. Reflexes had him taking a step back. Curiosity had him wondering if Dallas had just met his match.

Dallas cleared his throat. "Miss Carson, I'm certain you did nothing wrong—"

"I didn't say I did anything wrong," she corrected him as she stopped before him and tilted her face. The afternoon sunlight streamed in through the window, bathing her in a yellow halo. "You're angry because our trip was delayed, and I don't blame you for that. I'm certain you were concerned and that's enough to make anyone irritable. But when we saw the horses . . ." She sighed sweetly. "They were magnificent. If you'd heard Houston's voice when he said he'd come back for them . . . I knew they'd be gone, that he knew he'd never possess them. So I talked him into taking the time to capture them. We lost a few travel days, but we're here now."

She made it sound as though they would have been fools if they'd passed up the horses. Dallas was staring at her as though he couldn't think of anything to say.

"And the horses were so important now that Houston is breeding them."

Inwardly, Houston groaned. Why hadn't she stopped talking while peace was settling within the room?

"What?" Dallas asked, apparently finding his voice. He looked at Houston and winced. "You're breeding horses?"

"Thinking about it. I'm just thinking about it."

"That's not—"

He stopped Amelia's words with as cold a glare as he could muster. She lowered her gaze but not before he saw the hurt he'd put in her eyes. He'd forever be hurting her. It was his way, and he hated when it touched her. He needed to leave, but he couldn't leave without trying to put a smile back into those green eyes. "I like those clothes. Where did you get them?"

Grabbing the sides, she fanned out the skirt. "The cook brought them to me. He said they'd belonged to his wife."

"Hand-me-downs," Houston said quietly, knowing it was no longer his place to worry about the clothing she wore. Dallas had taken over that responsibility earlier in the day, when he'd led Amelia away from Houston's side, but he found himself worrying anyway.

"She won't be wearing hand-me-downs for long. I've already sent one of my men to fetch yard goods." He looked at Amelia. "There's a small settlement to the south of us. I can't guarantee that what he selects would be your first choice in materials, but until I can find the time—"

Amelia held up her hand, warmed by Dallas's consideration. "You don't have to explain. I'm quite grateful for what I have."

"Still, I put him on a fast horse so he should be back within three or four days."

"I'm sorry we lost most of the clothes you purchased me in Fort Worth. They were lovely."

Dallas furrowed his brow. "What clothes?"

"The clothes you told Houston to purchase for me."

"He didn't tell Houston to purchase you any clothes," Austin said.

"He did tell me to purchase her some clothing," Houston said in a low voice.

"I don't recall him saying anything about clothes."

"You weren't there," Houston said.

"I was there the whole time you were talk—"

With one swift movement, Houston grabbed

the scruff of Austin's shirt. Despite the boy's protest, Houston hauled him out of the room.

Dallas cleared his throat. "If you'll excuse me, I need to help settle this matter."

Amelia pressed her hand just above her pounding heart. "Certainly."

As soon as he walked out of the room, the harsh whispering in the hallway increased in volume. If she were a gambler, she would have bet money that Dallas hadn't told Houston to purchase her clothing. He'd bought her clothing because she'd been carrying one small bag with everything she owned tucked inside. The "outfits" had been a gift from Houston, a gift he'd never planned to claim. She wondered how many other gifts he might have given her: her life, a Texas sunset. She smiled with the memory of him inside her tent, stripping down. She wished now that she'd watched the entire show.

The men trudged back into Dallas's office, each wearing disgruntled expressions.

"My apologies, Miss Carson," Austin said. "Seems I was wrong. Dallas did tell Houston to purchase you some clothes."

She glanced first at Houston, then at Dallas. Their jaws were firmly set. The lie, she supposed, was for her sake. "No harm done. I'm sure quite a bit was said . . . or thought to be said before Houston was sent to fetch me."

Houston settled his hat on his head. "I need to be goin'."

"The cook said supper would be ready soon. Surely you'll stay for the meal," Amelia said, hating the thought of his leaving.

Houston watched as sadness and nervousness warred within Amelia's eyes. He wanted to stay. He wanted to leave. He wanted a few minutes alone with her so he could explain what couldn't be explained.

"You'll stay. Miss Carson wants you here," Dallas said, his tone effectively putting an end to Houston's choices.

Weary from the journey, Houston nodded. "I'll stay."

"I'm so glad," Amelia said before she turned to Dallas. "I have something for you." Holding out her hand, she unfurled her fingers to reveal a gold pocket watch. "A small token of my affection. But it broke."

"Your affection broke?" Dallas asked.

Houston wished he hadn't heard the catch in Dallas's voice, but the sound brought home how much Dallas was depending on Amelia to marry him, to give him the son he wanted.

Amelia smiled softly. "No, the watch broke. I was carrying it in a hidden pocket in my skirt, and it got ruined when I jumped into the river. If you shake it, you can hear the water that's still trapped inside."

Dallas took the gift from her, held it near his ear, and rattled it. "Well, I'll be. I'll treasure it always."

Amelia blushed. "But it no longer keeps time."

Dallas smiled warmly. "No, but it'll remind me to stay off wild horses."

EVERY ROOM AMELIA had set foot in was huge: her bedroom, Dallas's office, the front parlor, and the entryway. The dining room, however, was the largest of all. A chandelier hung from the ceiling towering above. The walls were bare. The hearth empty. One large oak table with four chairs resided in the room with nothing else. The furniture in each room seemed oddly matched, as though Dallas's taste in wood and fabric ran along the same lines as his taste in women's hats. Amelia didn't know if she could ever feel comfortable in any of the rooms. They seemed incredibly cold, and she sensed that fires burning within the hearths would not warm them.

The chairs scraped across the stone floor as everyone took their seats, Dallas at the head of the table to her left, Houston to her right, and Austin across from her. She was struck with the beauty of Austin's eyes, a sapphire blue that any woman would have envied. His thick black lashes framed his eyes, drawing attention to them. She thought if women did come to the area as Dallas hoped, Austin would soon be married.

A door at the back of the room was kicked open, and the cook ambled in carrying a black cast-iron pot. His white hair stood out in all directions as though it had battled the wind and lost. A bushy white beard hid his mouth. Stains splattered his white apron. He brought the ladle out of the pot and spooned the stew into Amelia's bowl. "Ain't fancy, but it's filling."

She glanced up at him and smiled. "Thank you. And thank you for the loan of the clothes."

"Ain't no loan. They're yours to keep. Got no use for 'em anymore."

"Didn't know you was married, Cookie," Austin said.

"Years ago, boy, years ago. Little gal from Mexico." He placed stew in Dallas's bowl. "She up and died on me, but I kept some of her clothes. Used to take 'em out at night and just smell 'em because they smelled like her. But it's been too many years now. Can't smell her no more. Might as well let Miss Carson here get some use out of 'em."

"What was your wife's name?" Austin asked as Cookie filled his bowl until the stew dripped over onto the table.

"Juanita. Beautiful, she was. With black hair, black eyes, and red, red lips." He closed his eyes at a memory. "What those lips could do to a man." He ambled over to Houston. "If I keep thinkin' about her, I'm gonna have to hightail it up to Dusty Flats."

"Dusty Flats?" Amelia said.

What was visible of Cookie's cheeks turned as red as Juanita's lips might have been. He dropped the pot on the table. "I'll leave this with you. I ain't no butler." He went back through the door by which he'd entered, kicking it closed on his way out.

"Dusty Flats?" Amelia repeated. "Is that a town?"

Houston and Dallas both shifted in their chairs, their faces set. "It's not a town that a lady would go to," Dallas said.

"But it's got women," Austin said. "Or so I've heard." He stuck out his lower lip. "Can't get nobody to take me, though."

Dallas cleared his throat. "It's not proper conversation for the supper table."

"How come?" Austin asked.

"Because we have a lady eating with us."

Austin nodded as though what Dallas had said made sense to him, but Amelia could see confusion clearly reflected in the blue depths of his eyes.

"How do you like the house?" Dallas asked.

Amelia nearly choked on the stew. She took a sip of water, glancing down the table at Houston. He sat with his chair turned to the side. She had expected him to at least be comfortable with his disfigurement around his brothers.

"It's big," Amelia said, turning her attention back to Dallas. Those words were an understatement. The house was huge. Two stories of stone and—

"Adobe," Dallas said. "The house is built of adobe so it'll stay cooler in the summer. Gets hot here."

"Yes, that's what Houston told me. He said you can drop an egg on a rock and watch it cook."

"He said that, did he?' Dallas asked.

Amelia nodded, remembering so many things Houston had told her as they'd settled in each night, within each other's arms.

"Did he tell you that I designed the house? Made it look like a castle with turrets and such, like they have in England. Thought it would be good for defense."

She smiled. "No, he didn't mention that. He just said that he couldn't describe it. That I needed to see it. And now I've seen it. It's very unusual. Where did you learn about castles?"

He leaned forward with none of the hesitation Amelia had grown to expect from Houston when she asked him a question. "There was a fella in my company during the war who had come over from England. We spent many a night discussing the differences between our countries. When the war ended, he returned to England." He cleared his throat and eased back in his chair. "Apparently, he had placed some rather large bets on the outcome of the war. The South losing was not to his advantage."

"He sounds like an interesting character. Houston never mentioned him."

Dallas's gaze shot to Houston, then back to Amelia. "Houston never met him. I didn't meet Winslow until after Chickamauga." He slapped his hands on the table. "But he was fascinating. Although I used much of what he told me to design this house, it still needs a lady's touch. Give some thought as to what you'd like to see in the way of furniture and decorations. Maybe in the spring, we'll go back to Fort Worth for a visit."

"I'd like that. The town had so much energy."

"I wanna go, too," Austin said. "I bet the town has a lot of women. Houston, was there a lot of women in Fort Worth?"

"Wasn't there long enough to notice."

"If I'd just been riding through, I sure as hell would have noticed the women," Austin said.

Houston slapped Austin's arm. "Don't use that language around Miss Carson."

Austin stared at him. "What language you want me to use? Spanish?"

Houston grabbed Austin's shirt and hauled him out of his chair. Austin protested loudly as Houston dragged him out of the room.

Dallas sighed deeply. "If you'd be so kind as to excuse me?"

Amelia swallowed her laughter and nearly choked. A woman's touch was needed with more than the house. "Certainly."

Harsh whispers filtered in from the hallway along with the sound of a possible slap on the arm or shoulder, which resulted in a young man's fervent objection. The brothers stayed in the hallway outside the dining room longer than they had stayed in the hallway outside of Dallas's office. When they finally returned, they had all set their jaws into uncompromising lines. They took their seats.

She wanted to hug Austin; his face was that of a boy trying desperately to become a man.

They ate in silence, Houston and Dallas concentrating on the meal. Amelia could see thoughts flickering across Austin's face as though he was trying to decide what he could say without being hauled out of the room. Suddenly, his face lit up like the candles on a Christmas tree.

"Dallas is gonna buy some of that new fencing."

Houston looked up at his older brother. "That barbed wire?"

"Yep," Dallas acknowledged.

With that, the conversation ended, and the meal continued in silence.

Chapter Fourteen

$\mathcal{A}$melia drew the remnants of a blanket over her shoulders. Dallas had torn the woolen blanket in half, the easiest way he knew to give her something that resembled a shawl.

The sun was easing over the horizon, painting the sky in lavender, the land in shadows. Beside her, Dallas matched his pace to hers, leaning on a cane, his limp slight. She thought that without the limp, he would be able to cover twice as much ground as she.

He stopped walking and pointed toward the setting sun. "See where the sun is going down? That's where my land ends."

He met her gaze. She didn't know if she'd ever seen a more handsome man, and she thought her heart should be tripping over itself with his attentions as he took her hand.

"When you wake in the morning, look out your window. Where the sun comes up is where my land begins." He brought her hand to his warm lips, his mustache tickling her flesh as he steadily held her gaze. "You're all that I imagined," he said quietly.

Her heart did trip over itself then, pounding fast and furious as though she were running, as though she wanted to run. She could think of nothing clever to say. Her tongue grew thick and useless. "I imagined you with blue eyes," she said, cringing with the inane comment as soon as the words left her mouth.

He raised a dark brow. "Blue eyes?"

She nodded. "Houston told me they were brown. And that you had a mustache. And that you cast a tall shadow." She glanced at the ground where his shadow stretched out behind her. Smiling self-consciously at her babbling, she looked up. "And he was right."

"I can't imagine Houston doing as much talking as it sounds like he did bringing you here."

"Only because I asked questions. He doesn't volunteer the information, but if you ask, he'll answer. Besides, it was a long journey."

"I'm sorry I wasn't able to come after you." He released her hand and leaned on the cane. "It was stupid of me to try and break a horse the day before I was to leave."

"Especially a black horse with a wavy tail and mane."

"I beg your pardon?" he asked, his brow furrowing deeply.

"Houston explained that a horse's coloring often tells him about its temperament. A black horse with a wavy tail and mane is usually mean-spirited."

"He said that, did he?"

"Yes. I don't remember what all the other colors mean, but he knows. You should ask him." She heard a horse whinny and glanced over her shoulder to see Houston in the corral, gathering the mustangs. "Is he leaving?"

"I imagine."

"I need to say good-bye."

"Why don't you run ahead and I'll catch up?" Dallas suggested.

"Thank you." The dust rose up around her as she ran to the corral. Houston was leaving, and she might not see him before she was married. She couldn't bear the thought. She skidded to a stop near the corral as Houston tied the last of his horses together.

He climbed over the railing and walked toward her, removing his hat to hit the dust off his trousers. She wanted to comb the hair off his brow.

"Enjoy your evening stroll?" he asked as he stopped before her.

"Yes. It was nice. Dallas is nice."

"Nice?" He smiled. "I'm sure he'll be glad to hear that you think he's nice."

"The ranch is huge."

"Yep, and you ain't even seen all of it. A man could travel for days without leaving Dallas's land."

"That's what we did, isn't it?" she asked. "Traveled for days on his land?"

"Three days."

"You could have signaled him sooner."

"Could have. Should have, but then I did a lot of things while traveling with you that I shouldn't have done."

She was grateful for every one of them. The memories would hold her for a lifetime, even if the man standing before her didn't. "I don't suppose there's a chance that some creature might haul the house away if we leave it unattended?"

He laughed, deeply, richly, and the warmth returned to Amelia's heart, a warmth that had disappeared when she'd moved from his side that morning.

"No, I don't imagine any critter is gonna haul the house away."

"It's . . . it's . . ."

"I told you that you needed to see it."

"Why do you think—"

"A castle for his queen," he said, his smile easing away. He touched a finger to her cheek. "You're his queen."

"And if I don't want to be a queen? If I just want to be a wife?"

"He'll let you do that as well. One thing about Dallas, he's loyal to a fault. If you're by his side, he'll give you everything."

"Why didn't you tell him you don't think the barbed wire is a good idea?"

He narrowed his gaze. "What makes you think I don't think the barbed wire is a good idea?"

"I traveled with you for well over a month, shared your food, shared your bed—"

"Don't you dare tell Dallas that!" he hissed. "He'd tan my hide and hang it out to dry. You didn't share my bed, you just slept beside me."

"Is that all you think I did?" she asked.

"That is all you did."

"I came to care for you."

"You'll come to care for Dallas even more. You just haven't had much time with him."

"I'm going to miss listening to you snore at night."

"Amelia—"

"I'm going to miss you."

"I'm not that far away. If you need something, you can send Austin to fetch me."

"And you'll come?"

"I'll come."

She heard approaching footsteps and turned. Dallas and Austin walked toward her, Austin with a loose-jointed walk as though he hadn't a care in the world, Dallas stiffly as though he carried the burden of the world upon his shoulders.

The brothers stopped before her, and she felt a tension rise within Houston.

"I'll send word when the preacher gets back," Dallas said.

"I'll be waitin' for it," was all Houston said, and Amelia realized she wouldn't see him again until the day she married his brother. A keen sense of loss ricocheted through her.

"Austin and I will sleep in the bunkhouse until the preacher arrives," Dallas said.

"The bunkhouse!" Austin exclaimed, horror laced through his voice. "Why do we have to sleep in the bunkhouse?"

"Because it wouldn't be proper for an unmarried woman to sleep in a house alone with two men," Dallas explained, his voice strained.

"Why not? Houston slept with her—"

Houston grabbed Austin by the shirt and

hauled him out of hearing range. Amelia thought she had heard material rip this time. The poor boy was going to need a sturdier shirt.

"You'll have to excuse Austin," Dallas said, drawing her attention away from the two men engaged in a heated discussion. "He hasn't had any women in his life and his education in certain matters is lacking."

"Houston said you're hoping more women will move out here once we're married."

He slipped his arm around hers and began walking toward the house. "I am hoping that this part of Texas will become more developed over time. My father told me once that some men are content to walk where others have gone." He turned and faced her. "I'm not one of those men. My aspirations and dreams are grander." He flushed, something she didn't think this man did often. "I know I sound like I'm full of myself, but we have an opportunity here to build an empire whose foundation is made up of dreams, hard work, and determination. I want you to share it with me. I want our children to inherit it."

He leaned down and kissed her on the brow as a brother might a favored sister. "I'm glad you're here. Sleep well."

He limped off the porch, leaving her to watch the fading sunset alone.

"DALLAS? DALLAS?" AUSTIN whispered harshly.

Staring hard at the wooden beams running the length of the bunkhouse ceiling, his mind on weighty matters, Dallas sighed heavily. "What?"

"I don't recollect ever hearin' Houston laugh

before. I didn't realize it until I heard him laugh this evening. You ever hear Houston laugh before?" Austin asked.

Dallas swallowed hard, fighting to push back the guilt. "He laughed a lot when we were boys . . . before the war."

"I'm thinkin' that you're right. Bringing women out here is gonna be a good thing. They sure make everything look prettier."

"Yeah, they do. Now, get yourself to sleep. We got business to tend to tomorrow. Can't stop working just because we've got a woman in the house."

"If you decide you don't want her, I'll take her."

"I'm not giving her up. Signed a contract saying I'd make her my wife if she traveled out here. A contract is like giving your word. I've never broken my word."

He slammed his eyes closed, knowing he'd find no sleep tonight. No matter what the cost, no matter who paid it . . . he'd never broken his word.

SLEEP HAD BEEN as elusive as the shadows hovering in the room, changing with the flickering flame from the lantern. Each time sleep drew near and Amelia grabbed it, she'd find herself searching for the feel of Houston's arms, the sound of his breathing, and the scent of horses and leather that was part of him. She'd awaken with a jolt, alone. She so hated being alone.

Sometime during the night, she'd slipped out of bed, draped a blanket over her shoulders, moved to the window, and welcomed the company of the stars. They had served as her canopy for so many nights, brought with them vivid memories of a man she didn't understand. She thought she could ask Houston questions through eternity, but his carefully guarded answers would forever keep her from understanding him fully.

She was certain that she meant more to him than he let on, thought it possible that he may have fallen in love with her, knew she'd come to love him. She wondered why he didn't act on his feelings. She wasn't married to his brother. Surely Dallas would understand if she had a change of heart. She didn't fear Dallas, but she sensed that Houston was wary of him, as though he thought his brother might strike out at him if he spoke the wrong words or took the wrong action. She wondered how much Dallas resembled his father. Houston had not been fond of his father. She wondered if he saw his father when he looked at Dallas.

In the predawn darkness, she sighed and listened to the steady clack of the windmill Dallas had built. Soon the sun would touch the earth, throwing its glow over Dallas's land. She hoped the sight would bring joy to her heart, would replace this mourning of a loss she couldn't identify or explain.

She heard a thump in the hallway. Her first thought was that Houston had sneaked in to see her, but she didn't think that would be his way. He'd said once that he always took the easy way. As much as it pained her, she had to acknowledge that for him, leaving her was easier than claiming her.

She heard the bump again. She rose from her chair and tiptoed across the room to the hearth, where the embers from the dying fire glowed red. She picked up the smallest log in the stack beside the fireplace and crept to the door.

She opened the door slightly and peered out. She saw a shadow moving out of one of the far rooms. She couldn't remember if that room was another bedroom. The person was carrying something. She stepped into the hallway and held the log like a club, hoping she had the strength to carry out her threat if the thief tried to bolt. "Stop right there!"

The culprit turned, stumbled back, hit the door, and fell into the room from which he'd just come. Amelia rushed down the hallway, her heart thudding madly. She skidded to a stop and stood over the prone figure, trying to decide if she should hit him now or cry for help.

"Miss Carson! It's me! Austin."

She scrutinized the darkness, barely able to discern his features. She could hear his heavy breathing. She had no doubt frightened him as much as he'd frightened her. She lowered her raised arms. They quivered as they relaxed against her side. "What are you doing here?"

He scrambled to his feet. "Come to get my violin. Dallas didn't give me no time to get my belongings. You scared me to death."

She laughed with a crazy sort of relief. "You scared me, too."

"Sorry about that. Didn't mean to." He tilted his head. "Miss Carson, you want to come watch the sunrise with me?"

"Will Dallas be there?"

"No, ma'am. He done headed out with some of the men to check the south range. I'm supposed to watch out for you today."

"Let me get dressed."

She hurried into her room and considered putting on her own clothes. She had washed them last night, but she had enjoyed the freedom she'd felt wearing the loose skirt and blouse. She slipped into the clothes, wrapped the makeshift shawl around her shoulders, and walked back into the hallway. Austin was plucking a string on his violin.

He shoved himself away from the wall. "Come on," he said, taking her hand and leading her down the stairs and through the house to the back porch.

He released her hand and dropped to the top step. She settled in beside him, leaning against the beam. "Dallas said that where the sun comes up is where his land begins."

"Yes, ma'am. He has a hell—excuse me, heck—of a lot of land." He leaned toward her. "Can I say heck?"

She smiled. He had lived in a world dominated by men. She didn't expect him to change his habits overnight, wasn't even certain if he should. "You can say whatever you want. I don't mind."

"Oh, no, ma'am. I'm used to seeing Dallas angry, but I ain't never seen Houston angry. I don't want to say nothing that's gonna make Houston angry, so I gotta practice talking to a lady like she's supposed to be talked to. And I sure as hell, excuse me, heck, ain't gonna mention that you slept together. I thought he was gonna tear me in two."

Amelia scooted toward him slightly, clasped her hands together tightly, and rested her elbows on her thighs. "Dallas and Houston don't seem to talk to each other much."

"No, ma'am. They surely don't. They never have as long as I can remember."

"But they talk to you?"

"Yes, ma'am. It's kinda funny. When it's just me and Dallas, he talks to me like I imagine a father would talk to a son, explaining things real patient-like. When it's just me and Houston, he talks to me like I figure brothers would talk to each other, but I never see him and Dallas talking that way. When it's the three of us, it's just best to keep quiet."

"Did you know that Houston was breeding the mustangs?"

"Oh, yes, ma'am. He told me. When he needs help, he lets me help him."

"Dallas never helps him?"

"Oh, no, ma'am. Dallas ain't never even been out to Houston's place. When he needs Houston, he just sends me out there to fetch him."

"Why?"

"I reckon 'cuz he needs to talk to him."

Amelia smiled at the boy's innocence, an innocence that was belied by the revolver he wore strapped to his thigh. She wasn't certain if she'd ever grow accustomed to the abundance of guns and the ease with which young men carried them. "No, I mean why doesn't Dallas go out there?"

Austin shrugged. "Busy, I guess. Least that's what Houston says. Sometimes I think it bothers him that Dallas ain't never been out there. I asked him about it once. He said Dallas has empires to build. He's got no time for the little things, but visiting family don't seem like a little thing to me. But I'm just a kid, so what do I know?"

She placed her hand on his arm. "I think you're very close to being a man, and I think you know a lot. Could you take me to Houston's place?"

"Sure could. It's just two whoops and a holler away. As soon as the sun finishes coming up, we'll head out. If you won't tell Dallas, I'll show you what the sun sounds like when it's coming up."

"Why would he mind?" she asked, taking her hand off his arm.

He lifted a shoulder. "Cookie is a fiddle player, and he taught me to play some songs. Dallas don't mind those. But I hear songs . . . Dallas says they ain't manly so I just play 'em when he's not around. Since he ain't here, you want to hear the one that I think sounds like a sunrise?"

Amelia wrapped her arms around herself and settled against the beam. "I'd like to hear it very much."

Austin shifted his backside on the porch, brought one leg up and stretched the other one out. He slipped the rounded end of the violin beneath his chin and picked up the bow. He pointed the bow toward the far horizon. "Watch the sunrise."

Amelia turned her attention to the distance, but as soon as she heard the first low strain of music, her attention drifted back to the boy sitting on the porch with her. He'd closed his eyes and swayed slightly in rhythm to the music he created. The melody rose softly in pitch just as the sun did. She could see the sunrise without watching it, could feel its warmth without touching it, could sense its power as it brought light to the land.

How could Dallas not encourage the boy to expand on his gift? If he played this beautifully after taking lessons from a cook, she couldn't imagine how well he would play if he had proper lessons. Dallas Leigh needed more than a wife. He needed someone who could teach him that life was composed of more than hard work.

The music drifted into a hushed whisper. Austin opened his eyes, tears shimmering within the incredible blue depths.

"That was beautiful," Amelia said softly.

Austin sniffed and blinked until the tears disappeared. "Dawn is my favorite time of day, but I got a song for the sunset, and for all the seasons. They just sorta come to me. Like yesterday, when I saw you for the first time, a song just went into my head, but I ain't had a chance to try it out yet."

"I'd like to hear it when you're ready to play it for me."

He smiled broadly. "I'll do that, as long as Dallas is off with the men." He stood and tucked the violin beneath his arm. "You ready to head out to Houston's place?"

She tried not to appear too eager as she stood, but the truth was: She couldn't wait to see Houston again.

HE WAS STANDING on the front porch of a small log cabin, his left shoulder pressed against the beam, his gaze focused on the horses milling around in the corral. He wore no hat, and the wind blew through his black hair much as it blew through Amelia's blond tresses. She'd worn her hair pulled back, a strip of cloth keeping most of it in place, but much of it had worked itself free.

"Maybe we should yell so he'll know we're coming in," Amelia suggested, anxious to have him turn and see her, wondering if he would be as pleased to see her as she was to see him.

"Won't do no good. He can't hear from that side," Austin said.

Stunned, Amelia stared at Austin. "He's deaf?"

"Only on the left side. When he was wounded during the war, he lost his sight and hearing on that one side. Always figured that was why he sat with his right side to us, since his hearing ain't so good."

Austin's reasoning made sense, but Amelia didn't think it was correct. Near the end of their journey, Houston had never turned his face away from her. But she had whispered her heartfelt endearment near his left ear. She realized now that he hadn't been ignoring her. He simply hadn't heard her words, although she now understood that his hearing them would not have altered the journey's end.

As they neared, Houston turned slightly and shoved his hands into his trouser pockets. The morning was cool, but he wore no duster or hat. She was certain he'd expected no company.

"What brings you out?" he asked as he stepped off the porch.

"Dallas took the men to the south. He told me to watch Amelia. She wanted to see your place," Austin said as he dismounted.

"Oh, she did, did she?" Houston asked, his lip curved up slightly on one side as he placed his hands on her waist and helped her dismount.

The warmth of his touch shot clear down to her toes. His hands lingered, his fingers flexing as though he knew he should let her go, but couldn't bring himself to do it. She wanted to step forward, lean against him, and feel his arms close around her.

As though reading her thoughts, he shook his head slightly and stepped away from her. "Not much to see. House, corral, shed. Nothing fancy."

"A woman doesn't always need fancy," Amelia said softly.

"But she should have it just the same."

"You gonna let Amelia watch when a stallion mounts a mare?" Austin asked.

Houston turned swiftly to grab Austin, but he ducked just as quickly, backing off, his fingers splayed before him. "What'd I do now?"

"You don't talk breeding around a lady," Houston said, his voice low.

"Makes no sense. You can't say nothin' around a lady. What's the point in sharing your life with her if you can't speak what's on your mind?"

"I'm not gonna marry her and neither are you. And you need to call her Miss Carson."

"Why? Dallas told me last night that she'll be

my sister by marriage. I wouldn't call my sister Miss Leigh."

Houston reached to pull down a hat that wasn't on his head. Then he spun around and faced Amelia. "What do you want him to call you?"

"I'm hoping Austin will come to think of me as a sister so I'd truly prefer for him to call me Amelia."

"Fine." He waved his hand in the air. "Fine. Call her Amelia."

Austin released a whoop. "Hot diggity damn! That's the first time I've won an argument!"

Houston pointed his finger at his brother. "No swearing!"

Wearing a broad smile, Austin raised his palms as though warding off an attack. "I just forgot. Won't do it again."

"See that you don't," Houston mumbled.

"Can I ride Black Thunder to the bluff and back?" Austin asked.

"Black Thunder?" Amelia asked.

"Yeah, he's over here," Austin said, grabbing her hand and pulling her toward a distant corral, leading their horses behind him. "He ain't gelded, so Houston has to keep him apart from the mares."

The black stallion threw his head back and trotted around the enclosure. In a separate enclosure nearby, the palomino stallion whinnied.

"He's beautiful," Amelia whispered. The horse's black coat shimmered in the morning sun.

"I named him," Austin said.

"Why Black Thunder?" she asked.

"Because he runs so fast and so hard that he sounds like thunder rolling over the plains." He glanced over his shoulder. "Ain't that right, Houston?"

Reluctantly, Houston had followed them over, cursing himself for wanting to see Amelia's face when she caught sight of the stallion. He'd never given much thought to raising horses until he'd seen this black stallion on a rise. He'd pursued him for two years, wondered at times if he was a phantom, a horse of legend . . . until he'd captured him with Austin's help. He hadn't had a mare worthy of the black stallion until now.

Until Amelia had convinced him to pursue the palomino's herd. He'd carefully made his selections, choosing the mares that would service his black stallion.

"Yep, he's fast, but he's not saddle broke," Houston said.

"I love ridin' him bareback," Austin said, rubbing a hand up and down his thigh. "I can feel his power, his strength . . . Please? Amelia can wait here. I won't be long. Just a short fast ride."

Houston felt as though he was trapped between a stampeding herd and a huge abyss. What he wanted and what he knew was right were warring. Amelia looked at him, her green, green eyes filled with hope, and he couldn't say no, couldn't send her on her way, even though he knew it was best.

"Just don't be gone too long," Houston said, gruffly, offering himself a compromise.

"I won't," Austin assured him. He handed the reins of his horse and Amelia's horse over to Houston, grabbed the hackamore bridle off a post, and slipped through the railings.

The horse snorted and pranced. Amelia sidled up against Houston. "He's black. Isn't he dangerous?"

"All horses are dangerous if you don't handle them right, but he's not mean spirited."

She smiled as Austin slipped the bridle over the horse's snout, wrapped his fingers in the long black mane, and threw himself over the horse. The horse bucked once, and Austin hollered, his smile brighter than the noonday sun.

Houston pulled back the gate, and the horse with rider sprang forth, churning up the dirt as they headed out. Houston slapped Austin and Amelia's mounts, urging them into the empty corral. He closed the gate.

"I was thinking about working with the mare today. Need to get over to the other corral so she can start getting used to my scent again."

"Can I come with you?"

Houston nodded. He walked to the corral, Amelia at his side. Sweet Lord, it felt right to have her there with him, to smell her scent, to see her shadow touching his. He crossed his arms over the top railing, and the horses scattered to the far side of the corral.

"They don't trust us yet," she said quietly.

He thought now might be a good time to make sure the woman understood there was no "us," would never be an "us." But the morning was peaceful, the breeze slight, and she looked so pretty standing beside him watching the horses that she'd helped him capture.

He should have explained to Austin why a man would want a woman in his life. It had little to do with the physical release his body craved. It had everything to do with every memory he had of her from the moment she'd first stepped off the train in Fort Worth until he'd watched Dallas kiss her last night. It had to do with the softness of her voice, the way she believed in him when no one else ever had.

"They'll get used to us again in time," he said.

She turned her attention away from the horses, her delicate brows drawn together in a furrow. "Why didn't you tell Dallas that you were breeding mustangs?"

He averted his gaze, deciding it was easier to watch the horses than her. "I might not have any success at it. Dallas has seen enough of my failures."

"Such as?"

"You don't want to know."

"I don't want to know or you don't want to tell me?"

He forced himself to meet her gaze. "I don't want to tell you."

"You don't trust me," she said simply. "You're like the mustangs. You don't trust easily."

"Look what happened when they finally decided to trust us. We betrayed them."

"And you think I'll betray you?"

"No," he said, unable to stop the ragged edge in his voice. "I think you'll hate me."

Chapter Fifteen

꧁꧂

Austin returned late in the morning, while the breeze was still cool. Amelia wouldn't have minded spending the entire day with Houston, watching him work with the palomino mare, but she sensed that Austin was ready to move on.

As they rode back to the ranch, Amelia found herself intrigued by the young man riding beside her. Full of untamed energy, he had a restlessness about him. She supposed it had to do with youth. Something more exciting was always waiting just ahead, in the next mile, in the next moment.

Amelia drew her horse to a halt. "What in the world is that?"

Austin sidled up next to her. "What?"

She pointed toward the reddish-brown beast. Austin's eyes nearly bulged out of his head. "It's a cow. Ain't you never seen a cow before?"

She shook her head. It looked nothing like the cows of Georgia or the ones she'd seen grazing at John and Beth's. "Not one like that. Those horns look dangerous."

"They are dangerous. From tip to tip, the horns can grow as long as some men are tall. Longhorns enjoy a good stampede, too. Dallas keeps his cattle spread out over the range so they're less likely to stampede. You wanna see Dallas at work?"

"You know where he is?"

"Sure. He's gathering his cattle down on the south end, marking 'em so they'll be ready come spring."

She realized too late that she should have sought out Dallas first thing that morning, instead of Houston. When she had begun this journey, her mind was filled with thoughts of Dallas. Somewhere along the way, Houston had taken his place. "I'd like to see him working."

"Come on, then."

They rode at a gallop with the breeze circling around them. She thought she might never understand how men could look out over the land and know exactly where they were. More cattle became visible, dotting the countryside.

Then she saw what she thought must have been a whole herd, a sea of brown and red. It didn't take her long to spot Dallas. He rode through the herd obviously with a purpose. She watched as he maneuvered his horse, maneuvered the calf away from the center of the herd.

"He rides well," Amelia said.

"Yep. He's got men to do that but every now and then, he does it himself." Austin removed his hat and waved it in the air.

When the calf broke through to freedom, another cowboy lassoed it. Dallas rode past the bawling calf and caught up with Austin and Amelia. "What are you doing out here?"

"Took Amelia out to see Houston. Discovered she didn't even know what a longhorn was so figured she ain't never seen a roundup. Thought I'd show her."

Dallas nodded and glanced over his shoulder. "They're smaller in the fall. Come spring, you can hardly see for the dust the cattle stir up."

"Houston said you had two thousand head of cattle."

He smiled. "At last count."

"I thought a ranch would feel like a plantation, have its grace and charm."

"You don't find the smell of burning cowhide and the ruckus of bawling cattle charmin'?"

She laughed lightly. "I find it fascinating, but nothing like what I'd expected. It's so big. I think it takes a special breed of men to tame it."

"That it does."

"Houston mentioned that you were that sort of man."

A blush swept down Dallas's face, disappearing behind the red bandanna he wore wrapped around his neck. "I'm having a hard time believing how much that man talked. Reckon I got some catching up to do."

A tinny sound filled the air. Amelia looked toward its source: the chuckwagon. With a metal bar, the cook was hitting a metal triangle.

"Are you hungry?" Dallas asked.

Amelia smiled. "As a matter of fact, I am."

"Austin, go fetch us a couple of plates."

As Austin rode to the chuckwagon, Dallas

dismounted and helped Amelia off her horse. He removed his vest and set it on the ground. "It's not fancy, but it'll protect your skirt somewhat."

"Thank you," she said as she lowered herself to the ground.

"Think we're having beefsteak today," he said, dropping down beside her.

"I suppose when you raise cattle, you always have meat to eat."

"Yes, ma'am, we do."

She sighed, her mind suddenly blank. Asking questions of Houston had come so easily. She couldn't think of a single thing to ask the man she was going to marry.

"Do you—"

"I've never—"

She laughed, he smiled as their voices bumped into each other.

"Go ahead," he said.

"No, you go first."

"All right." He yanked a spear of grass out of the ground and slipped it between his lips. "I was just gonna say that I've never had a girl before so you might need to prod me from time to time if you need or want things."

"You've never had a girl?"

He flung his arm in the direction of the cook. "No, ma'am. As you can see, my company is made up of men and cattle."

"But you've been to a brothel."

He sat straighter. "I beg your pardon?"

"Houston said that sporting women don't charge you, so I'd assumed you'd had a woman."

"I meant I've never had a steady girl." He leaned

forward until she could see her reflection in the brown depths of his eyes. "Did Houston mention that I stopped visiting brothels when I got your first letter?"

"No, he didn't tell me that."

Dallas stretched out beside her, raised up on an elbow, and smiled. "Why don't you tell me everything he *did* mention?"

DALLAS RODE HIS horse hard, with the cold midnight wind circling him, and his temper hotter than a branding iron straight out of the fire.

Houston said . . . Houston thought . . . Houston had told her . . .

Dallas had spent the afternoon and early evening hearing about everything Houston had ever said to Amelia. Dallas had known Houston for twenty-eight years and his brother had never in his whole entire life talked that much! Never!

Not when he was a boy working the cotton fields, not when he was beating a drum for the Confederacy, not when they'd traveled back to Texas . . . Never!

Dallas hadn't planned to break his leg, but when he had, sending Houston after Amelia had seemed the right decision.

He'd known Amelia would be safe with Houston. Houston kept to himself, had since after the war. Dallas had moments when he felt regret over that . . . and a measure of guilt. Sometimes, he wondered if his actions on that fateful night had been self-serving. He'd never gone back on his word in his life, but he often wondered if the price of keeping his word had been worth it.

He shoved the unsettling thoughts back into the dark corner of his heart that he reserved for regrets, and set his spurs against his horse's sides.

A rough ride usually calmed him. But tonight, nothing was working. He kept hearing Amelia's voice, speaking Houston's name so softly, as though she liked the way it sounded or enjoyed saying his name. As though she spent time thinking of him . . .

He drew his sweating horse to an abrupt halt and listened to the beast's breath wheeze into the night. He wasn't a man who usually abused his animals, and any other time, he would have dismounted and asked no more of the horse than he asked of himself.

But this time he had a burning inside him that couldn't be contained. He urged the horse forward at a slower gait. He saw the lantern hanging on the front porch of the log cabin, a lantern to welcome strangers and friends alike. He hadn't expected Houston to be so accommodating.

He drew his horse to a halt just beyond the front porch and gazed at the simple log structure. Judging by the size, he didn't think it could be more than one room. It reminded him of . . . home.

Home before the war. Home, where his mother would flap her apron at them when she discovered them sticking their fingers into her precious sugar or honey. Home, where his pa would let him herd the few cattle they owned instead of making him work in the fields. He'd hated the fields, hated the cotton. Sitting on a horse with the scent of cattle riding the wind was preferable any day to tearing up the land and breaking his back to do it.

He dismounted, pushed the memories aside, and pulled on the tether that harnessed his anger. He took no pains to be quiet as he stepped on the porch and pounded the door so loudly he was certain he'd wake the dead.

If his brother didn't get his butt out here, that was exactly what he'd be—dead.

Sleeping on a pallet against the corral fence, Houston had awoken to the sound of hooves beating the earth unmercifully. His first thought as he saw his brother riding in like hell's vengeance was that something had happened to Amelia. His heart had matched the rhythm of the horse's gallop, and although the evening air was cool around him, he'd broken out in a clammy sweat.

He'd thrown off the blanket, scrambled to his feet, and would have gone tearing across the yard like a madman if Dallas hadn't brought his horse to a grinding halt, and then sat there as though he'd come in from a leisurely Sunday ride.

Now his brother was banging on his door loud enough to start a stampede.

"Goddamn it, Houston! Open the door!"

A memory flickered through Houston's mind of a time when they were boys: They'd been swimming in the cold creek. Dallas had left the water, claiming it was time to go home, ordering Houston out of the creek, always ordering him around. That day, he hadn't been in the mood for orders. Taking a deep breath, he'd gone under the water and swam to a place where the shadows were deep. He'd come up for air just as Dallas was stomping his boots into place. Then Dallas had looked out over the creek and started yelling for him. Houston had held his silence, hard as it had been, until Dallas had finally plowed back into the creek, slicing his hands through the water like he was Moses and could part the waters of the creek to reveal his brother. Houston had crept out of the water and moseyed over to where his clothes were. He'd sat there quietly waiting until Dallas stopped his thrashing and called out his name again.

"You might try lookin' a little to your left!" Houston had yelled. "I might be over there!"

Dallas had spun around so quickly that he had lost his balance and slid beneath the water. He'd come back up sputtering and angry.

They'd wrestled, as boys were prone to do, until the laughter took over, and they both agreed it had been a fine day. They'd come home covered in mud, smiling as they told the story. Unfortunately, their father hadn't shared their enthusiasm for the prank. Houston had received a lecture on the evils of crying wolf and had been sent to bed without his supper. But it had all been worth it to see the surprise on Dallas's face when he'd turned around, and the horror in his eyes when he'd realized he was going down.

Oh, yeah, it had been worth it.

Dallas's pounding hadn't abated as he yelled once again, "Houston, open the goddamn door!"

Houston stepped silently onto the porch, eased his arm beneath his brother's pounding fist, grabbed the latch, and shoved the door open. "That what you wanted?" he asked.

Dallas jerked back as though someone had just roped him and given him a sharp tug. His breathing was labored, and Houston was certain if it had been daylight, he would have seen fury within his brother's dark eyes.

"Where in the hell were you?" Dallas demanded.

"Sleeping by the corral."

Dallas turned toward the corral, and Houston almost imagined he could see the horror on Dallas's face. He couldn't stop himself from adding, "I saw you the minute you rode in."

"Then you should have spoken up, let me know you were about."

"But watching was so much more fun."

"I didn't give you anything to watch."

Houston could have argued against that statement, but decided to let sleeping dogs lie. "Has something happened to Amelia?"

"No, she's fine. I just . . ." Dallas cleared his throat. "I've just never been out to your place before."

"It looks better at night," Houston said, a bad feeling in his gut. It wasn't like Dallas to have difficulty finding the right words, and the man never explained his actions. Never. "What'd you do to Amelia?"

Dallas jerked his head around. "I didn't do anything to her, but I'd like to know what you did."

Houston narrowed his gaze. "What do you mean by that?"

Dallas took a step forward. "I mean every sentence she utters has your name in it. Houston said this . . . Houston thinks that . . . You'd think the two of you were one person. She's telling me things you think like she's an authority on what goes on in your head."

Houston shrugged. "You travel with a person, you get to know him."

"How well did you get to know Amelia?"

Houston's gut reaction was to plow his balled fist right into the center of his brother's perfect face. Instead, he did what he always did. He took the easy path. "Why don't you head on home, and I'll forget you ever came out here tonight?"

"Answer me, goddamn it!"

"I just did. Now get the hell off my land."

"You bedded her, didn't you?"

Like most cowboys, Houston had never before hit a man. Guns were a man's way, not fists. His brother's face felt like a wall of stone when Houston's tightened fist made contact with it. The pain shot up his arm as Dallas stumbled back and fell off the porch. Houston leapt off the porch and planted his foot squarely on his brother's chest. Dallas grunted and wrapped his hands around Houston's ankle. Houston pressed down.

"I told you to stay off that goddamn horse, but you wouldn't listen! And I paid the price for your stubbornness. For forty-three days I traveled through hell, wanting that woman like I've never wanted anything in my life. For forty-three days, I drew your goddamn brand in the dirt to remind myself that she belonged to you, that she deserved the best of men. Think what you want of me, but never for one goddamn minute think less of her because you forced her into my company." He jerked his foot back. "She went through hell to get to you: snake, storm, flood, hunger, and cold, and she never once complained. She's a woman of courage, Dallas, and by God, if you don't worship the ground she walks on, I'll find her a husband who will. Now, get the hell off my land."

Without looking back, Houston strode to the corral and crossed his arms over the railing. He was shaking badly and his legs felt like the thick mud of a bog. He thought they might buckle under him at any moment. That would certainly ruin the effectiveness of his tirade. He thought he might even be sick.

He heard Dallas's horse whinny and then he heard the pounding of hooves. He slid to the ground and leaned back against the fence post. His father had been a violent man, quick to raise his voice and fist in anger. Houston had never wanted to be like him. He'd kept his temper to himself, letting it gnaw at his insides, never letting it show for fear of what it might do.

Well, now he knew. He was just like the man he despised.

WITHIN THE DEPTHS of slumber, Amelia heard her name whispered frantically. She struggled through the haze, squinting against the light burning in the lantern. She could see a slender form hovering over her bed, a young man with worried eyes. Austin.

Her heart slammed against her ribs. Bad news

always came at night. Houston. Something had happened to Houston. She jerked upright and grabbed his arm. "What's wrong?"

"Dallas got hurt."

"Dallas?" Her momentary relief gave way to panic and guilt. Her first waking thought should have been of Dallas. Scrambling out of bed, she wrapped a blanket around herself.

"It ain't bad," Austin explained, "but I think it's gonna need stitching."

She rushed to the chair by the window and knelt beside the green dress she'd been trying to repair. She grabbed her scissors and cut the thread before slipping the needle from the cloth. "Where is he?" she asked as she spun around. Caught off guard, she stared at Austin, who had pressed her pillow against his face.

Guiltily, he dropped her pillow to the bed. "Your pillow don't smell like mine."

"Do you want to take it?" she asked.

He hooked his thumbs on the waistband of his trousers and ducked his head. "Nah, I'd best not. The men might laugh at me. That sweet smell would surely get noticed in the bunkhouse. It's rank in there, just like old meat."

She made a quick mental note to sprinkle some fragrance in his room once he moved back into it after she and Dallas were married. "Where is Dallas?"

"Oh!" He jumped, his arms flailing out. "This way."

She followed him to the barn. Dallas was sitting just inside the doorway, his head pressed back against the wall, his eyes closed. Dust coated his clothes. Blood trailed slowly down his bruised and swelling cheek.

"Oh, my goodness, what happened?" Amelia exclaimed as she knelt beside him.

His eyes flew open, and he glared over her shoulder at Austin. "I told you to get the cook."

"I know, but I figured you probably just forgot that we had a woman here to tend to our needs."

"Amelia, go back to bed," Dallas ordered. "I'll get Cookie."

He started to rise, and Amelia placed her hand on his shoulder. "I'll take care of you, but we'll need to move to the kitchen."

"That wouldn't be proper."

"Why not?"

"Because we're not married, and it's the dead of night."

She sighed. "You're hurt. You're the man I'm going to marry. Surely the men who work for you know that I can trust you in my kitchen."

She could see the arguments running through his mind. She thought she might never understand the way a man thought. "It makes no sense that I can travel across the state with your brother and not damage my reputation, but helping you in a time of need will mark me as a loose woman."

He averted his gaze and struggled to his feet. "All right." He pointed a menacing finger at Austin. "This goes no further than you and me."

Austin nodded, but Amelia saw the confusion in his eyes, a confusion she understood.

"Dallas will be all right," she assured Austin as they walked to the house.

Once inside the kitchen, Dallas pulled a chair out from the table and dropped his aching body into place. Austin hitched up a hip and sat on the table.

"Make yourself useful and build a fire in the stove for Amelia. We'll be needing warm water."

Austin slid off the table and went about the task, dropping three logs in the process. Dallas had a feeling Austin had grown sweet on Amelia. He couldn't blame the boy. They were a young man's feelings, no threat to him.

He watched as Amelia warmed the water. He'd been so grateful to finally see her in person when she'd first arrived at the ranch that he hadn't given a lot of thought to what she'd endured in getting here. He should have. He should have grilled Houston for an accounting of every day—

"How did you get hurt?" she asked as she set a bowl of warm water on the table and sat beside him. She dipped the cloth into the water and gently dabbed at his cheek.

Humiliation swamped him. He would have preferred a bullet to a fist. "I fell off my horse."

Her hand stilled, and she searched his face. He kept it as still as stone, knowing she was looking for the truth, hoping she didn't find it. He'd never lied before, and he had no idea if he was covering it up.

"I couldn't sleep. I go riding when I can't sleep."

She smiled softly. "Well, then, I'm certainly marrying into the right family. You don't sleep. Houston doesn't sleep. I don't sleep." She glanced at Austin. He'd returned to his spot at the end of the table. "Do you sleep?"

"Not in the bunkhouse. Too many men snoring. Dallas is the worst. You won't get any sleep at all after you marry him."

"If I can sleep through Houston snoring, I can sleep through anyone snoring."

"I'm probably louder," Dallas said, wondering what had prompted such a childish response. He'd never felt competitive where Houston was concerned. He'd always known he was the better of the two. His father had drilled that lesson into him, every chance he got, pointing out Dallas's strengths and Houston's weaknesses.

Her smile increased. "I won't hold that against you." She withdrew the needle from her sleeve. "I think I should sew that up."

He nodded toward Austin. "Go get the whiskey."

Austin hopped off the table and headed for Dallas's office. Amelia continued to dab at his face, so gently. Before he could think, he'd cradled her cheek in his palm and carried his lips to hers. She sighed in surprise, and he slipped his tongue inside her mouth.

She returned the kiss timidly, almost as though she were afraid. Lord, he didn't want her to be afraid, not of him, not of anything. He drew back and studied her face. So innocent. He was ashamed of his earlier doubts. He'd deserved the punch Houston had given him; deserved it and a lot more.

"It's gonna be a long two months," he said.

She blushed prettily, so damned prettily, that for the first time, he saw the journey through his brother's eyes. And he didn't like what he saw. Not one damn bit.

LONG BEFORE DAWN, Amelia sat on the back porch, waiting, hoping that she was wrong.

She smiled as Austin appeared through the darkness, his long legs carrying him toward the back porch, his violin tucked beneath his arm.

"Mornin'," he said as he sat beside her and positioned his violin beneath his chin.

"Did Dallas ride out with the men?"

"No, ma'am. He rode out right after we left you. Said he had some business to take care of."

Panic swelled within her as she imagined exactly what that business might entail. She shouldn't have waited. She should have ridden out by herself. "Will you take me to see Houston?"

Grimacing, he tapped the bow on the violin. "Dallas told me not to take you out to Houston's place."

Her panic increased as she stood. "Then I'll go alone."

Austin jumped to his feet. "You can't do that."

"I need to see how badly Houston is hurt."

"What makes you think he's hurt?"

She tilted her head and studied him, wondering when it was that people lost the innocent way they viewed life. "I've seen Dallas ride. He didn't fall off his horse."

"Then what happened?"

Reaching up, she brushed the dark hair from his youthful brow. He ducked his head in embarrassment at her attentions. "I think he and Houston got into a fight."

"Houston? Ah, no, ma'am. Houston wouldn't have hit him. Houston never fights. Maybe Dallas ran into some cattle rustlers and just wanted to spare you the worry."

"Then why did he tell you not to take me to see Houston?"

"I don't know. He's not a man I question."

"I know that you're probably right, and I'm probably wrong, but I need to see Houston."

He sighed heavily. "What if I just went to check on him?"

"No, I need to see him."

"All right. I'll get our horses."

She heard him muttering oaths as he strode away. If she was right, she expected to be muttering a few of her own before the day was over.

"See? He's just fine," Austin said as they brought their horses to a halt at the edge of Houston's property. "He wouldn't be inside the corral working with the palomino if he wasn't."

"I want to see him more closely."

She started to urge the horse forward, but Austin snaked out his hand and grabbed her arm.

"We can't go ridin' in there while he's alone in the corral. We spook that horse, and she'll pound Houston into the ground."

"All right, I'll walk."

She dismounted, only to find Austin barring her way.

"You know, you are more stubborn than Dallas ever thought about being. Let me tie these horses up over at that bush and I'll walk with you. If we don't do this right, we'll get him killed."

"I know how to approach a wild mustang. I was with Houston when he rode into the herd."

Using his thumb, he tipped his hat off his brow, his blue eyes wide. "He took you with him? Into the herd?"

She smiled at the memory.

"God damn it! He never took me. He always made me wait by the corral he'd built for them so I could close the gate. How come he took you?"

"I guess he couldn't leave me alone."

"What'd it feel like?" he asked in awe. "What'd it feel like to be in the middle of all them horses?"

"Wonderful." She put her hand on his arm. "Let me see if Houston is all right, and then I'll tell you all about it."

"Wait here," he ordered before taking the horses back to the bush.

Amelia turned her attention back to the corral. Without a shirt or hat, Houston stood in the center of the corral, leading the palomino on a rope. The horse trotted in a circle.

The animal was beautiful, graceful, and carried herself proudly as though she knew her ancestors were of the best stock. Houston would be able to get a good price for her, enough that he could expand his small operation, breed more horses with earnestness.

She imagined the joy that would be found in working beside a man, helping to build and shape his dream. Dallas had already built his empire, realized all but one of his dreams. Amelia would give him his final dream: a son. She would find joy and happiness in their child. Through the years, she would guide him so, like his father, he would be a man whom other men respected and admired.

Yet, she couldn't help but wonder if a small part of her would always yearn for more.

Austin rejoined her, and together, they slowly approached the corral. She couldn't stop herself from admiring Houston's lean form. As sinewy as that of the mustang, as powerful, his muscles rippled over his back, over his chest, along his arms as he guided the horse.

As they drew nearer, she could hear the gentle timbre of his voice as he encouraged the horse. She thought the man could tame a snake if he set his mind to it.

"He doesn't look like he's been in a fight," Austin whispered, leaning low so she could hear him without disturbing the horse.

No, he didn't look as though he'd been in a fight. She could see no bruises on his face or body. She could only see the magnificence of his stance. He was in his element here, with his horses. She supposed some men were simply meant to be loners, simply preferred their solitude.

He caught sight of them then, and her heart misbehaved as it always did when he gazed upon her with such intensity. She wished for an insane minute that she was a horse, that he could love her as he did his mustangs.

With a gentle guiding hand, he slowed the horse to a walk, then brought it to a halt. He removed the rope halter and gave the horse a slap on the rump before walking toward Amelia.

The horse turned about and nudged Houston's backside. Smiling broadly, Houston reached into his pocket and withdrew an apple. The horse took it and trotted to the far side of the corral.

Houston continued on and climbed over the railing.

"What brings you out here?" he asked as he grabbed his shirt and shrugged into it.

She resisted the urge to capture the bead of sweat that trailed down his chest until it found refuge behind the waistband of his trousers.

"Amelia didn't believe that Dallas fell off his horse last night and busted his face," Austin said.

Houston began to button his shirt, his gaze lowered as he concentrated on a task he should have been able to perform in the dark. "It's not unusual for a man to fall off his horse when he's riding at night. Especially when there's no moon. Horse drops a leg into a prairie dog hole, and he throws the rider."

She placed her hand over his, and he grew still. "How did you bruise your knuckles?" she asked.

He lifted his gaze. "Fell off the porch."

"How'd you do that?" Austin asked.

"A hell of a lot of falling going on around here," she said before she spun around, the anger seething within her.

"I didn't think women were supposed to swear," Austin said.

"Take Black Thunder for a ride," Houston said.

"But I wanna hear—"

She heard a gentle scuff that she was certain was Houston tapping Austin's head.

"Goddamn it!" Austin cried.

"Stop using that language around Amelia."

"Why? She uses it around me."

She heard Houston's exasperated sigh and fought back the tears burning her eyes.

"Please take the horse for a ride," Houston said in resignation.

"Will you take me into the herd with you the next time you go after wild mustangs?" Austin asked.

"Yes."

"All right. I won't be gone long."

"Fine."

She watched as Austin ran to the corral. She waited an eternity for him to mount the horse and gallop out of sight. She felt Houston's hand come to rest on her shoulder. She couldn't stop herself from turning and stepping into his embrace. He closed his arms around her, and she laid her head against his chest, relishing the steady beat of his heart.

"Dallas came here last night, didn't he?"

His arms tightened around her. "Dallas has his life planned out in detail. He's just a little frustrated right now because some of those details didn't go as planned. Once you're married—"

She lifted her gaze. "I don't love him. I don't know if I'll ever love him."

He released his hold on her and stepped back as though she'd suddenly sprouted poisonous fangs. "You knew you wouldn't be marrying for love when you placed your ad."

"Because at the time, I didn't know what it was to love, how precious a gift it is."

"If it's a gift, then it can be given away, and you'll find a way to give it to Dallas."

"I've already given it away. I can't take it back. But you don't want it, do you?"

She saw anguish reflected in the depths of his

gaze. "It's not that I don't want it. It's that I don't deserve it."

"Why?"

"Ask Dallas. It's the reason he can't stand the sight of me."

Chapter Sixteen

Sitting astride his horse, Dallas gazed at the tower, admiring its simple design as he admired all works of man that harnessed nature. He found comfort in the steady pounding of the hammer as Jackson worked to finish the wooden structure. Dallas already had three windmills bringing up water on his land. His first had been built where he'd always planned to build his house so he could gift his wife with the luxury of pumped-in water.

He, his brothers, and the men who worked for him had slept beneath the stars before Amelia had accepted his offer of marriage. Her simple words, "I would consider it an honor to become your wife," had set Dallas on a course toward establishing stability. He'd built the house that he had thought about for years: something grand, worthy of the family who would live within its walls. He had erected a bunkhouse to add to the feeling of permanence that Amelia's letters had stirred in him. The future would find a kitchen next to the bunkhouse to replace the chuckwagon because eventually the cook would become as stationary as the cattle.

The barbed wire would see to that. It would bring dramatic changes to their lives, just as the expansion of the railroads continued to do. Dallas fought a constant battle to stay ahead of the changes, to make decisions that wouldn't leave him trailing in the dust. He had to be the best. His father would accept no less.

Dallas shifted his backside over the saddle. He wanted to carry his son to the top of the windmill so together they could look out over all the land that he had tamed. He wanted to teach his son to appreciate nature, to understand its weaknesses, to respect its strengths. He wanted to love his son unconditionally, as his father had never loved him.

Everything he owned, all that surrounded him, he had gained through his own efforts, his own persistence, his willingness to take chances when other men held back. If he could obtain a son on his own, he would, but he was a man who acknowledged his own limitations.

He needed a wife in order to have a son. He needed Amelia. And whether or not she knew it, she needed him.

He hadn't been tactful when he'd confronted Houston last night. When Houston's fist had plowed into his face, Dallas had thought his brother intended to claim Amelia for his own. Instead, he had threatened to find her another husband. If Houston harbored feelings for Amelia, they didn't run deeply enough to overshadow Dallas's desire for a son.

As for Amelia's feelings . . . After receiving her gentle ministrations as she had repaired the damage inflicted to his cheek, Dallas had decided it was simply her nature to care about people. He would see to it that she never regretted taking him as her husband.

And the sooner she became his wife, the sooner these needless doubts would stop distracting him from the concerns of running his ranch. "Jackson!"

The pounding stopped, the silence reverberating through the air as the man at the top of the tower tilted back his hat. "Yeah, boss?"

"Need to talk to you."

Dallas eased his stallion forward as Jackson nimbly climbed down the sturdy structure. His legs were as long as a longhorn's, his body as wiry. Dallas admired his agility and respected him for doing his job when no one was around to watch him. It was the trait of a good cowboy; a trait all the men who worked for him possessed. He might know nothing of their pasts, but he knew how they worked.

The man hit the ground with both feet and swept his hat from his head. "Yes, sir?"

"I need you to go find the circuit preacher."

Jackson's jaw dropped. "What about the windmill?"

"I need a son more than I need water."

"You won't be thinkin' that if we get hit with a drought."

Dallas raised a dark brow, and the man settled his hat over his dark hair. "Yes, sir. I'll find him."

"When you do, bring him and yourself on up

to the house. I'll want all the men there for the wedding—for Amelia's sake."

"Yes, sir."

Dallas prodded his horse into a gallop. This time next year, he'd be sharing that windmill and all the land surrounding it with his son.

AN INCREDIBLE FREEDOM swept through Austin as he stood at the edge of the bluff and stared across the craggy rocks below to the far horizon. Here, his dream seemed attainable. Here, he could voice his heart's desire aloud, and it didn't sound foolish with only the wind to listen.

Someday, he'd find the courage to tell his brothers. Or maybe he'd just leave, and when he'd realized his dream, he'd return to share the glorious moment with them. He knew once he'd proven himself, they wouldn't laugh, but until that moment of success, he feared their lack of faith or interest might destroy what he hoped to have.

One violin . . . created by his hands . . . that would make the sweetest music ever heard.

Rising in crescendo, soft as a spring breeze, strong as a winter storm, the gentle strains flowed through his heart, his mind, so clearly . . . so clearly and so loudly that he didn't hear the scattering of rocks soon enough. Black Thunder snorted and pawed the ground as Austin spun around.

He was a dead man.

He balled his hand into a fist to keep it from reaching for his gun. He'd never drawn on a man . . . much less six.

"Howdy, boy." His lips raised in a sneer, the bearded man leaned forward and crossed his arms over the saddle horn. "Nice horse you got there."

"Ain't worth nothin'. He ain't saddle broke."

The man laughed. "I can break him. Could break you if I wanted."

Austin didn't doubt that for a second as his gaze dropped to the man's big beefy hands. He had a godawful feeling in the pit of his stomach that the man liked to draw out killing. "Look, mister, I don't want no trouble."

The man's grin spread like an evil plague. "That's good, boy, 'cuz I don't neither." He drew his gun from his holster and five other guns were quickly drawn.

Austin's mouth went as dry as dust, his heart pounding so hard and fast that he could hear little else.

"Mead, get the horse."

A man built like a bull climbed off his horse, lumbered over to Black Thunder, and grabbed the dangling reins. The horse jerked his head up and the man yanked hard, pulling the horse after him.

Without warning, the bearded man fired a bullet near Austin's feet. Austin jumped back. The man laughed.

"Just keep goin' back, boy."

Austin held up his hands. "Mister, I'm standing on the edge of a cliff. If I go back—"

"I know, boy. You can holler all you want on your way down."

He again fired at the ground, the bullet spitting up dirt between Austin's boots. Austin scrambled back.

"The next one's going to take your big toe with it, the one after that your knee."

Austin heard the explosion, jumped back, and found himself surrounded by nothing but air and demented laughter.

COWBOYS WEREN'T MEANT to walk. Aching and sore from his head to his toes, Austin dropped to his backside and jerked off his boots.

He'd gone over the edge of the cliff, grabbed a scraggly bush; and clung tenaciously to it, his toes searching for a hold on the side of the rocky gorge. He'd waited until he heard the riders galloping away before he'd started working his way up.

He'd been walking for hours, the sun beating down on him, the dry wind whipping around him, and the dust choking him. Standing, he drew his gun from his holster and fired it into the air, realizing too late that he might alert the horse thieves to the fact that he'd survived.

Angrily, he swiped at the tears streaming down his face. He should have taken a stand. He shouldn't have allowed those men to run off with Houston's best horse. He should have pulled his gun—he would have been killed for sure.

He should have been paying attention, not daydreaming. If Dallas and Houston discovered what had happened today, they would never trust him again, would see him as the boy they thought he was instead of the man he was becoming.

He'd been irresponsible and stupid. Dallas was always lecturing him on the dangers that abounded out here, where they were isolated from the law. He'd taught him how to use his gun. Austin just hadn't had the guts to test that knowledge.

He saw two riders in the distance. He aimed his gun, his intent to kill them both. He dropped his hand to his side when he recognized Houston and Amelia. They'd no doubt grown worried and ridden out to find him.

He wiped the fresh tears from his cheeks. He'd rather face the horse thieves again than Houston.

Houston and Amelia brought their horses to a halt. Houston was out of his saddle and grabbing Austin's shoulder before Austin had time to blink back any more tears. "Are you hurt?" Houston asked, his voice ragged with concern.

"No, just bruised. I wasn't paying attention." He sniffed, wishing to God he wasn't crying like a baby. "Black Thunder hit a prairie dog hole. Snapped his leg in two. I had to shoot him."

Houston jerked his head back as though Austin had just slapped him. "Where is he?"

Austin hadn't expected him to want to see the horse. He rubbed his finger beneath his nose, buying himself some time while he thought of another lie. "I heard coyotes. I don't think you want to find him."

"No, I don't reckon I do." Houston removed his hand from Austin's shoulder and walked past him.

Austin turned to watch his brother come to a stop and drop his chin to his chest. He knew

Houston was hurting, and his guilt increased because he had no idea how to ease his brother's pain. He was startled when Amelia took hold of his hand.

"Are you all right?" she asked.

"Yep. I didn't mean to lose the horse."

"He knows that."

She strolled to Houston and he wrapped his arm around her, drawing her against him.

Austin didn't think they were talking, just holding each other as though that was enough. He wished Amelia had kept touching him, but he figured Houston needed her more right now. Austin couldn't remember how he'd felt when he'd lost his ma, he just knew the ache stayed with him, always there as though a part of him was missing. He imagined Houston was feeling that right now, and he was glad Dallas had brought a woman out here to ease their hurts because he and his brothers sure as hell knew nothing about giving comfort. A glare, a shout, a slap upside of the head was all they knew.

Amelia tipped her lovely face up and said something to Houston, and Austin would have sworn the man smiled. He drew Amelia closer until it looked as though they were one person before he moved away from her and walked back to Austin, Amelia strolling along behind him.

"I appreciate that you put an end to Black Thunder's suffering. Putting a horse down ain't an easy thing to do."

The tears welled back up in Austin's eyes. "What'll you do for a stallion now?"

"As Amelia so kindly reminded me, I've got

the palomino. Come spring, you and me will go find another stallion. I'll take you into the herd with me then."

Austin felt as though Houston was rewarding him for an action that he should have punished him for. "You don't have to take me into the herd."

"Said I would. A man's gotta keep his word. Why don't you mount up behind me, and we'll get you home so Amelia can tend to your cuts and scrapes?"

Austin nodded in mute agony. His conscience had him feeling lower than a snake's belly.

As NIGHT FELL, Amelia sat on the front porch, lanterns on either side of her providing the light by which she worked, using patience, care, and delicate stitches to mend the torn green silk, wishing she could mend the tear in her heart as easily.

Her mother had told her once that it hurt to love a man. Her mother had been crying at the time. Amelia had decided then that she would never love a man who'd hurt her.

Yet she had fallen in love with a man who was determined to hurt her as his way of protecting her. She didn't think she'd ever feel this yearning for Dallas.

She would care for him and grow fond of him. She would be a good wife, a wonderful mother to his children. She would gain his respect, his trust, but never his love.

And he would never hurt her. It was impossible to hurt someone who had given her heart to another.

She heard the mournful strains of the violin serenade the night. She would have joined Austin on the back porch, but she sensed that he needed to be alone. He hadn't wanted her patience or her attentions when they'd returned to Dallas's house. If she didn't know better, she'd think he was trying to punish himself for something that wasn't his fault.

She had admired the manner in which Houston had handled the loss of his horse: without blaming Austin. She knew Houston was hurting tonight, had lost one corner of his dream. She wished she could be with him to ease his pain, but her place was here, waiting on the porch Dallas had built for her, waiting on the future that she had once anticipated.

Dallas was the man to whom she had given a promise, a promise she would keep no matter what the cost to her heart. He didn't deserve her doubts or the betrayal of her feelings.

Austin's music drifted into silence just as Amelia saw the rider coming in . . . at long last. She'd been waiting for Dallas, needed to speak with him. He rode to the house, dismounted, and wrapped the reins around the railing.

His spurs jangling, he stepped onto the porch. He wore a vest over his light brown shirt, chaps over his dark brown trousers. He swept his hat from his head and knelt beside her, his large tanned finger touching the green silk. "What's this?"

"One of the dresses Houston purchased. It got torn when the wagon overturned, but I can fix it."

Furrowing his brow, he rubbed the silk cloth

between his callused fingers. "It doesn't have any ribbons or bows."

She secured the needle in the cloth. "It's really a simple evening dress, but I think it looks quite elegant when I'm wearing it."

He looked up and the light from the lanterns shimmered over his black hair. "Don't ladies like frilly things?"

She thought of the hat he'd sent her and tried to find the right words. "We like some frilly things. It depends on the occasion."

"You must have been grateful, then, when that raccoon took off with your hat."

"I was . . . I was greatly relieved."

"Too many ribbons, huh?"

"Too many birds," she confessed.

He nodded sagely and smiled. "Think a rattlesnake would have been better?"

"If I had opened that box and seen the head of a rattlesnake, I'm not certain I would have come."

The smile eased off his face. "Why didn't you tell me you were doing without? I would have sent money."

"Your letters were comfort enough."

His fingers skimmed along her cheek. "Too proud. I could always sense that in your letters. We're well suited to each other, Amelia, and after waiting so long to finally have you here, two months seems like an eternity. I've sent one of my men to find the circuit preacher. Hopefully within the month, we'll be married."

She held his gaze. If she could not have a marriage built on a foundation of love, she at least would insist that it be built on trust and honesty. Lies from the past, hers and his, she would forgive and forget. But their future demanded a stronger foundation. "I want your word that you will never again lie to me."

He clenched his jaw. "You saw Houston today?"

She nodded. "He wouldn't tell me why he hit you, but I suspect it had something to do with me. I don't imagine he told you that during the time we were together, he was always respectful of me and loyal to you."

"No, he didn't mention that, but I'm beginning to see that's the way it was."

"He became my friend, and I'd like to think that I became his. You're his brother, and yet I don't understand why you didn't know he was raising mustangs, why you never went to his home before last night—"

Dallas surged to his feet. "He never asked! Not once. He likes his solitude, and by God, I owe him that if that's what he wants."

"But you sent him to fetch me."

"To protect your reputation. No one would question your reputation knowing you'd traveled with him."

"Because of his disfigurement?"

Dallas had the grace to blush. "That and his temperament. He keeps to himself, or at least he did until he made this journey."

She lowered her gaze. He knelt beside her and touched her cheek. "Amelia, I need a wife that people will respect."

She lifted her eyes to his. "I need a husband who won't lie to me."

His fingers curled away from her face as he

averted his gaze, staring into the darkness beyond the porch. "I need you, Amelia, and I want you happy." He shifted his gaze back to hers. "Give you my word that I won't lie to you again."

His large palm cradled her cheek, just before his lips touched hers. The kiss was tender, gentle, everything that Houston's had not been.

Her remaining nights, her remaining days, she would be kissed like this, would feel this warmth with no heat, would feel safe, secure, content. She prayed it would be enough.

He moved his mouth from hers and smiled. "Sweeter than last night's kiss."

She rubbed above her lip. "Your mustache tickled."

"Do you want me to shave it off?"

"No!" She touched her hand to his cheek. "It suits you."

"My father had a mustache." He shook his head. "I suppose Houston told you that as well."

"No, he never spoke much about your father."

"Well." Dallas stood and rubbed his hands on his thighs. "I thought we'd celebrate your arrival tomorrow evening. Kill the fatted calf. Give you a chance to get to know my men."

"I want you to invite Houston."

"He won't come."

"Invite him anyway."

He crossed his arms over his chest and leaned against the porch beam. "If it'll please you—"

"It will."

The low strains of the violin filtered through the air again. The sound almost broke Amelia's heart.

Dallas turned his head to the side. "What's that noise? Sounds like somebody dying."

"Austin is playing his violin. I think he relies on his music to help him handle things that upset him."

"Why is he upset?"

She sighed deeply. "Houston had a black stallion. Austin rode it this afternoon, and it dropped a foot in a prairie dog hole. He knew the horse was important to Houston, and I think he feels guilty because he had to shoot it."

"He shouldn't feel guilty. That's a hazard that comes from riding out here. You accept it."

"Maybe you could talk with him. You're his brother, but he sees you as his father. He wants desperately for you to notice that he's becoming a man."

"How do you do that?"

"Do what?"

"Make a man tell you what's on his mind?"

She smiled softly. "I care enough to ask."

DALLAS STOOD WITHIN the shadows and listened, truly listened, to the music for the first time in his life. He imagined he could actually feel Austin's grief hovering around him. When Austin stopped playing, the air was still fraught with the sound, lingering on the breeze. Austin dropped his head back against the beam. Dallas could barely make out his brother's features in the darkness.

"Austin?"

Austin jumped to his feet. "I didn't know you were here. I wouldn't have been playin' if I'd known you were here."

Dallas heard the terror reflected in Austin's voice. Good Lord, Dallas expected to strike the fear of God into the men who worked for him, but not his family. He'd never wanted his brothers to fear him the way he'd feared his father.

"Well, then, I'm glad you didn't know I was here. I've never heard anything so . . . so—"

"Unmanly?"

"On the contrary. I've never heard any music that had the strength to strip emotions bare. You've got a gift there." He cursed the darkness because he couldn't tell if Austin had relaxed his stance. "Ma used to play songs that were low like that, but I don't guess you'd remember that."

"Nah, I don't."

"That's her violin."

Austin lifted the violin closer to his face. "It is?"

"Yep. It was Houston's idea to keep it. Said he thought you had Ma's long fingers. Never expected you to play better than she did."

"Never expected you to think I played good at all."

"Well, then, I reckon we both surprised each other tonight."

Austin's grin shined through the darkness. "Reckon we did at that."

Dallas stepped closer to his brother. "Amelia told me about Houston's stallion."

Austin's smile disappeared into the night. "I should have been paying closer attention."

"A man can't anticipate all that's gonna happen in life. If we always knew what the next moment would bring, we'd never look forward to it coming."

"Houston needed that horse."

"A horse can be replaced. A brother can't. We're damn grateful you didn't break your neck."

"Houston said we'd go lookin' for some more mustangs come spring."

"And you'll find them."

"Still, if I'd been paying attention—"

"Don't get into the habit of looking over your shoulder and thinking about what you should have done. Regrets make one hell of a shaky foundation on which to build a life."

WITH THE SOFT light of dawn bathing the morning, Dallas dismounted and walked his horse toward Houston's corral, wishing he hadn't given Amelia his word that he wouldn't lie. He had a feeling she'd question him about inviting Houston, so he was obligated to ask, even though he knew his brother wouldn't come.

He watched as Houston led the palomino around the corral with a hackamore, a blanket thrown over its back. A saddle straddled the corral railing. Dallas had seen Houston break enough mustangs to know Houston would get the horse accustomed to the weight of the saddle before he gave it the weight of a man. He'd just never realized his brother planned to breed them. He thought his brother would enjoy a measure of success with this venture, and he ignored the pain that came from knowing Houston hadn't wanted to share his plans.

Dallas rested his arms over the corral fence. If Houston had seen him arrive, he was doing a damn good job of pretending he hadn't. Dallas held his patience in check, although he had business to tend to and didn't have all day to stand around while his brother worked.

Houston removed the halter and blanket. He walked to the corral and slipped through the slats, presenting Dallas with his profile. Dallas stared at the horse. "Looks like a good horse."

"Will be when I'm done with her."

"How much you want for her?"

"She's not for sale."

"You can't build a business that way."

Houston crooked his elbow and placed it on the railing. "You can't build an empire that way, but then I'm not interested in empire building."

"There's nothing wrong with empire building."

"Nothing wrong with it at all if that's what you want. It's just not what I want."

Dallas shook his head, wondering why some men dreamed of great accomplishments while others were content not to dream at all. "I'm having a celebration this evening in honor of Amelia's arrival. She wanted me to invite you. Consider yourself invited."

"Tell her I appreciate the invite, but I've got other plans."

Dallas mounted his horse. "I told her you wouldn't come. Reckon we both know why."

He prodded his horse into a hard gallop. When he'd left Houston at the hospital, he'd been swathed in bandages. When he'd returned, Houston had been wearing a shirt. He'd never seen him without one since and hadn't realized how badly his body had scarred.

When Houston's place was no longer in sight,

Dallas slid off his horse, dropped to his knees, and threw up.

HOUSTON HADN'T PLANNED to come.

Celebrations and hordes of people weren't his style. Even when he helped Dallas herd his cattle north, Houston stayed on the outer fringe of the herd, circled the cattle at night, and kept his own counsel.

When he wasn't herding cattle, his evenings were spent sitting on a porch, listening to night creatures come to life: the chatter of crickets, the occasional howl of a lonesome wolf. Sometimes, he whittled.

Mostly, he just sat and sought the peace that always eluded him, taunted him just beyond reach. If he thought about the past, the nightmares would come; if he thought about the future, the loneliness eased around him. He'd learned to be content with the present, taking each day as it came.

Damn Dallas for making him yearn for a future different from the one he'd accepted as his due.

Yet, here he stood, his left shoulder pressed against the cool adobe as he watched the men milling around. He could smell the beef cooked over a mesquite fire, the coffee, and the beans.

He could hear the deep-throated guffaws of the men. He could hear the sweet, gentle laughter of a woman. She was walking beside Dallas, her arm wrapped around his. They made a pretty picture: the gallant ranchman, the genteel lady.

Dallas was smiling broadly, looking happier than Houston had ever seen him.

Amelia was as lovely as ever. Wearing the green dress they'd purchased at Mimi St. Claire's, she looked like a queen.

"Dallas said you weren't coming."

Houston jerked his head around and met Austin's gaze. "Changed my mind."

"I was afraid maybe you got to thinking about it and decided you needed to be mad at me about Black Thunder."

"I'll admit I was saddened to lose him, but he's bound to have sired a colt or two somewhere. I'll find him."

"I'll help you," he said eagerly.

"I was counting on that."

"I won't let you down this time."

"You didn't let me down before."

Austin looked away as though embarrassed. "I'm gonna get something to eat. You wanna come with me?"

"No, I won't be staying that long."

As Austin walked away, Houston turned his gaze back toward Amelia. She saw him, and her face lit up with such wondrous joy that it hurt his heart. He shoved himself away from the wall, his long strides eating up the distance between them. He told himself that he was trying to save Dallas some discomfort, but he knew in his heart that he just wanted to be near Amelia a little sooner.

He'd hurt her feelings yesterday morning, not for the first time, and probably not for the last, yet she'd comforted him when he'd lost his stallion and welcomed him now with a fierce hug before running her hands down his arms and slipping her fingers around his.

"We're so glad you came."

"I can't stay long," he said, focusing his gaze on Amelia, avoiding looking at his brother, knowing his brother was as grateful as he was that they had a woman to stare at instead of each other. Sometimes, he missed the easy camaraderie he'd shared with Dallas before the war. During the war, they had traveled side by side along different paths that had taken them away from each other.

Dallas cleared his throat. "We've got beef to eat."

"I ate before I came."

Dallas's lips thinned, and Houston knew he'd given the wrong answer. He was always giving the wrong answers, doing the wrong things. He'd never been able to please his father, and he sure as hell couldn't please his brother.

Dusk was settling in, and he thought about heading back home. He'd only have a sliver of a moon by which to travel tonight. It was a good excuse. He'd seen her. She looked happy. That was all he cared about.

A lanky cowboy, whose legs bowed out, approached and removed his hat. "Miss Carson, Cookie said he'd tune up his fiddle if you'd honor us with a dance."

Amelia blushed prettily and gave a quick glance to Houston, before looking at Dallas.

He smiled with regret. "I can't dance proper with this healing leg, but that's no reason for you not to enjoy the music."

She looked at Houston, and damn it, he knew she wanted him to step in for his brother, but if he didn't set limits for himself now, he'd forever be stepping in where he shouldn't.

"I never learned how to dance," Houston said, grateful he had an honest excuse not to hold her within his arms, wishing he didn't have any excuse.

Her face fell momentarily before she brightened and spun around. "Well, then, I'm most grateful that you asked me . . . Skinny, isn't it?"

The cowboy's face split into a grin. "No, ma'am. Slim."

"Oh, yes, Slim. You'll have to tell me how you came by that name," she said as she slipped her arm through his and followed him to an area near the corrals.

Houston could have sworn her attentions had the cowboy growing two inches. As the couple approached, the men let out a whoop and formed a big circle. Cookie climbed on a wooden box, slipped the fiddle beneath his chin, and started playing a fast, little tune. Slim hooked his arm through Amelia's, skipped her around, then released her and stepped back, clapping and stomping his foot as another cowboy pranced into the circle, slipped his arm through hers, repeated Slim's previous movements, then backed out of the circle, giving another man a chance.

Houston smiled at Amelia's surprised expression and the smile of pure delight to which it quickly gave way.

"Imagine she was expecting something closer to a waltz," Dallas said, a wide grin shining beneath his mustache.

"Reckon she was."

Dallas leaned on his cane. "Thought you had other plans for the evening."

"Got to thinking about it and figured if Amelia sent the invite, I'd best come. She's not a woman you want to rile."

"So I'm learning." Dallas shifted his stance. "I'm thinking of setting aside some land for a town. A woman needs certain things. I aim to see that Amelia gets them."

A town would bring more people. Houston hated the thought, but he hated more the idea of Amelia doing without. "When I was in Fort Worth, I heard talk of them taking the railroad farther west. If it stays on the course they've set for it, I'd say it's gonna hit the southernmost portion of your spread. You'll need the railroad to bring the businessmen."

Dallas nodded slowly. "Makes sense. I'll keep that in mind. Speaking of Fort Worth, I don't think I ever thanked you proper for going to fetch Amelia for me."

Houston slipped his hand inside his duster pocket, his fingers trailing over threads that were becoming worn. "I'd planned to shoot you when I got back."

Dallas jerked his head around, then turned his attention back to the dancers. "Why didn't you?"

"Lost a case of bullets when the wagon overturned, so at the moment I don't have any to spare."

Dallas's laughter rumbled out. "Then I'd better hope that preacher gets here before the supplies. I think you care for Amelia too much to make her a widow."

Houston watched as Austin, with his gangly arms and legs, took a turn at dancing with Amelia. Dallas was right. Houston cared for her too much to make her a widow . . . too much to make her his wife.

Chapter Seventeen

During the ceremony tomorrow, do you think I should stress that a husband should not beat his wife?"

Amelia scrutinized the minister who had just spoken, a man who leisurely hitched up his hip and sat on the porch railing, his long black coat opening to reveal his pearl-handled revolver. "I hardly think that will be necessary," she assured him.

Reverend Preston Tucker nodded slowly. "After speaking with Dallas earlier, I didn't think so, but a wedding ceremony is more for the woman than the man. Most men I know would consider the deed done with little more than a 'Do you?' followed by 'I do' and a handshake."

"Incredibly romantic."

"Romance is seldom involved out here. I've performed several ceremonies involving mail-order brides. Some women feel more comfortable if I stress how they should be treated."

"I feel fairly confident that Dallas will treat me just fine."

He studied her as one might a bug beneath a rock, his blue eyes penetrating. Dressed all in black—black shirt, black trousers, long black coat—he appeared relaxed, and yet he left the distinct impression that he was ever alert, ever watchful. He reminded her more of a gunfighter than a preacher.

His full lips lifted into a smile that she thought could tempt any woman into sinning.

"Something's bothering you," he stated simply.

"I was just wondering if you planned to wear the gun during the ceremony."

He slowly stroked the revolver strapped to his thigh. "No, I just wear it when I'm traveling. It bothers you, though. Perhaps I bother you."

"I just never expected to see a man of God wearing a gun."

"Life is different out here, Miss Carson. It's still considered a wilderness. Renegades and outlaws run rampant. Frontier justice often becomes more of an injustice. I have no intention of meeting my Maker before I'm ready."

"Would you kill a man?" she asked.

He averted his gaze and squinted into the distance. "Somebody's coming."

Amelia followed the direction of his gaze, and her heart leapt with joy. "It's Dallas's brother."

She rushed off the porch and crossed the yard, keeping her distance as Houston brought Sorrel to a halt. He was leading the palomino beside him.

"You've tamed her," she said, a hint of question in her voice.

"Yep."

Cautiously, she approached and rubbed the horse's neck. "She's so beautiful. She'll give you a fine herd of horses to sell."

"I doubt that." He leaned down and extended the reins toward her. "She's yours."

She stared at the leather strips threaded through his long, tanned fingers. She took a step back. "I can't accept her as a gift."

"She's your wedding gift. The saddle, too. It's not a woman's riding saddle, but it was the best I could find on such short notice."

She touched her fingers to the detailed etching worked into the fine leather. The saddle was as beautiful as the horse, not something he'd simply run across.

"I've grown used to riding in men's saddles," she said.

"Figured you had, what with all the riding you do with Austin."

She looked up. "I'm getting married tomorrow."

"I know. Dallas sent word to me this morning."

"That's Reverend Tucker on the porch."

He glanced toward the porch and touched a finger to the brim of his hat in acknowledgment. "He looks like a gunfighter."

Amelia laughed. "That's what I thought."

"Did I ever tell you that I like the way you laugh?" he asked, his voice low.

She placed her hand over his, slowly threading her fingers through the reins, relishing the roughness of his palm against hers. "Take me for a ride."

He straightened. "I'd best not."

"Please. I think you should be with me the first

time I ride Palomino so she'll understand that she's changing owners."

He smiled as though secretly pleased with himself, and she wished she could have a lifetime of his smiles.

"I didn't name her Palomino."

"Golden?"

His smile increased. "Nope."

"Mustang?"

He shook his head. "I named her after the woman who'd be riding her."

She laughed. "Amelia?"

His smile slipped away. "Valiant."

Tears stung her eyes. "Please take me for a ride."

Whatever good sense he might have possessed must have left him because he dismounted and walked around to her. "We won't go far," he said.

She nodded. "That's fine."

"We won't stay gone for long."

"That's fine."

He cupped his hands together and bent down. She put her foot within his palms, and he hoisted her up. She settled into the saddle as Valiant sidestepped, snorted, and shook her head.

Houston grabbed the reins and spoke in a low voice near the mare's ear before moving aside and mounting Sorrel. He glanced at Amelia. "Let's test her speed and endurance, but I'll set the pace."

She could only nod as she began to hoard away all the images that would make up the memories of their last ride.

AMELIA REMOVED HER socks and shoes and dipped her feet into the cold water of the springs. She hadn't expected their short trip to take them this far, but it seemed appropriate to finally have the chance to say good-bye properly and to say it here.

Houston was stretched out beside her, raised on an elbow, watching her as though he'd never again have the opportunity to look at her. And perhaps he wouldn't. At least not in the same way.

Tomorrow, she would become his sister by marriage. Leaning forward, she slipped her fingers into the water until they were wet enough, then she lifted them out and flicked them toward Houston. He turned his head aside as the water sprayed over him. Then he met her gaze.

"You didn't ask Dallas why he won't look at me, did you?"

"No." She tilted her nose slightly, daring him to ask.

"Why?"

"Because you've told me time and again that you take the easy way. Asking Dallas would have been the easy way for you. I deserve better than that."

He smiled sadly. "And I'd never give you better than that, Amelia."

"And you think he will?"

"I know he will."

She turned away, wondering why she was trying to push herself into the life of a man who obviously didn't want her. She couldn't explain why she loved him, why she wanted to be part of his life, his dreams.

"Accepting Dallas's offer of marriage seemed so right before I met you. Now, I no longer know what is right. I wanted to be a wife. I wanted to escape the memories from the war. I never expected to find love."

He gently grazed his knuckles over her cheek. "You should have expected to find love. There's so much about you to love."

She had never wanted anything as desperately in her life as she wanted to hear him voice aloud his love for her. Just three words. Three simple words. Yet, she knew he would never say them. To do so would force them to acknowledge a dream they could never possess, would condemn them to years of wondering what might have been.

She placed her hand over his and rubbed her cheek against his rough palm. "Will Dallas love me?"

She watched his throat work as he swallowed. He shifted his gaze to the waterfalls, his voice raspy when at last he spoke. "Yeah, he will."

She could hear the rush of the water as it spilled over the rocks, her moments with Houston flowing by as quickly. Never again would she be alone with him, to look upon him with a longing that should have never entered her heart. She had so much that she wanted to say to him, but she knew the words would only make their leaving this peaceful sanctuary more difficult, so she locked them away, hoping a day would come when she would forget that she'd ever thought them.

"I imagine this place is beautiful in the spring," she said softly.

"Yep. It's a lot greener then, and the flowers come up."

"Will Dallas bring me here to see it?"

"I don't know if he knows about it." He glanced at her. "I'll give him directions."

"How did you manage to find it?"

He shrugged. "Just happened upon it one day."

"Sometimes, life gives us the most unexpected gifts, doesn't it?"

Houston wanted to tell her that she had been an unexpected gift, along with her laughter, her smiles, and her courage. He didn't think he'd ever receive anything finer than the days he'd spent with her as they'd traveled from Fort Worth. "Yeah, it does," he said quietly.

INSIDE DALLAS'S BARN, Houston removed the saddle from Valiant's back and swung it over the slats of the stall. She was a good horse. She had a good temperament. She'd serve Amelia well.

He smelled Amelia's sweet scent before he heard her gentle footsteps. He'd put off saying good-bye as long as he could. Words failed him as they always did. He wanted to thank her for the sunshine she'd brought into his life, for the memories that would linger.

And he wished to God that he'd made different choices in his life.

"Take a dare or tell me the truth," she said softly behind him.

He swallowed hard, knowing he was damned either way. He turned slowly, memorizing the slant of her brow, the tip of her nose, the blush in her cheeks. "Dare," he rasped.

"Kiss me as though you loved me."

She stood valiantly . . . his heart-in-her-eyes woman. He had but to tell her the truth to put out the fire of love, to replace it with the cold ashes of disappointment. It should have been easy, but dear God, he didn't want her to hate him, to know him for the man he really was.

So he held his silence and played the game with her rules. He framed her face between his large hands, tilted her face slightly, lowered his mouth to hers, and plunged into hell.

She whimpered softly and leaned into him, her arms moving up to snake around his neck. He tried to be gentle, wanted to be tender, but all he could think about was her warm mouth greedily mating with his. His arms moved down until his hands were roaming over her slender back, pressing her closer to him, until her soft curves met the hard planes of his body.

God, he wanted her. He wanted her here in the hay beside the horses. He wanted her beneath the stars on a warm, sultry night, beneath a pile of blankets when the snow was falling. He wanted her sleepy smile in the morning, her contented smile at midnight.

He wanted to see her flesh when she took off her clothes and ran the damp cloth over her body. He wanted to see everything that existed behind the shadows.

He wanted to make her laugh. He never wanted to make her cry. He never wanted to hurt her.

He drew back, his breathing labored, his heart pounding so hard he thought surely she could feel it. But her breathing matched his and her eyes, her eyes of clover green, were searching his face, searching for what he could never let her see.

"I'll take a dare," she whispered hoarsely.

He touched his trembling thumb to her quivering lip. "Find your happiness with Dallas."

He edged past her, and without looking back, walked out of the barn. He hadn't given her the farewell she deserved, but then nothing he gave her would ever be what she deserved.

AMELIA SAT ON the back porch and stared at the moon, incredibly large, shimmering in the night sky. Every so often, clouds slowly rolled before it with a touch that she imagined was as light as Houston's.

She wanted his love, but more she wanted his trust. She had seen the ugliest part of him and accepted it. Why couldn't he accept it?

"Amelia?"

She glanced up at the shadowed figure. The clouds waltzed past the moon, illuminating Dallas, his hands stuffed into his pockets. He ambled to the porch and leaned against the beam. "I couldn't sleep," he said. "Figured I'd better not risk a horse ride tonight."

Pressing on her skirt, she slipped her hands between her knees. "I couldn't sleep, either."

He hunkered down before her and draped his hands over his knees. "Thinking about tomorrow?" he asked.

She laughed self-consciously. "Yes. You?"

"Yep."

She squeezed her hands between her knees to stop their trembling. "I guess people have gotten married who knew each other less than we do."

"My pa met my ma the day he married her."

"I wonder if your mother was as afraid as I am now."

"I won't hurt you, Amelia."

"But I might hurt you. I don't know if I'll ever be able to give you my heart."

"I'm not asking for your heart. Just your hand, your loyalty, and your respect."

The warmth flared through her cheeks. "And a son."

"That would please me greatly."

"What will we name him?"

He smiled broadly in the moonlight. "What would you like to name him?"

Amelia shrugged. "I don't know."

"Well, we have a few months to think about it. It will be your choice, but I'd like a strong name. Sometimes, all a man needs is his name to make his mark on the world."

"Mark," she said quietly. "We could name him Mark."

"Short for Marcus?"

She nodded. He smiled. "Marcus it is. Marcus Leigh." He looked into the distance. "All of this is for him, Amelia. His legacy."

He brought himself to his feet. "I'd best let you get some sleep." Reaching down, he took her hand and pulled her to her feet.

"My pa told me once that love is something

that grows over time. I think that'll be the way of it with us." He kissed her palm, his mouth warm, his mustache soft. "Until tomorrow."

Amelia wrapped her arms around the beam and watched him disappear into the night. She pressed her hand against her stomach. Marcus Leigh.

She would love the child, respect and honor his father, and forget that his uncle had the ability to curl her toes.

HOUSTON SAT ON his front porch and listened to the night. The wind blew cold around him, but it wasn't nearly as cold as his heart.

He rubbed a hand over his unmarred cheek. Fate had been cruel enough to leave a portion of his face unscathed so he would forever be reminded of what he would have had . . . had he chosen differently.

Unmercifully, he pressed his fingers to his scars, slowly tracing every ridge, every valley, every section of knotted flesh. Each served as a testament to the man he was.

The man he would always be. The boy he had been.

"Dallas, I'm scared."

"Don't be. Ain't nothing to fear but fear itself. That's what Pa says."

"I don't know what that means."

"It just means don't be afraid."

But he had been afraid. Thirteen years later, the fear still hovered around him, the memories strong enough to catapult him back in time.

Houston could hear the roar of the cannons,

feel the pounding of the earth. The land had been so green, so pretty at dawn. Then it became blackened, red, and torn. The air hung heavy with smoke and the shouts of angry men, brave men, scared men, dying men.

Houston Leigh buried his face in his hands and did what he'd been too afraid to do thirteen years before.

He wept.

THE FRIGID WINDS whipped through near dawn. At Dallas's insistence, the men left the herd unattended on the range while they crowded inside the parlor, shoving and elbowing each other like children anxious to get outside.

A fire blazed within the hearth, but its warmth could not penetrate the chill seeping through Houston's bones. He stood beside Reverend Tucker, waiting for the hell to end, for decisions and choices to be taken out of his hands.

The men fell into silence as Amelia walked into the room, Dallas at her side. She again wore the green silk dress. He'd never asked Dallas for payment, wouldn't have accepted it if it had been offered. Everything he'd ever given her was his way of apologizing for intruding in her life.

If the value of a gift was based upon what it meant to the giver, he was about to give her the finest gift of all: his brother as her husband.

Dallas stood on one side of Amelia, Houston on the other. Austin fidgeted beside Houston in a brown jacket he'd outgrow before he had the need to wear it again.

Outside, the wind howled and the sky turned gray.

Inside, the fire crackled, and Reverend Tucker asked one and all to bow their heads in prayer. As his voice rang out, Houston studied the woman standing beside him. She hadn't looked at him as she had walked into the room, and he couldn't blame her.

They'd traveled through hell together and survived. She'd clambered out of it. How could he drag her back into it?

Reverend Tucker ended the prayer and spoke about marriage, commitment, and duty. Houston stopped listening to the words. They weren't for him. They were for Amelia and the man standing on the other side of her.

Then Reverend Tucker's voice was pounding through his head, reverberating around his heart. "If anyone knows why these two should not be joined in holy matrimony, speak now or forever hold your peace."

Amelia turned her head slightly, caught, and held Houston's gaze. He wanted to tell her. God help him, he'd rather have the disappointment in her eyes than the hurt.

She turned away, and he knew that she'd said farewell at that moment, that there would be no turning back the hands of the clock. For her, he'd held his silence, would forever hold his peace.

As Dallas took Amelia in his arms and kissed her, Houston plunged into the darkest depths of hell.

THE WINDS WERE cold as Houston stood on the back porch, his duster flapping around his calves. He should head out before it got much darker, taking Austin with him so the newly married couple could have some privacy.

He heard the door open and glanced over his shoulder to see Amelia. "It's cold out here. You'd best stay inside."

"Don't I have a say in where I stand?"

He smiled at her comment, but he had no desire to tease her back. She'd do what she wanted, just as he'd done what he had to do. He turned his attention back to the horizon.

She walked to the edge of the porch, briskly rubbing her hands up and down her arms. He wanted to take her into his embrace and warm her. Instead, he shrugged out of his duster and wrapped it around her. She closed it tightly around her.

"Marcus," she said softly.

He glanced at her. "Marcus?"

She nodded. "That's what we're going to name our first son. We'll call him Mark because Dallas expects him to make his mark on the world."

"With Dallas as his father, I imagine he will."

Her knuckles turned white as she clutched his coat. "I'm nervous about tonight. I don't have any women to talk to . . . and I . . . I always considered you . . . a dear friend. I was hoping maybe you might have some words of wisdom to share so I won't be afraid or disappoint him."

"You could never disappoint him."

"Unless I give him a daughter."

"Not even then."

Her cheeks reddened, but he didn't think it had anything to do with the cold chafing her skin.

"Will it hurt?" she asked quietly.

He felt as though he'd just been kicked in the gut by a mustang. What the hell did he know about a woman's first time? He knew whores. Their stench, their bodies that were always ready for a man, their outstretched hands asking for more money. He looked away. "Christ, I don't know."

A thick silence built between them.

"Thank you," she finally said and turned to go.

He grabbed her arm and looked at her, really looked at her for the first time, into the green depths of her eyes. He could see the terror. He pulled her against him, wrapped his arms around her, and touched his cheek to her soft hair.

"He won't hurt you," he said quietly. "If he can help it, he won't hurt you. The women I've known were so used . . . He'll kiss you . . . and he just won't stop."

"But kissing won't make a baby."

He slipped his thumb beneath her chin and tilted her face up, wanting desperately to remove the worry from her green eyes. He swallowed hard. "He'll lay his body over yours." He cradled her face, wishing he could cradle her body. "And he'll give what he always gives: the best of himself."

She smiled then, so sweetly with so much trust that his heart ached. "I'll miss you," she said quietly.

"You know where I live. If you need—"

She shook her head with a profound sadness. "No, this at long last is our final good-bye." She stretched up on her toes and kissed him lightly on the lips.

He couldn't stand it: the betrayal reflected in her eyes, the hurt, the disappointment. He'd rather have the hate. "I killed my father."

He released his hold on her and averted his gaze. She'd hate him now, hate him as he hated himself.

"I don't believe you," she said softly.

He laughed derisively. "Believe me, Amelia. For thirteen years, I've run from it. For thirteen years, the truth has stayed as close as my shadow."

"How did you kill him?"

"You want the gory details?"

"I want to understand how the man I traveled with could have possibly killed his father."

He stared into the distance, stared through the passing years. "I was his drummer. He gave the orders and the beat of my drum told the men what those orders were. In the thick of battle, you can't hear a man's words, only his dying screams and the sound of the drum. The smoke grows so heavy that it drops like a fog, surrounding you, burning your eyes, your throat, suffocating you until you can't see the man issuing the orders.

"But you can hear the beat of the drum. So wherever my father went, I had to be. When he rode into battle, I ran by his side, beating . . . beating my drum while bullets whistled past and cannons roared."

His mouth grew dry with the familiar fear licking at his throat. He could smell the smoke and blood. He could hear the screams.

"His horse went down, kicking at the air, screaming in agony. My father scrambled to his feet and pulled his sword from his scabbard. 'Let's go, boy!' he yelled.

"Only I couldn't. The man standing beside me fell. The ground exploded in my face. My father hollered at me again. I started to run. As fast as my legs would take me, I started running back to the place where I'd slept the night before.

"He came after me, yelling, 'By God, I won't have a coward for a son!'

"He grabbed my arm, jerked me around, but I turned away from him, struggling to break free. Suddenly, there was a loud explosion, a bright light, pain . . . and he was gone. And then there was nothing but blackness."

"That's when you were so terribly wounded?"

He laughed mirthlessly. "Yeah, I should have died, too, but I didn't. I prayed for death hard enough, but some prayers just aren't meant to be answered."

"You can't really believe you killed your father?"

"If I hadn't run, he wouldn't have died. I was just what he always said I was. A coward. A weak no-account excuse for a son."

"But you were a child."

"I was old enough. At fifteen, Dallas was marching into battle with a rifle in hand and men following him."

"You're not Dallas."

He finally turned from the past and met Amelia's gaze. "That's right, Amelia, I'm not. And that's why I held my silence. Because you deserve better than me. You don't deserve a man who runs from his own shadow, who's afraid of life."

She tilted her head, that familiar gesture like a puppy who is sizing up another dog and deciding if he can outfight him for the bone. "Does Dallas know that you prefer solitude and have an aversion to towns?"

"Yeah, he knows."

"Yet he sent you to fetch me anyway."

"He didn't have a choice. As much as he trusts his men with cattle, I'm not altogether sure he'd trust them not to take advantage of a pretty lady on a long journey."

"He could have sent Austin."

"Austin?" Houston chuckled. "Austin is just a boy."

A deep sadness swept over her features, tears welling in her eyes, as she laid her palm against his scarred cheek. "He's older than you were the last time you stood on a battlefield."

Her words slammed against him, stunned him, left him paralyzed. He had to have been older than Austin. Austin . . . hell, Austin had shaved for the first time that morning.

The door opened, and Dallas stepped onto the porch, Austin in his wake. Austin crossed the porch, leaned down, and bussed a kiss against Amelia's cheek.

"What was that?" Dallas asked.

Austin flushed. "I was just practicin'."

"For what?"

"Houston's taking me to a sportin' house tonight."

Houston shoved Austin's shoulder and fought to find his voice. "That's between you and me."

"What?" Austin stumbled down the steps. "I don't understand anything anymore. We wanted a woman here so bad, and now that we've got her, we've all gotta change. It makes no sense to me at all."

Houston stepped to the ground. Austin brought up his fists. "I'm tired of getting hit, yanked, and yelled at for being me."

Houston slowly shook his head. "I'm not gonna hit you. Go get your horse."

Austin's eyes widened. "You still gonna take me?"

"Told you I would. Now go get your horse."

Austin released a whoop and started running toward the corral. Houston turned to the couple standing on the porch. "Thought I'd get him out of your way for a couple of days."

" 'Preciate that," Dallas said as he removed Houston's duster from Amelia's shoulders and tossed it to him. He shrugged out of his own jacket and wrapped it and his arm around Amelia.

She glanced up at her husband and gave him a hesitant smile. Houston wished to God she didn't look so small standing beside his brother, so small, and so damn vulnerable.

Houston backed up a step and threw his thumb over his shoulder. "Reckon we'll be goin'."

"Take care," she said quietly.

"We will." He started walking toward the corral, stopped, and looked back over his shoulder.

Dallas was escorting his wife into the house, her back straight, her chin held high.

The Queen of the Prairie.

Chapter Eighteen

Dusty Flats wasn't much more than a hole in the ground, a place for cowboys to spend energy and money when they were trailing cattle. It boasted one cantina with a bathing room in the back; a general store with so little merchandise that people simply traipsed in, picked up what they needed, and slapped their money onto the counter; and a house filled to capacity with sporting women. No church, no school, no town hall.

Houston hadn't detoured by the settlement in years. He'd forgotten how dismal the place appeared at midnight, but it had what he needed to distract him from all the unsettling thoughts running through his head, and it had what Austin wanted. It'd do.

He brought his horse to a halt in front of the two-story wooden framed house and dismounted.

"This it?" Austin asked as he slid off his bay gelding and absently wrapped the reins around the hitching rail.

"Yep."

Bending at the waist and peering through the dust coated windows, Austin paced the rattling wooden porch. "Ain't much light. What if they're closed?"

"They're not closed," Houston assured him as he stepped on the porch. He wondered if he'd ever been as young as Austin appeared now, ever held that much exuberance about anything. Houston had been eighteen the first time he had paid a woman for her services. He'd felt like an old man, with no excitement, no anticipation. Just something to do so he could say he'd done it. "You don't need much light for what we're gonna do." The door squeaked on dry hinges as he shoved it open. "Come on."

Austin bounded through like a puppy being tossed a bone. He swept his hat from his head, his eyes larger than a harvest moon as he took in the drab surroundings. The vacant seats of the wooden chairs had been polished to a shine by the backsides of all the cowboys who had sat waiting their turn over the years.

A woman with fiery red hair, violet eyes, and full lips painted blood red sauntered over and trailed her fingers from Austin's shoulder to his elbow and back up. She purred like a contented cat that had just lapped up the last of the cream, her smile one of appreciation.

"Hey, darlin'," she cooed in a voice as sultry as a summer night.

"Howdy," Austin croaked, his voice changing pitch three times. He'd latched his gaze onto her bountiful bosom which Houston thought might bust free of that shimmering red corset at any moment. He watched his brother's Adam's apple slide up and down and figured Austin was thinking the same thing.

"Maria still work here?" Houston asked.

The woman yelled over the din of a distant off-key piano. Maria shoved herself away from the lanky cowboy over whom she'd been draped and sauntered over, smiling when she recognized Houston.

She appeared older than he'd remembered, worn as thin as the wood on the chairs. The red paint she'd smeared on her cheeks didn't stop them from sagging and the dark circles beneath her eyes had little to do with the kohl she was wearing.

Because she knew him, had serviced him before, she placed her hand inside his thigh, embarrassingly close to his crotch. He was uncomfortable as hell blushing in front of his little brother.

"Been a long time, cowboy," Maria said in a weary voice. "I got that handsome fella over there interested in me. I don't know if double will make me forget him."

"Triple, then."

Her smile grew, but never reached her eyes as she wrapped her arm through his. "I'm yours."

He looked over his shoulder at Austin. "This is his first time. Be gentle with him."

The woman's throaty laughter spilled past her curved lips. "Ah, honey, I'm always gentle." She tugged on Austin's hand. "Come on, sweet thing."

"Shouldn't we talk first?" Austin asked, and the woman's laughter grew.

"Don't worry about him. Velvet will give him a time he won't soon forget," Maria said as she led Houston toward the stairs, leaving Austin standing and stuttering in the front parlor. "You want it the same as last time?"

The loneliness swept through him as he gave her his answer. "Yeah."

HOUSTON STEPPED ON the porch and drew in a long deep breath of the brisk fresh air. No smoke. No heavy perfume. No musky stench of stale bodies rutting like dogs.

The night air was clear, as clear as the stars twinkling above him. He thought he'd never again be able to look upon the night sky without thinking of Amelia curled in his arms.

He'd watched Maria undress . . . and felt nothing but a desire to leave. The woman's naked body hadn't been half as alluring as Amelia's shadow. He'd apologized for his lack of interest, paid her what he'd promised, and walked out without touching her. Since Amelia had come into his life, he was doing one hell of a lot of apologizing.

He crossed the porch and dropped to the top step where his younger brother was leaning against the porch post, gazing into the distance as though he'd fallen in love.

"Didn't take you long," Houston said as he settled against the opposite post. He chuckled low. "Course, as I recall, didn't take me long the first time, either."

"I didn't go with her," Austin said quietly. "I was thinking about Dallas and Amelia—"

"Well, don't," Houston snapped.

Austin turned his head slightly. "I wasn't thinking nothing personal or anything. I just thought all women were like Amelia, all clean and sweet smelling and smiling like they were glad to see me."

"There's a hell of a lot of difference between a sporting woman and a woman like Amelia."

"How come?"

Houston sighed with frustration. He didn't need or want this conversation tonight. Dallas was the one who had the vast experience with women. He should have done a better job of educating the boy. "Sporting women, well, they can be had for a price. A woman like Amelia . . . doesn't give herself lightly. Men don't fall in love with sporting women. But a woman like Amelia . . . when a man falls in love with a woman like Amelia . . . he does what's best for her, no matter what the cost to him."

"You ever fall in love with a woman like Amelia?"

"Once."

"When?"

He dug his elbows unmercifully into his thighs, welcoming the distraction of the pain. "Forever. Reckon I'll love her forever, till the day I die."

"What happened to her?"

"She married someone else."

"You loved her, but you let her marry some other fella? Why'd you do a fool thing like that?"

"Because it was best for her."

"How do you know it was best for her?"

Houston swiveled his head and captured his brother's gaze. "What?"

Austin shrugged. "What if what you thought was best for her wasn't what she wanted?"

"What are you talking about?"

Austin slid his backside across the porch. "I'm not learned in these matters so I don't understand how you know what you did was best for her."

"I just know, that's all. I just know." He surged to his feet, leapt off the porch, and began pacing across the lantern-lit path, into the darkness, then back into the light. Darkness. Light. His life before Amelia. His life after he'd come to know her. Darkness. Light.

He *had* done what was best for Amelia. She didn't need to wake up each morning next to a man who was afraid of the dark, afraid of the dawn, afraid of what the day might hold. She deserved better. He'd given her better.

Dallas feared no man, feared nothing. He hadn't run when the cannons were roaring and the bullets were whizzing past. He'd stood his ground and led the Confederate forces through the charge . . . over and over . . . in battle after battle.

Dallas was the kind of man Amelia deserved. Amelia with her courageous heart that had seen them through disaster after disaster. Amelia with the tears shimmering in her eyes, along with understanding.

Why had she looked at him with no judgment in her eyes, no revulsion after his confession?

He wasn't the hero Dallas had been. He never would be. He had run like a frightened jackrabbit and paid a heavy price: his father's life.

He had never talked with Dallas about that day. Sometimes, Houston would wonder if the battle had happened at all. Then he'd stop to water his horse at a pond. Within the clear still waters, he'd see his reflection, a constant memento of how his father had died.

He knew his face served as a reminder for Dallas as well. For months after Houston had been wounded, Dallas had preferred to stare at his mud-covered boots rather than meet Houston's gaze.

Amelia should have averted her gaze as well. She should have been appalled and horrified. The woman kept her heart in her eyes and that was all he'd seen reflected there: her love for him.

He skidded to a dead halt and stared hard at Austin. The boy's chin carried so many nicks from his first shave that it was a wonder he hadn't bled to death. He was a year older than Houston had been when he'd last stood on a battlefield. Sweet Lord, Houston had never had the opportunity to shave his whole face; he'd never flirted with girls, wooed women, or danced through the night. He'd never loved.

Not until Amelia.

And he'd given her up because he'd thought it was best for her. Because he had nothing to offer her but a one-roomed log cabin, a few horses, a dream so small that it wouldn't cover the palm of her hand.

And his heart. His wounded heart.

He yanked the reins off the hitching post and mounted his horse.

Austin came to his feet. "Where you goin'?"

"Back to the ranch."

THEY RODE HARD through the night. Houston wasn't at all certain what he would say to Amelia, what explanation he could give Dallas.

He'd held his silence, sacrificing his right to say anything. She had pledged herself to Dallas, had become his wife. Vows Houston thought he'd ignored thrummed through his head with the rhythm of the pounding hooves: to love, honor, and obey . . . until death parted them.

He only knew that he had to see her, had to talk to her, and had to understand why she hadn't turned away from him, repulsed by his confession. Good Lord, if he didn't know better, he'd swear she had looked as though she loved him more.

Would a night in Dallas's arms sway her heart away from Houston? And if it didn't, what difference would it make? She could already be carrying the son that Dallas wanted so desperately.

Black smoke billowed in the distance, darkening the brilliance of the dawn. The familiar panic and the accustomed fear settled into Houston's gut. He urged his horse into a faster gallop, with Austin following him like a shadow.

"What is it?" Austin yelled behind him.

"Trouble!"

His horse tore up the ground with the intensity of the gallop. Houston leaned low, pressing

Sorrel to ride with all her heart. Good judgment told him to slow as he neared Dallas's home, but the eerie silence urged him on.

Someone had reduced the barn to smoldering embers and the corral to broken planks of wood. With black soot and sweat smeared over their faces and clothes, the men milled around in front of the house as though lost.

Houston jerked his horse to a halt. "What happened?"

Slim lifted a shoulder and a vacant gaze. "Don't know. We were all in the bunkhouse drunk as skunks after celebrating the wedding. We heard a gunshot. Got outside, but it was too late to do any good. Barn was on fire, horses gone. The boss is still out cold. Cookie's with him. Jackson took off at a run to find some help, but on foot, it'll take him a week to reach another ranch. The rest of us ain't no good without a horse beneath us."

"Amelia? What about Amelia?"

Slim dropped his gaze. Houston dismounted and grabbed the man by the shirtfront, pulling him up to eye level. "Where's Amelia?"

Slim shifted his gaze to the other men. They stepped back. Houston shook him. "Goddamn it! Is she hurt?"

Slim swallowed. "We don't know where she is."

Roughly, Houston released his hold on Slim, his heart pounding so hard, he was certain every man in the state could hear it. "She has to be here. Find her! Now!"

"She's not here," a seething voice echoed from the doorway.

Dallas stumbled down the steps and leaned against the beam for support, breathing heavily, blood trailing near his temple.

Houston placed a steadying hand on his brother's shoulder. "You've been shot."

"It's just a crease. That's the least of my worries right now. God damn horse thieves took Amelia." Dallas pushed away from the porch. "I'm going to get her back. Nobody takes what belongs to me, by God. Nobody. Austin, I'm taking your horse."

Austin scrambled off his horse so quickly that he lost his footing and his backside hit the dirt. In an unsteady gait, Dallas headed toward the gelding. Houston knew it was determination alone that got his brother up into the saddle.

"I'm coming with you," Houston said as he mounted Sorrel.

"Suit yourself. Austin, you're in charge here till we get back."

Austin's eyes widened. "Me?"

"You got a problem with that?" Dallas asked.

Austin shook his head vigorously. "No, sir."

"Good. Any orders you give are coming from me, so don't give any orders I wouldn't give."

"Yes, sir. We'll get the corral rebuilt. Reckon you'll be bringin' the horses back."

"Damn right I will. Along with my wife."

DALLAS HAD A reputation for protecting what was his. In his wildest dreams, Houston never would have thought anyone would be fool enough to try and take what belonged to Dallas Leigh, but as he was discovering, the men who had taken

Amelia were fools. They left a trail that a blind man could have followed.

"They're not too cautious," Houston observed.

"Since they took all the horses, I don't imagine they expected anyone to come after them for a day or so. That mistake will cost them dearly."

They caught up with the horse thieves near dusk. They were ensconced in a canyon, smoke spiraling from their campfire. Houston and Dallas climbed the bluff and crawled on their bellies to its edge.

"I count six," Dallas said. "We could pick them off from up here."

Houston took Dallas's word for the number. His gaze was trained on Amelia. From this distance it was difficult to measure, but he didn't think she looked hurt.

"They might take it into their heads to use Amelia as a shield," Houston said.

"True enough, but it looks like there's only one way in. We'd make easy targets if we went that route," Dallas said.

"And we'd put Amelia at risk if we go in there with our guns firing. She's sure to get hurt."

"Then what would you suggest?"

"I go in alone."

Dallas jerked his head around.

"If I can get close to her," Houston continued, "I could at least protect her while you fire from up here. If I can get my horse close enough to her, maybe I can get her up on it, and we can ride out."

Dallas clenched his jaw. "She's my wife."

"But they know what you look like. Besides,

you're a better shot than I am and my horse is faster. Figure I can go in there claiming to be an outlaw looking for a place to hide." He lifted a corner of his mouth. "My face ought to convince them I'm telling the truth."

Dallas flinched and gazed back into the canyon. "I don't want the two of you trapped in there. I won't start shooting until you can get your horse close to her. Use the diversion to get her on the horse and get her out of there. I'll take care of the thieves."

"See that you do."

"It'll be night soon. We need to work fast. If anything goes wrong . . ." Dallas's voice trailed off.

Houston grabbed Dallas's coat and jerked him around. "Just make sure Amelia comes first. No matter what happens, she gets out of there alive."

AMELIA HAD NEVER been so terrified in her entire life. She hugged the rocky canyon wall wishing she could melt into it and disappear. If she survived, she didn't think she would cherish her green wedding dress or its memories.

The ropes chafed her wrists, her jaw still ached. When she didn't think anyone was looking, she'd tried to gnaw the knots loose. Her attempt had earned her a flat-handed slap and tighter knots.

She saw a man, his arms raised, walking into the canyon leading a horse. Two men sauntered behind him, rifles trained on him giving them the advantage and a false arrogance. She recognized the weathered hat, the dusty black coat, and the horse. Houston didn't look at her or call out to her with reassurances. Perhaps he had no reassurances to give. Or perhaps he was simply biding his time. He seemed remarkably calm for a man who had just walked into a nest of vipers. She kept her gaze locked on him, watching for any small signal that would indicate he had a plan to rescue her.

"What have we got here?" the man she knew to be leader said as he came to his feet, his hand resting easily on the butt of his gun.

Houston walked farther into the camp, hoping to give Dallas sight of the two men behind him. He didn't know how to signal to him that another man was guarding the entrance.

"He was just ridin' in, pretty as you please, whistlin' some song like he owned the place," one of the men who had been tailing him said as they both stopped walking sooner than Houston would have liked. He didn't know if Dallas could see them from his vantage point at the top of the bluff.

"I do own the place," Houston said, trying to imitate the authority Dallas always carried in his voice. "Or at least I do when I'm lookin' for a place to hide out for a couple of days." He squatted, lowered his arms, and warmed his hands before the fire, praying no one could see how badly they were shaking. "I don't mind sharin' the place, though."

The man he assumed was the leader narrowed his eyes. "You hidin' from the law?"

"I'm hiding from anyone who's looking for me."

The man scratched his scraggly beard and chuckled. "Know that feeling. You got a name?"

"Dare."

"Dare?" the man asked, incredulously.

Houston came slowly to his feet, used his thumb to push his hat up off his brow, and met the man's gaze. "You got a problem with that?"

"Nah, ain't got no problem with it at all." He held out his hand. "I'm Colson. These here are my men."

Ignoring the outstretched hand, Houston glanced quickly around the canyon. A makeshift corral held the stolen horses. The other horses were saddled and lightly tethered to the brush growing out of the rocks. They could be mounted in the blink of an eye and riding west a half-blink later. "You seem to have a lot more horses than you do men."

"We collect 'em whenever fortune smiles on us. Can always find a man willing to pay for good horseflesh."

"And the woman?"

Colson laughed knowingly. "Reckon men are willing to pay for that, too."

"Reckon they are. Mind if I have a look-see?"

Colson rubbed his chin. "Not as long as all you do is look. She'll be keeping me warm tonight."

"Understood," Houston said as he fought the urge to plow his fist into that ugly face. He damned the men for taking his revolver. Thank God, they'd left his rifle in the scabbard, although he didn't know if it would do him much good in these close quarters. An idea came to him. He turned back to Colson, hoping the smile he gave the man looked as mean as it felt. "Mind if I have me a little innocent fun? I like to hear women scream."

Colson narrowed his eyes. "What do you mean by innocent?"

Houston jerked his head toward Amelia. "The way she's worked her way into that crack, I figured she ain't given any thought as to what's in there with her. Women hate things with tiny legs. Just thought I'd mention them to her."

Colson squatted before the fire. "I don't think she's the type to scream over a little bug, but it don't bother me none if you have your fun."

Houston walked as calmly as he could toward the far corner of the canyon, grateful no one objected when Sorrel followed him. He was going to reward the horse with a whole basket of apples if they lived through this night.

Amelia had wedged herself into a large crack in the canyon wall. She carried a fresh bruise on her cheek, and it was all he could do not to turn around right then, yank his rifle out of the scabbard, and start shooting.

As he neared, he called out, "Little lady, scorpions and snakes sure do love to hide in the cool cracks." He mouthed "scream," and bless her heart, she did.

She released an ear-splitting scream as she catapulted out of the crack and lunged into his arms. The men surrounding them guffawed. A shot rang out.

As the thieves scrambled for cover, Houston wrapped his hands around Amelia's waist and hoisted her into the saddle. She grabbed the horn. He mounted behind her and urged Sorrel into a gallop as a second shot ricocheted off the rocks.

"What the hell?" someone shouted.

Houston heard several more shots ring out. Particles of rock flew through the air, showering over them as they raced toward the entrance. Men hollered. Horses whinnied. All hell was breaking loose behind them, but he rode on without looking back.

He held Amelia as close as he could, using his body as a shield around her as much as possible as they tore through the mouth of the canyon. He heard a bullet whisper past his ear.

He kicked Sorrel's sides, prodding her into a faster gallop. He saw the setting sun glint off a rifle and he kept riding. He heard the retort of more gunfire. He didn't know how much time Dallas could buy them. He feared it wouldn't be enough.

He felt a sharp bite in his arm. He glanced back. Three riders were galloping fast and furious from the mouth of the canyon. Leaning forward, he pulled his rifle from the scabbard. He looked back over his shoulder. The three riders were gaining on them. A horse with two riders couldn't outrun a horse with one, no matter how fast he was.

"Take the reins!" he yelled.

Awkward as it was with her hands still bound, Amelia did as he instructed. His thighs hugging the horse, he pulled Amelia flush against him. "'Keep riding!"

He took one last breath filled with her faint sweet scent. "I love you."

With fluid motions, he released her, grabbed the back of the saddle, shoved hard, and propelled himself off the galloping horse, away from the pounding hooves. He hit the ground, rolled into a kneeling position, brought his rifle up, and fired.

Amelia had heard Houston's words as though he'd whispered them in a field of flowers instead of on the open plains as they were riding hell-bent to get away. And then she had felt him leaving her . . . forever.

Against his wishes, she jerked back on the reins, fighting to bring the galloping horse to a staggering halt. She whirled Sorrel around just in time to see Houston shoot the second of three riders. The remaining rider fired his rifle. Houston jerked back, his arms flailing out to the side.

"No!" she cried, her heart screamed.

Another retort of gunfire filled the air, and the last rider slumped forward before tumbling from his saddle. Amelia urged Sorrel into a gallop, a litany of prayers rushing through her mind. She drew the horse to a halt where Houston had fallen. She scrambled out of the saddle and fell to her knees beside him.

Bright red blood soaked through his shirt. "No," she whispered, tears welling in her eyes. "No, no, no." Ignoring the pain as the rope bit into her wrists, she ripped off a portion of her petticoat and pressed it against the wound, desperately trying to staunch the flow of crimson. The white cotton rapidly became red.

Houston opened his eye. She touched her palm

to his cheek. "Don't you die on me. I'll never forgive you if you die on me."

"I didn't run," he rasped.

"But you should have, you fool! You should have stayed with me!"

A corner of his mouth tilted up. "That would have been the easy way. You deserve better than that."

He sank into oblivion, his breathing shallow. A shadow crossed over his face. Amelia jerked her head up as Dallas dropped to his knees, knife in hand, and began to cut away Houston's shirt.

"Why in the hell didn't he stay on the horse? I wasn't that far behind—"

"He had something to prove to himself," she said quietly, the tears coursing down her cheeks.

Chapter Nineteen

━━━⟡⟡⟡━━━

*I*n his entire life, Dallas had never met the next moment without a plan of action, had never known what it was to feel useless, without a purpose. He sure as hell felt useless now, and he didn't know what to do about it.

He'd gathered up the stolen horses and had left the men he and Houston had killed to the buzzards and coyotes. He hadn't been cruel out of vengeance, but he had recognized that time was rapidly becoming his bitter enemy. The bullet had entered and exited through Houston's shoulder, leaving a relatively clean wound, but two gaping holes through which the blood could flow. And flow it did.

As much as Dallas had hated to do it, he'd wrapped a rope around Houston to keep him from falling out of his saddle. They'd ridden through the night, keeping the horses at a slow, steady walk, their planned destination the ranch. Near dawn, when Houston's cabin had come into view, Dallas had decided not to push his luck.

He had carried Houston, unconscious, into

his log cabin and laid him as gently as he could in the bed. He'd helped Amelia clean, sew, and dress the wound, his admiration for her growing as her competent hands handled each task with efficiency. She'd grown pale, her hands had trembled from time to time, but her jaw had been clenched with determination, her eyes challenging death.

She was one hell of a woman.

When Dallas had decided he'd done all he could for the moment, he had left his brother in Amelia's care while he'd raced to the ranch, horses in tow, to give orders to his men, sending four men in opposite directions to scour the countryside for a doctor. He'd sent another man to find Reverend Tucker, praying harder than he'd ever prayed in his life that he wouldn't need the preacher's services.

Austin had returned to the cabin with him. They would have taken turns relieving Amelia as she tended to Houston's needs if she had let them. As it was, they simply sat in the shadows and worried.

It hurt. It hurt to watch his brother lying so still as though he were simply waiting for death's arrival. It hurt to watch Amelia hovering over Houston, wiping the fevered sweat from his brow, his throat, his chest, talking to him constantly, softly, gently. Always talking to him about his horses, his dream of raising them, and how she didn't want to be part of a dream that died.

Amelia Carson was everything Dallas had wanted in a wife. A survivor, someone with a willingness to reach out to the future. She was full of grit, determination, and courage.

He thought he'd never forget the way she'd looked riding back for Houston: fearless, angry, terrified. Or the depth of despair he'd seen reflected in her eyes as she'd knelt beside Houston and tried to stop his blood from spilling into the earth.

Dallas rose to his feet, stretched the ache and tightness out of his back, and walked to the hearth. He took a wooden bowl off the mantel, bent down, and ladled the simmering stew out of the pot. Houston's house was about as simple as a man could make it: a table with one chair, a bed, a wardrobe, a chest, a small table by the bed, and a stack of books. No mirrors. Not one goddamn mirror.

Straightening, he glanced over his shoulder at Austin, who was sitting on the table since Dallas had confiscated the chair. He was surprised the boy's elbows hadn't created holes in his thighs. He looked as though he was awaiting a hangman's noose. "You want to check on his horses?"

Austin shot to his feet and bobbed his head. "Yes, sir." He headed out the door.

Dallas crossed the room and knelt beside the bed. "You need to eat."

Amelia gave him a weak smile. "I can't get his fever to break. Where's the doctor?"

"I sent my men to find one. It's as hard to find a doctor as it is to find a wife." He spooned out a bit of stew and lifted it up. "Come on. Eat for me."

"I'm not hungry."

"Then eat for him." He tilted his head toward

Houston. "'You won't do him any good if you get sick."

She opened her mouth, and he shoveled in the stew. Licking her lips, she took the bowl from him. "I am hungry after all."

He watched her eat, this woman he'd married, this woman who wasn't fully his wife. She had been as skittish as a newborn filly on their wedding night. He'd decided to take her for a walk, hoping to help her relax. Instead, he'd lost her.

Or maybe he'd just failed to acknowledge that he'd never had her.

When he'd confronted Houston with his accusations weeks ago, he'd convinced himself that Houston had felt nothing more than lust for Amelia. He'd closed his mind to the possibility that Houston might have fallen deeply in love with Amelia.

That she might have fallen deeply in love with Houston.

He had measured their love against what he knew of love . . . which was nothing at all. He understood loyalty, honor, and the value of keeping one's word.

Regardless of his feelings for her, Houston had never claimed Amelia. For whatever reason, he had held his silence as she and Dallas had exchanged vows. And with his silence, he had forsaken Amelia and given his own vow to forever hold his peace.

She handed the empty bowl back to Dallas, her brow furrowed so deeply that he thought her face would always reflect the strain of the past few days. "Thank you."

He unfolded his body. "I'm going to step outside for some fresh air. Holler if you need me."

He set the bowl on the table, crossed the room, opened the door, and stepped into the night. He'd never felt so damn useless in his entire life. At least when Houston had been wounded during the war, Dallas had been able to take some action, he'd been able to do something.

He bowed his head. For thirteen years, he'd been fighting the guilt, never knowing if the decision he'd made that fateful night had been the right one. Every time he looked at Houston, he was reminded of the actions he'd taken and questioned his own motives for doing what he had done.

Dallas had always assumed Houston was self-conscious about his disfigurement, had distanced himself from Dallas because Dallas had kept his word. He hadn't let him die.

Now, he wondered if whatever demons had forced Houston off his horse to face those outlaws alone were also responsible for his preferring solitude over the company of others.

From his pocket, Dallas removed the watch Amelia had given him, held it to his ear, and shook it vigorously. He could hear the water swirling inside. He couldn't repair the token of her affection, he couldn't force Houston to claim her, but he could do all in his power to love her as she should be loved.

Deep, gut-wrenching sobs interrupted Dallas's thoughts. He walked to the edge of the porch and glanced around the side of the house.

Austin sat on the ground, his arms folded

over his drawn-up knees, his head resting on his arms, his shoulders shaking with the force of his grief.

Dallas had never seen a man cry. His father had raised him to believe that tears were the domain of women, certainly not something a man ever let slide down his face. Awkward and out of his element, he approached. "Austin?"

Austin jerked his head up. In the moonlight, Dallas could see tears streaming along Austin's cheeks, pooling around his mouth.

"Houston is gonna die, ain't he?"

Dallas dropped to his haunches. "I doubt it. He doesn't like to get on Amelia's bad side, and he'd certainly do that if he died."

Roughly, Austin rubbed his hand beneath his nose. "It's my fault."

"Don't go thinking that."

Austin scrambled to his feet. "But it's true. If you look through those horses you brought back, you'll find Houston's stallion. They stole him from me."

Dallas slowly brought himself to his feet. "But you said—"

"I lied! They snuck up on me, and I was ashamed that I let them do it, that I didn't try and stop them from taking the horse. If I'd a-told the truth—"

"Stop it!" Dallas roared. "Stop it. You don't know what would have happened if you'd told the truth. It might have made no difference at all." He held up a hand to stop his brother's protest. "I'm not gonna say that you should have lied because, by God, you should have told us the truth. But you can't let what happened eat at you. It's done." He sliced his hand through the air. "It's done."

Just like his marriage to Amelia. It was done.

Austin sniffed. "Shouldn't you punish me or something?"

Dallas shook his head. "You're nearly a man now. No man goes through life doing everything right. A man who wallows in his mistakes is destined to have a miserable life. Learn from what you did and become a better man because of it."

Austin straightened his shoulders. "I will. I won't let you or Houston down again."

"Good. Now see after those horses."

"Yes, sir."

"Dallas!"

Amelia's cry had Dallas charging around the corner of the house and bursting through the door, Austin hot on his heels. His heart slammed against his ribs at the panic reflected in her eyes.

"Houston started thrashing, calling for you. He's going to tear open his wound."

"God damn it. Austin, fetch me a rope." He strode to the bed and grabbed one of Houston's flailing arms. "Be still, God damn it."

Houston latched onto his shirt, pulling him down. "Dallas, I'm scared."

Dallas would have sworn he was meeting the gaze of a fifteen-year-old boy. "Don't be," he rasped. "I won't let nothing happen to you."

"Swear?"

Dallas swallowed hard. "Give you my word."

Houston loosened his hold and sank back into oblivion.

Austin burst through the door. "I got the rope."

"We don't need it now," Dallas said quietly. He lifted his gaze to Amelia's.

"You were both back at the war," she said softly.

"The night before he was wounded. You think he would have asked for my word if he had known my keeping it would give him the life he's had all these years?"

"You should ask him. You might be surprised by what he thinks."

"I'd rather not know."

It was near midnight when Amelia shook Dallas's shoulder to wake him. "He's shaking, and I can't find any more blankets."

Dallas looked toward the bed. Shaking? Houston was trembling as though someone had thrown him into an icy river. "Hell, he hasn't a goddamn thing around here."

He bolted out of the chair and nudged Austin's foot. Disoriented, Austin opened his eyes and stared at him.

"Ride home and gather up all the blankets you can. I'll get some wood, build up the fire, and see if we can warm him that way."

He followed Austin out the door and headed for the wood pile. Thank God, Houston had wood. The man's Spartan life was starting to wear thin.

He gathered into his arms as much wood as he could carry and stormed back toward the house.

He shoved open the door, stepped inside, and came to a dead stop.

Houston was no longer trembling. He lay perfectly still, his face a reflection of contentment.

He no longer needed a fire or blankets for warmth. Amelia, curled against his side asleep, was giving him all the warmth he needed.

AMELIA AWOKE DRENCHED in sweat, Houston's sweat. A blanket had been tucked around her. Lifting her head, she searched the room until her gaze fell on Dallas as he sat in the shadows beside the bed.

"He was cold," she stammered. "I couldn't get him to stop trembling."

"I know."

She moved the blanket aside and climbed out of the bed. "I think his fever's breaking."

"Good. I'll get you some fresh water. He'll be thirsty."

Ignoring her own sweaty discomfort, Amelia began to wipe the beaded sweat from Houston's body. Not until he grabbed her wrist did she realize he was awake. She smiled softly. "You gave us quite a scare."

"Dallas?"

"He's fine."

"Horses?"

"Austin's been taking care of them."

"I . . ."

She watched him swallow. "Let me get you some water."

He nodded slightly. Turning, she took the tin

cup Dallas was holding, slipped her hand beneath Houston's head, and touched the cup to his lips. "Drink slowly," she ordered although in his weakened state, she didn't know if he had much of a choice.

When he had drained the cup dry, she set it aside and took his hand.

His Adam's apple bobbed. "I can smell you," he croaked.

She trailed her fingers along his brow. "Austin brought the blankets from my bed."

"What do you wear that makes you smell so sweet?"

"Magnolias. They grew on our plantation."

A corner of his mouth crooked up. "Maggie. That's a good name for a girl. Name your daughter Maggie." His eye drifted closed.

"I will," she whispered in a broken voice.

She felt a strong hand with long fingers come to rest on her shoulder. She glanced up at Dallas. He shifted his hand slightly and squeezed her neck. She rubbed her cheek against his roughened hand. "I think the worst is over," she said.

"He'll be weak for a while and probably ornery as a bear. I'm tired of feeling useless. I need to get back to the ranch and take care of business."

She rose from the bed. "You weren't useless. I couldn't have managed without you and Austin."

He touched her cheek. "I think you would have managed just fine. If you want to stay here until he regains his strength, I'll come by and check on you from time to time."

"I'd like to do that, if you don't mind."

He brushed his lips across her forehead. "Just get him strong enough to realize those dreams he has. I didn't even know he had any."

HOUSTON LAY IN that damn bed for two long days trying to regain his strength just enough so he could crawl to the table. He wished to God he hadn't told Amelia that he loved her before he'd jumped off the horse, but at the time he'd figured it was safe to reveal his heart because he didn't think he had a snowball's chance in hell of surviving.

He wished to God he'd kept his mouth shut when Amelia shaved him without meeting his gaze and fed him without asking him one god-damn question.

He wished he'd kept the words to himself when she prepared herself for bed each evening in silence. She'd perch her hand mirror against a bowl on the table, separate the strands of her braid, and slowly brush her hair until it glistened in the firelight from the hearth. She'd weave the strands back together, then check the flame in the lantern, and without so much as a "sleep well," she'd retire for the night . . . curling up on a pallet on the floor.

He'd watch her in the hours past midnight and listen to her soft, even breathing. He wanted her in his bed, beside him, in his arms.

But he'd given up the right to ever hold her again—forever. Because he'd been afraid. As always, because he'd been afraid.

And now she hated him. Not for the cowardice he'd shown thirteen years before when he'd been a boy, but for the cowardice he'd shown now, as a man.

Ignoring the pain in his shoulder, the weakness in his knees, Houston crawled out of bed and reached for the clothes Amelia had left on the table. He'd slipped into his trousers and was awkwardly buttoning his shirt when she stepped into his house, carrying a bucket of water. She set the bucket down, walked across the room, brushed his hands aside, and buttoned his shirt.

"You ever gonna look at me or talk to me again?" he asked.

"It's harder now. I wish you hadn't said what you did before you leapt from the horse."

"Yeah, so do I, but I didn't think a man should die without ever having said the words."

"So it's only because I was there that you spoke the words to me. Any woman would have done," she said softly, meeting his gaze only for the instant that a flame might flicker.

He slipped his finger beneath her chin and tilted her face. "No. I was more afraid that I wouldn't be able to stop the men, and you'd die without ever knowing that I loved you."

She balled up her fists, tears welling in her eyes. "Damn you. Damn you for telling me now, when it's too late."

"It was always too late for us, Amelia. You promised yourself to Dallas. He's not a man who gives up what belongs to him."

"What belongs to him? You think if I lift up my skirt, you'll find his brand on my backside? I'm not a possession, Houston. I'm not something to be owned."

"You're his wife."

"Yes, now I'm his wife. And do you know what I discovered? That you lied to me. You told me that my needs were based on lust. I won't deny that a part of that was true, but the greater part of my needs came from the love I held for you. I don't feel those needs when Dallas touches me. I just feel empty."

Her words tore through him. He knew the emptiness that came from being with someone you didn't love. He had thought Dallas would have the power to hold the emptiness at bay for her.

She suddenly laughed mirthlessly. "On the other hand, I suppose I should be grateful. I would have hated being married to a man as vain as you are."

"Vain? You think I'm vain?"

She spun around, waving her hand in a circle. "You don't have a single mirror in this whole house. You hide your face beneath the shadows of your hat."

"You think I don't have mirrors because of this?" he asked, dragging his hand down the left side of his face.

She nodded, her movements jerky.

He pointed to his right eye. "It's this I don't want to see. When I meet my gaze, I see the man who lives inside here." He hit his chest, grimacing as the pain shot through his shoulder. "What's inside here is uglier than anything you're looking at right now."

"You don't know the man who lives inside of you," she said angrily. "You only know the boy, the fifteen-year-old boy who ran. You won't let him go; you won't let him grow up! You see yourself as a coward because you don't meet your reflection in the mirror. You don't see the man you've become, you only see the boy you were. You jumped off the back of that horse because you thought you had something to prove—"

"I jumped off that horse because I was afraid. Afraid Dallas couldn't stop those men, afraid you'd be killed. Every decision I make in life is based on fear. The thought of you dying scared me more than the thought of me dying. That's why I jumped. I always take the coward's way."

She shook her head sadly. "The coward's way. You held me through a storm that could have easily killed us both; we fought a raging river; we captured wild mustangs—"

"I wouldn't have done any of those things if you hadn't been by my side."

"Yes, you would have. Because that's the man you've become. You just don't know yourself as I do. *Dare* to look in a mirror sometime, and you'll see the man I grew to love."

The door opened. Amelia jumped back, swiping the tears from her cheeks. Houston met Dallas's gaze as he walked into the house, Austin in his wake.

"You're out of bed," Dallas said, his gaze shifting between Houston and Amelia.

Houston nodded, searching for his voice. "Yeah, I'm feeling stronger."

"Then you won't mind if I take Amelia home."

"No, no, I don't mind at all. She's your wife. You should take her home."

"Then I'll do that." He held out his hand.

Amelia slipped her hand into Dallas's, and Houston felt as though a herd of mustangs had stampeded over his heart.

When the couple closed the door behind them, Houston sank to the bed.

"You sure you're feeling all right?" Austin asked.

"Yeah."

Austin scraped the chair across the floor, turned it, and straddled it, crossing his arms over the back. "I owe you an apology for Black Thunder."

"We've already discussed this. We'll get a new stallion in the spring."

Austin shook his head. "You must not have taken a good look at those horses in the canyon, the ones those horse thieves had."

"No, I was only thinking about Amelia and getting her out of there."

"Black Thunder was there. Dallas brought him back. I put him in his pen."

Houston rubbed his shoulder, the ache intensifying. "What do you mean he was there and now he's here? You shot him."

"Nope, I lied."

Houston stared at his brother, wondering when he'd stopped being a boy. Austin swallowed.

"The thieves took me by surprise and stole Black Thunder. I was ashamed that I didn't try and stop them. It didn't matter that there was six of them and only one of me or that they had their guns out and I didn't. I thought I'd let you down. Figured you'd never trust me again if you knew what had happened. So I lied. And because I lied, you got shot."

"I didn't get shot because you lied—"

"If I'd told the truth, you would have gone after them. They never would have taken Amelia."

"We don't know that. You can't start second-guessing what might have happened."

"Dallas said the same thing, but I needed to hear it from you."

"Well, now you've heard it, so take Black Thunder and head on back to the ranch."

"Take Black Thunder?"

"Yep, he's yours. I'd like to borrow him from time to time, of course, but he belongs to you."

"Why?"

Houston leaned forward. "Because I don't want you spending the rest of your life thinking I blame you for what happened. It wasn't your fault."

Austin laughed. "You don't have to give me the horse. Dallas told me that a man who wallows in his regrets lives a miserable life. I got a dream that I want to hold in my hand. I ain't planning on doing any wallowing."

"Take the horse, anyway."

Austin stood. "All right, I will." He walked to the door and stopped, his hand on the latch. He gazed back over his shoulder. "That woman you love . . . Do I know her?"

Houston forced himself to meet his brother's gaze. The boy only knew one woman, if he didn't count the whores in Dusty Flats. "Yeah, you do."

"She never left your side, not for one minute."

"She should have."

"Well, I'm not learned in these matters, but I'd like to think if a woman ever loved me as much as that one loves you . . . I'd crawl through hell to be by her side."

Chapter Twenty

Houston sat at his table, running his fingers back and forth over the cloth Amelia had embroidered for Dallas, a gift he'd kept for himself.

He'd tried to sleep after Austin left, but Amelia was still here with him. He could smell her sweet magnolia scent filling his house, filling his bed.

He wondered how long it would be before her fragrance faded, before he became like Cookie, living on memories until they became so worn with the years that they would be discarded carelessly as hand-me-downs. Houston had already spent thirteen years wallowing in the regrets of his youth. He had a lifetime ahead of him to flounder in his latest regrets.

Whether intentional or not, she'd left her mirror on the table, glass side down.

He could see her so clearly, holding the mirror, smiling at her reflection. How simple an action, how difficult a step after all these years. The rippling waters of a pond always gave a distorted image with no depth, no clarity.

A mirror would give a clearer reflection and if he looked deeply enough, it would drag him back into the past. If he looked long enough, perhaps it would set him free.

Houston's mouth grew dry as his gaze shifted between the mirror and the flowers she had sewn with delicate stitches and pink thread.

With a trembling hand, he wrapped his fingers around the handle of the mirror, lifted it from the table, and held it before him.

IN THE FADING evening light, Amelia stood on the balcony and pulled her shawl more closely around her. Somewhere, out there, where the wind blew free and wild mustangs surrendered their freedom, lived a man with the heart of a fifteen-year-old boy.

How in God's name had Houston's mother allowed her husband to take her sons off to war? How did any woman let her son go off to war, regardless of his age?

The war had claimed so many boys, even those it hadn't killed. She wondered how differently her journey with Houston might have ended if he hadn't marched onto a field of battle before he'd ever shaved.

The hairs on the nape of her neck prickled as the cool breeze rushed past. She heard a small hushed movement and turned to see Dallas leaning against the wall, studying her, his gaze intense, penetrating.

He needed only one step to span the distance separating them. He touched his knuckles to her

cheek, and she couldn't stop herself from stiffen-
ing. His hand fell to his side. "I've never forced a
woman. I'm not going to start with my wife."

Reaching out, she wrapped her hand around
his and shook her head slightly. "You won't have
to force me."

He eased closer until only a whisper's breath
separated their bodies. "Do you love Houston?"

"I'm your wife."

"I know whose wife you are. I'm asking if you
love Houston."

The tears flooded her eyes. She squeezed them
shut, battling the river of sorrow. "Once." She
opened her eyes and met his gaze.

"Why did you marry me?"

She took a deep breath. "I had nothing in
Georgia. No home, no family. You offered me a
chance to have a home, a family, and a dream."

"In other words, I asked and Houston didn't."

She gave him a tremulous smile. "You asked.
He didn't."

He held out his arms. With quiet acceptance,
she laid her head against his chest as he enfolded
her in his strong embrace. She cared for him. She
liked him. Perhaps, in time, her heart would flut-
ter when he neared, her skin would tingle when
he touched her, and her toes would curl when he
kissed her.

He slipped his finger beneath her chin, tilted
her face, and brushed his lips over hers before
lifting her into his arms and carrying her into
their bedroom.

Dallas's warm mouth settled over hers as she

sank into the bed. His kiss was . . . nice. His hand cradled her breast. Nice. He groaned and laid his body over hers. Lean, strong . . . nice.

The door burst open and banged against the wall. Dallas came off her like a fired bullet. He grabbed his revolver out of the holster dangling from the bedpost and put himself between her and the door, his breathing heavy. "What is it?"

Amelia scooted back against the headboard, pressing her hand above her beating heart, her breath catching in her throat.

She peered around Dallas. Houston stood in the doorway, his legs spread wide. He stared at his brother. "I need to talk to you."

Dallas slipped his gun back into his holster and wrapped his hand around the bedpost, his knuckles turning white as he faced his brother. "Can't it wait until morning?"

"No." Houston's gaze shot to Amelia, then back to Dallas. "No, it can't."

Dallas tunneled his fingers through his hair and glanced at Amelia. "Will you excuse me?"

She could do little more than nod.

DALLAS STOOD BEFORE the window in his office, the whiskey he'd poured himself forgotten as he watched the woman standing beside the corral Austin had made the men rebuild. Dallas had known she'd slip out of the house and go to the corral. He wondered how long it would be before he knew her as well as Houston did. The palomino approached, nudged her arm, and she pressed her face against the mare's neck.

He could hear Houston pacing behind him.

For a man who had wanted to talk so desperately, he'd suddenly grown eerily quiet.

Dallas turned and, for the first time in years, didn't flinch when he met his brother's gaze. "You should sit down before you fall down."

Houston brought his pacing to a halt and held onto the back of a chair. "I can stand."

"You wanted to talk?"

Houston nodded, his fingers tightening their hold on the leather. "I'm in love with Amelia."

"And when did you decide this?"

"It just came over me somewhere between Fort Worth and here."

Dallas strode across the room and threw his glass of whiskey into the hearth. The shattering glass did nothing to improve his mood. "Then we've got ourselves one hell of a situation here." He spun around. "Why in God's name didn't you say something before we were married?"

"Because I thought she deserved better than a coward."

Dallas felt as though Houston had just punched him in the gut. "What?"

"She's got more courage in her little finger than I've got in my whole body. I figured she deserved someone who didn't run from his own shadow."

"What are you talking about?"

Houston surged across the room and slapped his hands on the desk. "What? After all these years, you want me to say to your face what you know in your heart? I'm a coward. A worthless, no-account excuse for a man. You know it, I know it. That's why you can't stomach the sight of me. If I could undo what I did, I would. But

I can't. God knows I try every night when I go to sleep, reliving that day, wishing I'd followed like I should have, but when I wake up the past remains as it was."

"You sound like Pa."

Houston dropped into the chair, closed his eye, and rubbed his brow. "I don't expect you to ever forgive me for killing him. Hell, I haven't forgiven myself."

"You think I hold you accountable for Pa's death?"

Houston lifted his despair-filled gaze. "Figured that was why you couldn't stand to look at me. Because you knew I'd killed him. If I'd had any backbone, I'd have struck out on my own, spared you the sight of me—"

"Oh, Jesus." Dallas sank into his chair and buried his face in his hands. "Oh, dear Lord." Then he threw his head back and laughed, a dry humorless laugh. "I thought you avoided me because you regretted what I'd done."

"What in the hell did you do?"

"I played God."

THE NIGHT FOLLOWING a battle was always the worst. The cries of wounded men echoed through the darkness, the stench of blood thickened the air.

Dallas stepped over a corpse and knelt beside a young soldier who was holding nothing but the torso of his best friend. "Jimmy?"

Jimmy looked at him blankly. "Can't find his legs. He'd a hated bein' buried without his legs."

"I'll help you look for his legs after I find Houston. You seen him?"

Jimmy wiped a bloody hand over his tear streaked face before pointing his finger. "They're putting the dead over yonder."

Stacking them like cords of wood, one body on top of the other. Dallas had found his pa there, but he couldn't think about that now, had to ignore the pain knifing through his heart.

"Houston's not there."

"Did you check the hospital tent?"

"Yep, he wasn't there, either."

Jimmy pointed a finger. "They left the dying over there."

Dallas's stomach tightened, and his jaw tingled. Lord, he wanted to throw up, but not here, not in front of a soldier. He placed his hand on the man's shoulder. "We'll whip them Yankees tomorrow."

He struggled to his feet and wove his way among the dead who had yet to be moved, until the moaning hovering around him grew louder. So many men lay in the clearing. He might have never found Houston if he hadn't spotted the battered drum.

He knelt beside his brother. Houston was a bloody mess, lying so still, so pale even in the moonlight. Dallas worked the drum away from his brother and threw it with all his strength and pent-up anger into the nearby brush. He slipped his arms beneath Houston's still form and struggled to his feet. He ignored the cries of men wanting water, wanting help as he wended his way toward the hospital tent.

No light burned inside. Using his shoulder, he nudged the tent flap back. The moonlight spilled inside. He judged the distance to the table, walked inside, and laid his brother on the table in the darkness as the tent flap fell back into place.

Houston made no sound. Dallas went outside and quickly returned carrying a lantern. He hung it on a beam and studied his brother in its golden haze. Houston's breathing was shallow, his bloodied chest barely rising as he took in air. The anger swelled within Dallas, and he stormed out of the tent.

He raced across the compound, and without ceremony, barged into a physician's tent. "Dr. Barnes, I got a man that needs tending." He shook the sleeping man. "I got a man that needs tending!"

The doctor opened his eyes and released a weary sigh. He was still dressed, blood splattered over his clothes. Sitting up, he dropped his feet to the ground. "Where is he?"

"In the hospital tent. We need to hurry."

Dr. Barnes rubbed his face before rising to his feet. "Let's go."

He didn't walk fast enough to suit Dallas, but at least he was coming. Dallas threw back the tent flap and hurried to his brother's side. Houston hadn't moved, but he was still breathing. Dr. Barnes moved around to the other side of the table.

"Dear God."

"I need you to fix him," Dallas said.

Dr. Barnes lifted his weary gaze. "Son, he's better off dead."

"I gave him my word I wouldn't let him die."

Dr. Barnes shook his head, regret filling his eyes. "I've spent my time saving men with facial wounds like this, only to have them kill themselves once they're strong enough. Those that don't kill themselves end up living alone, not wanting people to see them." He placed his hand on Houston's brow. "I won't be doing him a favor if I tend his other wounds. My time would be better spent sleeping so I'll have the strength to save those worth saving tomorrow."

Dallas pulled his revolver from its holster.

"I gave him my word that I wouldn't let him die. I've never gone back on my word." He leveled his gun at the center of the doctor's chest. "I'm givin' you my word now that if he dies, you'll be keepin' him company in heaven."

"Don't do this, son."

"I ain't your son."

"I know it's hard to let go of those we love, especially when they're so young, but I give you my word that death is better for him."

"I ain't interested in your word. I'm only interested in mine. Now, fix him."

In resignation, the doctor sighed, reached behind him, picked up a pair of scissors, and began to cut away what remained of Houston's gray jacket. Stoically, Dallas stood and watched as the doctor worked. Two hours. Two long torturous hours of staring at his brother's mutilated flesh.

"I've done all I can do," Dr. Barnes said as he finished wrapping the last bandage around Houston's' head. "It's up to him now whether he lives or dies."

Dallas lowered his shaking hand. "I appreciate what you did."

"I guarantee you that he won't appreciate it at all. In years to come when you look at his face, you remember the night you played God."

"HE WAS RIGHT," Dallas said with a heavy sigh. "I had to leave, go with my company, but when I came back, you weren't smiling. You wouldn't talk to me. When we were traveling home, you kept to yourself, hugging the shadows if we stopped in a town. I figured you wished I'd let you die. When I built the house for Amelia, you didn't want to live here, built yourself your own place. Figured you wanted nothing to do with me."

Houston could barely speak for the emotions clogging his throat. "I thought you wouldn't look at me because you knew I was a coward. I ran. If I hadn't run, Pa wouldn't have been killed."

"Sweet Lord, Houston, you didn't even have a gun to defend yourself, just a drum. If a soldier couldn't kill the man giving the orders, he'd do all in his power to silence the messenger. You were the messenger. I told Pa to give you a rifle, but he wanted someone to beat out his orders. You were a boy. Pa had no right to enlist you. I told him not to, but he wouldn't listen."

"You weren't much older."

"Not in years, but in temperament. I wanted to go. I wanted the glory that came with war. Only I discovered glory doesn't come with destruction. I thought I'd find it here, taming the land, building an empire, creating a legacy that I could hand down to my son."

Dallas's son. The foundation of his dream. Dallas had saved Houston's life—twice—and now Houston was asking him to sacrifice a portion of his dream so Houston could find happiness. "That brings us back to Amelia," Houston said quietly.

"Yeah, it does." Dallas shoved himself away from the desk and walked to the window.

Houston's chest ached more than it had when shrapnel had cut through it. He rose and joined his brother. "I owe you for keeping your word and not letting me die. The doctor was wrong. I never regretted that I'd lived. I only regretted that Pa didn't."

Dallas shook his head. "He had no right going after you. He had men to command. His place was to lead them. He wanted to shape you into the man he thought you ought to be. A battlefield wasn't the place to do it."

"You don't blame me at all?"

Dallas glanced at him. "It was his decision to run after you, stupid as it was. I loved him, Houston. I admired his strengths, but he wasn't perfect."

"I loved him, too," Houston said, for the first time realizing that he had indeed loved his father. "I just couldn't be what he wanted me to be."

"No fault in that. God help me, I'm his mirror image." Dallas looked back toward the corral at the woman still standing with the moonlight wreathed around her. He had never expected her to love him. He was too much like his father, a hard man to love, not truly appreciated until he was gone. Neither did he relish the thought of taking a woman to his bed, knowing she was thinking of another. Especially if that man was Houston.

"Give her a divorce," Houston said. "I swear to God I won't touch her for a month, not until she knows for sure whether or not she's carrying your son."

Dallas raised a brow. "It's highly unlikely that she's carrying my son, since we are constantly interrupted."

"Then give her an annulment."

"What in God's name makes you think she wants to marry you? You stood in my parlor and held your peace. You don't think that might have broken her heart?"

"She has every right to hate me, but at least let me ask her."

Guilt, misunderstandings, and regrets had given Houston thirteen years of solitude. Now, he had the opportunity to receive the love of a woman, something Dallas would never have. Any woman could give Dallas the son he wanted, but only Amelia had returned to Houston his smiles and laughter.

"I'll leave the decision up to Amelia," Dallas said quietly. "Let me talk to her. If she wants an annulment, I'll give her one. If she wants to marry you . . . I'll hold my peace."

A FULL MOON graced the heavens, its light illuminating Dallas's way as he approached the corral. Valiant skittered away to the other side, but the woman remained, gazing into the darkness beyond the corral.

Dallas crossed his arms over the railing. "That's a beautiful horse."

"Yes, she is."

"Houston has the patience of Job when it comes to horses."

"Yes, he does."

"You know what I was thinking about when I was walking out here?"

Shaking her head, she glanced at him.

"I was thinking about the last time I heard Houston laugh. We'd been swimming in the creek. I told him to get out, and while I was dressing, he hid in the shadows. When I looked up, I couldn't see him. I thought he'd drowned. Made a fool of myself, thrashing through that water, looking for him. He laughed so hard I thought he'd bust a gut."

She smiled softly. "I can't imagine that."

"No, I don't imagine you can. The next day, our pa went to war, dragging us along with him. I never heard Houston laugh again until the first night you were here. Fifteen years is a hell of a long time for a man not to laugh."

He trailed his finger along her cheek. "I don't need love, Amelia, but I think you do, and if you find it with a man who dreams of raising horses, know that you do so with my blessing."

Tears welled in her eyes, and a tremulous smile curved her lips. "I think if you'd come to Fort Worth to fetch me, I might have fallen in love with you."

He smiled warmly. "I'd think the fates had conspired against us if I didn't believe that we shape our own destiny. In my office is a man who wants to make you part of his destiny. I think it would be worth your time to listen to what he has to say."

HOUSTON SAT IN the chair, his elbows on his thighs, his shoulder aching unmercifully. He ran Amelia's cloth through his fingers, over and over. He knew every silken strand, every knot, every loop. It was all he'd have of her if she didn't come, and he had a feeling she wasn't going to come.

"Dallas said you wanted to talk with me."

He shot out of the chair at the sound of her gentle voice. He wadded up her cloth and stuffed it into his duster pocket. "Yeah, I did." He pulled her mirror out of his other pocket. "You left your mirror on my table." He extended it toward her.

"You can keep it," she said quietly. "We have lots of mirrors here."

"I'll keep it, then."

"Good. I'm glad."

He'd never rushed headlong into a battle, but he figured this time, it might be the best approach. "I spent a lot of time studying it. The back is real pretty with all the gold carving. Took me about an hour to gather up the courage to turn it over and look at the other side."

"And what did you see?"

"A man who loves you more than life itself."

Closing her eyes, she dropped her chin to her chest.

"I wouldn't blame you if you hated me. I haven't held your feelings as precious as I should have."

"I don't hate you," she whispered hoarsely. "I tried to, but I can't."

"Dallas is willing to give you an annulment."

Damn, the words were as ugly as his face, not at all what she deserved. He'd consider himself the wealthiest man in the world if he only possessed the words he thought she longed to hear, words worthy of her. He thought he could see a tear glistening in the corner of her eye. "Damn it, woman, look at me."

Slowly, she lifted her head. The sight of the tears welling in her eyes hurt more than the wound healing in his shoulder.

"I've had plenty of moments in my life when I've been scared, but I swear to you that I've never been as scared as I am right now. I'm afraid you won't take Dallas up on his offer for an annulment . . . and I'll have nothing in my life but the emptiness that was there before you stepped off that train in Fort Worth. I wouldn't blame you for staying with him. God knows I haven't done right by you—" He slammed his eye shut. "Ah, hell, this isn't what I wanted to say."

He slipped the mirror back into his pocket and sank down into the chair. He'd never felt so tired in his life. She rushed forward and knelt beside him.

"Are you bleeding?"

"No. Just need a moment to gather my strength."

"You shouldn't have come here tonight. You should have stayed in bed—"

"I couldn't. Every time I took a breath, I smelled

you." He wrapped his hand around hers, pressed a kiss to the heart of her palm, and held her gaze. "I've got a one-room cabin, a few horses, and a dream that's so small it won't even cover your palm. But it sure seems a lot bigger when you're beside me."

The moonlight streaming through the window shimmered off the tears trailing along her cheeks. "I've always wanted a dream that I could hold in the palm of my hand," she said quietly.

His heart slammed against his chest, and all the things he'd feared melted away. "I want you beside me until the day I die, Amelia. If you'll have me . . . as your husband."

She smiled softly. "I'll take a question."

"What?"

She raised a delicate brow. "A question." He swallowed hard, took her hands, and brought them to his lips. "Will you marry me?"

"Yes."

Joy overflowed within his heart, creating a sunrise bathed in love. "I'll take a dare," he rasped.

"Kiss me as though you love me."

"Woman, don't you know that I've always kissed you that way?"

Guiding her onto his lap, he took her into his arms and lowered his mouth to hers, kissing her tenderly, this woman of courage who would soon become his wife.

Chapter Twenty-One

*T*hey waited until spring, when the wildflowers formed a bright multicolored carpet over the plains.

Amelia stood beside the springs, listening to the babble of the water as it flowed over the moss covered rocks. Her dress of white lace and silk whispered in the breeze, a gift from Houston, one of many he'd brought her from Fort Worth. A gift to capture her memories.

In the years to come, she knew she would take it from the cedar chest, look upon it with fondness, and remember the first of the happiest days of her life.

She had intertwined her arm through Houston's, just as their lives would forever be joined. No brand would emblazon their union. Only the words they exchanged today.

She couldn't take her eyes off Houston as he stood beside her in his new brown jacket and woolen trousers. She thought he more closely resembled a banker than a man who spent the best part of his day with horses . . . and soon she hoped, the best part of his night with her.

The even, straight brim of his new broad-brimmed hat made her smile, and she wondered how long it would be before old habits crumpled it. Around the brim, he wore her linen of long ago, with its delicate embroidered flowers, faded and frayed. Through the eyes of her heart, she knew she'd never seen a more handsome man.

Reverend Tucker's melodious voice rang out as he once again spoke the words he'd said the previous autumn. Dallas stood solemnly beside her, and she wondered briefly if he was remembering the day she had become his wife or if he was mentally designing the layout of the town he planned to build. She hoped he was thinking of his town, and that it would bring him a wife.

Austin stood on the other side of Houston, smiling broadly, his sparkling blue eyes competing in beauty with the pond as the sun reflected off the rippling waters.

"If anyone knows of any reason why these two should not be joined in holy matrimony, let him speak now or forever"—Reverend Tucker held the gazes of the three men in attendance for the space of a heartbeat—"and I do mean *forever* hold his peace."

Amelia caught her breath and waited. She knew Dallas had the right to object. A part of her was saddened with the knowledge that she would not give him the son he desperately longed for; a corner of her heart would always be reserved for the memories of the short time that she had been his fiancée, and then his wife. And her love for him would grow over the years as he'd predicted, only it would be the love of a sister toward her brother.

Reverend Tucker cleared his throat. Amelia released her breath and repeated the vows she'd said once before, her gaze never leaving Houston's.

Reverend Tucker shifted his attention to Houston. "And if you'll repeat after me—"

"She's had those words given to her before," Houston said gruffly. "She deserves better than hand-me-downs. I've got my own words to say."

Lifting a brow, Reverend Tucker chuckled low. "Well, I've never heard my words referred to as hand-me-downs, but I suppose they are. I have no objection to you giving your own vows as long as your bride doesn't. Amelia?"

"I have no objections," she said, her heart thrumming with the rhythm of the falls. She imagined that they still carried the sound of Houston's laughter mingling with hers, and after today they would forever echo their vows.

Reaching around her, Houston cupped her elbow, tugging slightly until she faced him completely. He swept his hat from his head, the shadows retreating to reveal the craggy left side, the perfect right side that came together to form the face she loved.

He took the hand that wasn't holding the bouquet of wildflowers and stared at it, holding it so tightly that she thought he might crack her bones. Then his hold gentled. He slipped a gold ring onto her finger and lifted his gaze to hers.

"I'm not a brave man; I'll never be a hero, but I love you more than life itself, and I will until the day I die. With you by my side, I'm a better man than I've ever been alone. I'm scared to death that I'll let you down, but I won't run this time. I'll stand firm and face the challenge and work hard to see that you never have any regrets. You told me once that you wanted to share a corner of my dream. Without you, Amelia, I have no dream. With you, I have everything I could ever dream of wanting."

Tears burned her eyes as he glanced back at the preacher. "I'm done."

Reverend Tucker smiled. "In that case, I pronounce you husband and wife. With my blessing, you may kiss the bride."

Houston cradled her cheek, his gaze lovingly roaming over her features. "I love you, Amelia Carson Leigh," he said huskily as he lowered his lips to hers, sealing the vows with a sweet tender kiss, filled with the promise of tomorrow.

When he ended the kiss, she pressed her cheek against his chest, listening to the steady rhythm of his heart, gathering her happiness around her before she stepped away to face her brother by marriage.

Taking her hand in his, Dallas smiled warmly. "I never thought you'd look prettier than you did the day you married me, but you sure look prettier today. You wear love well, Amelia."

"I hope to say the same to you someday."

"That I look pretty?"

Standing on the tips of her toes, she brushed her lips over his. "That you wear love well."

"Don't hold your breath on that one," he teased.

"You could always order another bride," Houston suggested.

"Hell, no. I'll get my town built, and women will start flocking out here. Then I'll make a selection."

"Love isn't always that practical," Houston said.

"I'm not looking for love. I'm looking for a wife who'll give me a son." He glanced over Amelia's shoulder. "I'll build you a church in my town, Preacher, so I don't have to send my men chasing after you every time I need you."

"You do that, Mr. Leigh," Reverend Tucker said as he slipped his Bible into his coat pocket. "Meanwhile, I think my job is done here so I'm gonna get back to looking for a lost soul." He shook hands with the men and brushed a kiss against Amelia's cheek. "You be happy, now."

"I will."

He mounted a black stallion, and with little more than a gentle kick to the horse's sides, sent it into a flying gallop.

Dallas cleared his throat. "Well, reckon Austin and I ought to head back to the ranch."

"I need to give Amelia her gift first," Austin said. He walked over to his horse and returned carrying his violin. He sat on a boulder, stretched out one leg, worked the heel of his other boot into a crack in the rock, and rested the violin on his shoulder. "The first time I ever saw you, Amelia . . . well, this is what I heard in my heart."

The music began softly, little more than a soughing sigh. Amelia felt a touch on her shoulder and glanced up at her husband.

"Your wedding gift from me," he said as he stepped back and held out his arms. "A waltz."

Her eyes widened. "I didn't think you danced."

"Mimi St. Claire, proprietor and expert dress-maker, happens to give dancin' lessons." He reddened. "They cost more than the wedding dress."

"I love the wedding dress." She smiled as she stepped into his embrace, and they began to sway in rhythm to the music.

The lyrical strains of the violin wove around the falls, through the breeze, kissing the petals of wildflowers. They rose in crescendo, grand, beautiful, and bold, before drifting into silence.

Amelia and Houston waltzed while Austin tucked his violin under his arm. They waltzed after Dallas and Austin mounted their horses and rode away.

They waltzed until twilight, until it was time to go home.

THE CABIN WAS dark except for the fire burning lazily in the hearth. Houston had shoved the table to one side of the room and moved the bed closer to the hearth.

Amelia had imagined this night a hundred times since the evening Houston had asked her to marry him. She'd anticipated it, longed for it, but as she gazed at her full reflection in the cheval glass, she had a feeling her imaginings would pale in comparison to all this night would bring.

Her husband stood behind her, slowly releasing the buttons of her wedding dress. He parted the material and placed a kiss on her nape.

He met and held her gaze in the mirror, his

knuckles brushing along either side of her throat. "You haven't asked me a question all evening."

"I can't think of anything I need answered right now."

"You can't think of anything?"

She rubbed her cheek against his hand. "I'm having a hard time thinking of anything to say, much less to ask."

"I have a lot of questions that need answering."

He nibbled on her earlobe and trailed his tongue along the shell of her ear. She thought she might melt to the floor. "You do?"

"Mmmm-huh. I'd like to watch a shadow show without the canvas between us."

"It wouldn't be a shadow show without the canvas."

He smiled, one side of his mouth moving more than the other. "Exactly, but a lot of my questions sure would be answered without me having to ask them."

He stepped back and sat on the edge of the bed. She pivoted slowly and angled her chin. "What's good for the goose—"

"Understood."

Smiling serenely, she tugged first on one sleeve and then the other, watching as her husband's gaze darkened. The gown pooled at her feet, and she stepped over it, stepped nearer to him. Slowly she removed her undergarments. Her husband swallowed hard, his lips parted slightly, and he leaned forward.

Standing before him with nothing but the air surrounding her flesh, she was surprised she felt no self-consciousness. She cupped her breasts.

"You must have thought me terribly wanton the first time you saw me do this."

"I didn't think anything at all," he rasped as he came to his feet. He shrugged out of his jacket, tore his shirt over his head, and removed his trousers in one fluid movement. Then he was standing before her, cradling her cheek. "If you hadn't asked me questions, I think I might have made that whole journey without a clear thought in my head. The first time I saw you, I couldn't think of anything to say."

She trailed her fingers over his chest, admiring every aspect of his hard, lean body. "And now?"

"A question?" He smiled warmly. "God, I hope you like my answer."

His lips swept down to cover hers, his mouth hot, his tongue exploring hers as though he'd never kissed her before when he'd actually kissed her through the winter and the beginning of spring. She had come to know his kisses intimately, but they'd never promised all that he seemed to be promising her now. The kiss promised no end . . . only a beginning.

Groaning deeply, he trailed his mouth along her chin, nibbling as he went until he pressed his mouth against her ear. "Remember how I wanted to touch you?"

"As my husband, you have that right."

"Only if it's what you want."

"How could you possibly think I wouldn't want you to touch me?"

"Good, 'cuz I'm gonna touch all of you."

He moved his large hands up her sides and cupped her breasts, his thumbs circling the sensitive flesh until her nipples hardened. Moaning, she collapsed against his broad chest. He slipped his arm beneath her knees and lifted her against his chest. She had never felt more at home than she did as he carried her to the bed and gently laid her on the thick feather mattress, stretching his body alongside hers.

She loved the length of his body, the breadth of his shoulders. She trailed her fingers over the scars that ran along his face. "Can you feel that?"

"Barely." He took her hand and placed it over his beating heart. "But I feel that."

Then his body was covering hers, flesh against flesh, warmth against warmth. His mouth blazed a trail of kisses along her throat, traveling lower to circle the crest of each breast. She scraped her fingers through his hair until a leather strip barred further exploration. "Do you mind if I remove this?" she asked.

He lifted his gaze, and she watched as his Adam's apple slowly slid up and down. "If you want," he said in a strangled voice.

"I love everything about you, Houston. Everything."

"Even the ugliness."

"That's just it. I don't see any ugliness when I look at you."

He closed his eye as she untied the leather strip and gently removed the patch covering his face. He released a ragged breath before lifting his gaze back to hers.

"I think you're handsome as sin," she said softly.

He buried his face between her breasts. "You can't love me that much."

"I love you more."

"Oh, Lord." Houston thought he might weep. That'd be one hell of a manly action on his wedding night. His father would tan his hide—

Only his father wasn't here, and he wasn't the man his father had wanted him to become. But he was the man this woman loved.

She accepted his weaknesses and his scars, inside and out. The tears burned his throat, burned his eye as he raised his face from the soft pillow of her flesh. "I haven't got the words to tell you how much I love you, but I'm hoping I can show you."

He called on the skills he'd acquired while working with horses, hoping to tame her passions, bend them to his will, to her desires. He skimmed his hands along her body, from her shoulder to her tiny bare toes. Shadows waltzed over her flesh in rhythm to the dancing flames within the hearth. He relished the sight of her skin glowing beneath his fingers.

Years ago, he'd stopped dreaming, and when he began to dream again, all his dreams revolved around her. The feel of her beside him, beneath him, around him.

He fought against rushing to have all that he wanted, forcing himself to gift her with the patience he gave his horses. She meant so much more to him than his horses. Without her, they were nothing more than animals. With her, they were a dream waiting on the horizon, a dream they would touch together.

He kissed her deeply, inhaling the scent of magnolias that would forever remain in his bed.

Then he began to trail his mouth over her flesh, following the path his hands had blazed earlier.

He heard her sigh like the soughing of the wind. He took his time, allowing her to grow accustomed to the feel of his mouth on her breasts, suckling, taunting, before he trailed down to her thighs.

Slowly, leisurely, he kissed her intimately, passionately until she quivered beneath him.

"Houston? I need—"

He swirled his tongue along her sensitive flesh. "I want you to buck for me."

"Buck for you?" Amelia rasped, her fingers pressing against his face. "Oh, God." Sensations she'd never known existed swept through her: lightning flashed and thunder rumbled as he created a tempest within her. Her entire body curled as tightly as her toes, and then the storm exploded, raining pleasure and rapture throughout until she did buck like a wild mustang.

She opened her eyes to find him gazing at her, a smile of pure joy etched across his face. "You know there are some mustangs that can't be broken, but they're always worth the ride."

"I think you just broke me," she confessed breathlessly.

"Nope. You have too much spirit, Amelia. I'd never try to break you, but I always want you to enjoy the ride as much as I do."

With one long smooth stroke, he joined his body to hers. The pain was fleeting as her body instinctively tightened around him. Then he was riding her, she was riding him, two people with one destination.

The journey was like none she'd ever taken, none she'd ever dreamed of taking. She ran her hands along the taut muscles of his chest and back, kissed the dew from his throat, relished the sight of his clenched jaw.

His mouth swooped down, covering hers, kissing her, mating their tongues just as he'd mated their bodies. She whimpered, he groaned. Her breathing became shallow, his harsh.

His thrusts grew swifter, and she kept pace as the sensations stampeded through her until her body hurled her into an abyss of pleasure, and he arched and shuddered above her.

In awe, she languorously trailed her fingers over his glistening back.

He rubbed his cheek against hers. "I love you," he whispered on a tired breath.

"Those whores were fools for charging you double."

He chuckled low, lifted his head, and brushed a strand of hair away from her cheek. "I never gave them this. I never gave anyone this. I didn't know I had it to give." He held her gaze. "I want you to know that when I took Austin to Dusty Flats, I didn't touch a woman."

She pressed a kiss to the center of his chest. "I'm glad. Even though you weren't married to me at the time, I'm glad."

He rolled to his side and brought her up against him. She nestled against his shoulder, relishing the day's memories and the night's wonders before drifting off to sleep.

Amelia awoke several hours later, her body sore, her heart content. Houston's body was draped over hers, his leg slung over her thigh, his large palm cradling her breast, his breath blowing across her nape like the constant West Texas breeze. It took her a moment to recognize that she was not only surrounded by him, but by darkness as well. "Houston?"

"Mmmm?" he mumbled in a sleepy voice.

"The fire went out."

"Are you cold?"

"No, but there's no light."

"Want me to find the lantern?"

"Just hold me a little tighter."

"I can do better than that," he promised as he gently rolled her over and kissed her deeply, giving her what he would always give her from that night forward . . . the best of himself.

Don't miss the next captivating historical romance in Lorraine Heath's bestselling Sins for all Seasons series,

WHEN A DUKE LOVES A WOMAN

Gillie Trewlove knows what a stranger's kindness can mean, having been abandoned on a doorstep as a baby and raised by the woman who found her there. So, when suddenly faced with a soul in need at her door—or the alleyway by her tavern—Gillie doesn't hesitate. But he's no infant. He's a grievously injured, distractingly handsome gentleman who doesn't belong in Whitechapel, much less recuperating in Gillie's bed . . .

Being left at the altar is humiliating; being rescued from thugs by a woman—albeit a brave and beautiful one—is the pièce de résistance to the Duke of Thornley's extraordinarily bad day. After nursing him back from the brink, Gillie agrees to help him comb London's darker corners for his wayward bride. But every moment together is edged with desire and has Thorne rethinking his choice of wife. Yet Gillie knows the aristocracy would never accept a duchess born in sin. Thorne, however, is determined to prove to her that no obstacle is insurmountable when a duke loves a woman.

Coming Fall 2018 from Avon Books

TEXAS SPLENDOR

A man on a mission . . .

After five grueling years in a Texas prison, Austin Leigh is finally a free man. He can't wait to go home and be reunited with his sweetheart. But when he discovers she didn't wait for him and is now married, he becomes more determined to clear his name of the crime he never committed.

Meets the one woman who could offer him salvation—and love . . .

En route to the state capitol, he meets a young woman, Loree Grant, and her dog. When he learns that they have survived a mysterious tragedy, he is moved—and curious. And as he spends more time with the lovely, intriguing woman, he sees glimpses of a future he had thought was no longer possible as they both find a new lease on life—and a love that can overcome any obstacle.

NEW YORK TIMES BESTSELLING AUTHOR

LORRAINE HEATH

FALLING INTO BED WITH A DUKE
978-0-06-239101-8

Miss Minerva Dodger chooses spinsterhood over fortune-hungry suitors. But at the Nightingale Club, where ladies don masks before choosing a lover, she can at least enjoy one night of pleasure. The sinfully handsome Duke of Ashebury is more than willing to satisfy the secretive lady's desires. Intrigued by her wit and daring, he sets out to woo her in earnest.

THE EARL TAKES ALL
978-0-06-239103-2

One summer night, Edward Alcott gives in to temptation and kisses Lady Julia Kenney in a dark garden. However, the passion she stirs within him is best left in the shadows as she weds his twin, the Earl of Greyling. But when tragedy strikes, to honor the vow he makes to his dying brother, Edward must pretend to be Greyling until the countess delivers her babe.

THE VISCOUNT AND THE VIXEN
978-0-06-239105-6

Desperation forced Portia Gladstone to agree to marry a madman. The arrangement will offer the protection she needs. Or so she believes until the marquess's distractingly handsome son peruses the fine print . . . and takes his father's place! But because she begins to fall for her devilishly seductive husband, her dark secrets surface and threaten to ruin them both.